LooseId®

SO-ARM-613

ISBN 1-59632-151-2
ISBN 13: 978-1-59632-151-9
RATED: X-MAS
Copyright © 2007 by Loose Id, LLC
Cover Art by April Martinez

Publisher acknowledges the authors and copyright holders of the individual works, as follows:

TWICE BLESSED
Copyright © November 2004 by Rachel Bo
CHRISTMAS NOIR
Copyright © November 2004 by Barbara Karmazin
SPIRITUAL NOELLE (A SISTER Leashed Story)
Copyright © December 2006 by Jet Mykles

This book is an original publication of Loose Id®. Each individual story herein was previously published in e-book format only by Loose Id® and is a work of fiction. Any similarity to actual persons, events or existing locations is entirely coincidental.

Printed in the U.S.A. by
Lightning Source, Inc.
1246 Heil Quaker Blvd
La Vergne TN 37086
www.lightningsource.com

Contents

TWICE BLESSED

Rachel Bo

Prologue

Jenny tossed her hair, loving the way the wind whipped its eager fingers through her silken strands. Flying down I-80 from New York to California, toward a new city, a new job, a new way of life, Jenny felt genuinely alive for the first time in her life.

The radio began to buzz, and she fiddled with the dial, searching for a good hard rock station. That was one of the problems with these lonely stretches of highway -- no decent stations within range. Jenny's mind wandered as she made her way slowly through the frequencies. After working for six years as a nurse, she had finally chucked it all. She'd never wanted to go into nursing in the first place, but her parents had refused to pay for her to get a degree in an art-related field, which was where she felt she really shined. So Jenny, ever the dutiful daughter, went to nursing school, graduated with honors, and lived the life her parents wanted her to live.

She smiled as she heard the opening guitar riffs of one of her favorite songs. Turning up the volume, she belted out the lyrics along with the band. That was another thing her parents hadn't been able to understand -- her taste in music. For years, she'd only listened to the music she loved when out of the house. That's the way much of her life had been -- trying to conform to the vision her parents had for her, instead of being herself.

Once she entered the workforce, however, she discovered that she liked herself much better when she listened to her own desires. As the band on the radio sang about starting over, Jenny grinned. Being herself felt so good, she had started planning for something different barely two months out of college.

The song ended and Jenny tuned out the commercial chatter as she reflected on the past few years. It had been an exhausting time, but she had no regrets. She had picked up as much overtime as she could, and had taken night classes at the art institute. When she had her second degree in hand, she applied for an eclectic mix of jobs on both the east and west coasts.

In the end, it had all paid off with an exciting offer from a company in the entertainment industry -- a position that would capitalize on her lifelong interest in costuming and her excellent design and sewing skills. Her sample designs had landed her a job as a costume designer and seamstress with a fledgling company out in California.

Giving in to the overwhelming bubble of joy rising up inside, she let out a faint "Whoop!" It felt so good, she whooped again, laughing at herself as the wind snatched her voice, carrying it away.

The top was down on the red Mustang convertible she'd purchased as a reward for herself when she got the news, but the bright sun baked this stretch of road in Arizona, and the warm breeze did nothing to alleviate heat like an oven. *Of course, they just had to want me in August.* She caught a glimpse of her sun-pinkened cheeks in the rearview mirror. *There's nothing worse than driving across the country in the hottest month of the year.* Determined to prove her wrong, a trickle of sweat meandered between Jenny's shoulder blades, collecting at her bra strap, which clung damply to her skin. She squirmed and immediately amended her previous thought. *Unless it's a sticky bra.*

Jenny glanced in the rearview mirror. Her convertible and a blue truck several car-lengths distant were the only vehicles in sight on this deserted bit of highway. Jenny hesitated, then shrugged. The truck was too far back for anyone inside to see what she was doing, so she reached up under her shirt, deftly unclasping her bra.

Jenny held on to the wheel with her right hand. The sleeves of her oversized blouse were loose enough for her to slip her fingers inside. Switching hands back and forth on the wheel, she managed to slip off her bra and tug it out from beneath her blouse.

"Oh!" Jenny gasped and watched in disbelief as an errant gust of wind yanked the silk from between her fingers. Mortified, she followed the garment's progress as it floated away, dancing in the air, to land snugly up against the window of the blue truck. "Damn." Heat rushed to her cheeks.

To her dismay, a lean, brown, unmistakably masculine arm reached out the truck's passenger-side window and plucked her bra from the windshield. She watched, horrified, as the vehicle began to pick up speed. "Shit!"

Jenny divided her attention between the road and the truck coming up behind her. They probably thought she was some kind of freak -- that she'd tossed her bra at them on purpose. Oh, well; she could handle a few moments of intense embarrassment.

Then another thought occurred. What if these were not nice people? What if they tried to run her off the road or something? The little convertible could probably outrun them, but she wasn't sure. Some trucks nowadays could give a sports car a run for its money. They usually took a little longer to get up to speed, though. Maybe if she waited until they got right behind her, then floored the accelerator, she could lose them.

Jenny watched the mirror. "Just a little bit closer," she murmured.

With a sudden burst of speed, the pickup zipped into the left-hand lane and pulled up alongside her. A grinning bronze Adonis with the bluest eyes Jenny had ever seen leaned out the window, holding her bra. "You dropped something!"

Jenny felt the heat flare in her cheeks again. She snatched at the trailing end of her bra and "Adonis" let go, chuckling as she tucked the wisp of fabric into the side pocket of her purse. "Thanks!" She gave a little wave as she started to pull ahead.

"Hey, wait!"

She hesitated, but those damn blue eyes were too tempting, and she felt herself slowing down until the vehicles were even again.

"Is that all we get?" Adonis's twin, the driver, was glancing over at her now, hollering. "Where's our reward?"

Jenny glanced past the passenger to study the man holding the wheel. She found her attention riveted once more by a pair of brilliant blue eyes. How in the hell could there be *two* of this heart-stoppingly gorgeous man? The devil was definitely tempting her, and Jenny was in just the right mood to take him up on his offer.

Pulling her gaze back to the road, knowing she was being stupid, but unable to resist the imp of mischief that was urging her to play their game, she yelled, "What do you want?"

The two men shared a look, then flashed identical, dazzling smiles. "Give us a peek," Adonis hollered, pointing toward her chest with his chin.

The flush in her cheeks abruptly traveled downward, flooding her chest with heat, making her nipples tingle. Despite a quieter, saner voice in her head urging caution, she caught herself smiling back. They were so damn cute, with their shaggy, sun-bleached hair and dark tans. And the light dancing in their eyes was flirty and mischievous -- not dark or dangerous. Her instincts said these guys meant her no harm. And after working for years in a job she didn't like, because she hadn't had the backbone to buck her Dad and follow her dreams, Jenny had decided to never ignore those instincts again.

"What the hell?" she whispered to herself. At twenty-eight, she was still in fine shape, and it wasn't like she was ever going to see these guys again. She glanced ahead, then checked her rearview mirror again. They still appeared to be the only cars on the road. Quickly, before she lost her nerve, she unbuttoned her blouse with one hand, the wild wind whipping her shirt-tails back, exposing her bare breasts.

Two long, sharp whistles pierced the air. "I'm in love!" Adonis whooped, hanging out the passenger window.

"Hey!" A brown hand pushed the man back against the seat, and "Adonis 2" gave her a long, lingering inspection, his quick glances smoldering with desire. "Marry me!" he hollered.

"Hell, no." His passenger leaned out the window again. "Marry *me!*"

Jenny laughed, feeling confident and sexy and wicked and attractive and utterly free for the first time in a long while. "I'll marry you both," she said, grinning up at them. "*If* you can catch me!" With that, she floored the accelerator and flew down the highway, watching the blue truck dwindle to a bright dot in the distance. She took a deep breath and whooped, astonished at what she had just done, but feeling years of tension melt away like wax.

She focused on the road ahead, just in time to see that she was coming up fast on an eighteen wheeler. Jenny slowed down a little, fumbling for the buttons, fastening her blouse back into place.

She drove on for six more hours that day. With each glance in the rearview mirror, she told herself that she wasn't watching for an old, beat-up blue pickup. The handsome strangers never reappeared, and she spent the rest of her trip to California trying to convince herself that she wasn't disappointed.

Invitation

Jenny tucked her socks into her sneakers and set off down the beach, relishing the feel of cool, damp sand beneath her toes. There was a brisk breeze off the ocean today, and she pulled her windbreaker close around her, tugging up the zipper. Santa Monica in November beat New York in winter any day, but it could still get chilly, and the spray off the surf made it colder still. But Jenny always came to the beach when she needed to think.

In just two short hours, Hartmann Historical Designs was closing down for the holidays, and she still hadn't decided whether to accept her parents' invitation. After seven long years, her mom and dad had finally forgiven her for abandoning her career and coming out to California to live with the "beatniks." She giggled. Even for their own generation, her parents were a bit antiquated.

Her mother had called two weeks earlier, after Jenny had written them a letter explaining that she'd be at loose ends for six weeks, to invite her to spend that time in New York. Jenny was torn, however. For one thing, she liked the mild California winters. She had never missed the cold, rain, sleet, and freezing temperatures of a New York City winter. Now, the snow at the cabin in Connecticut, *that* she sometimes missed; but apparently her parents had a whirlwind round of party obligations this holiday season, and they were staying in New York.

Which was another reason why she was reluctant to go. She'd never been the social butterfly her parents were -- especially her dad. The idea of having to suffer through those interminable parties made her skin crawl.

But she missed her parents. She'd been surprised at the sudden surge of emotion that flooded her when she heard her mother's voice on the phone. In all these years, she'd had only Christmas and birthday cards from her parents, even though she'd written them letters faithfully, every few months or so, letting them know how she was doing. Hearing her mother's voice had brought tears to her eyes, and even her father had picked up the extension long enough to say hello and let her know that, yes, he wanted her there, too.

A wavelet that was more ambitious than the rest folded over Jenny's feet, and she worked her toes deep into the swirling sand. Who was she kidding? She had to go. She wanted to see them. They did love her, whatever they thought of her chosen career. And she loved them. And none of them were getting any younger.

Her mind made up, she veered toward a wooden bench and sat down to let her feet dry so she could tug on her shoes. Then she recovered her car from the parking lot and made her way back to work.

She opened the door to her office to hear Christmas music blaring on the radio, and to the sight of her assistant, Becca, dancing around the room and singing at the top of her lungs. When Becca caught sight of Jenny, she let out a squeal and ran over to grasp Jenny's arms and jump up and down. "We got it! We got it!"

Jenny knew immediately what she was talking about, but she couldn't quite believe it. "B&B Productions? We got it?"

"Yes!" Becca squealed, still jumping up and down. "Yes, yes, yes!"

Jenny closed her eyes as a flood of joy mingled with relief washed over her. Finally. They had finally managed to bag a contract with a powerhouse Hollywood company to do the costume design and production for a major motion picture.

"Darn it, Becca! I wanted to tell her."

Jenny turned at the sound of Carol Hartmann's voice. The robust, buxom blonde stepped into the room and gave Jenny a quick hug. "*You* did it," Carol insisted. "Michael said B&B loved your designs. It's written into the contract, at their insistence -- not that they had to twist *my* arm -- you're lead project designer, kiddo!"

"I can't believe it." Jenny sighed. "This is great!"

"What you won't believe is our budget, Jen. It's to die for! We've never had a contract like this. We're finally a major player!"

Jenny frowned, the reality of the situation finally beginning to hit her. "If we manage all right. We could still screw it up."

Becca laughed. "No way. I know you, Jen. You won't give any of us any peace once this project gets under way. You'll sew every stitch yourself if you have to." She put one arm around each of her bosses. "Everything's going to be fine!"

Carol smiled. "Becca's right, Jen. I want you to use this time off to relax. I need you back here in January, fresh and focused. Carlos is coming in our first day back so you can go over the fabric orders with him, and I'm advertising for additional seamstresses to help carry the load. I'll hold the best apps for you to look over when we get back, then we'll set up some interviews."

Jenny nodded confidently, though her head was already filling with images of possible disasters. "Okay. I'll be ready." She grinned wryly. "I guess it's a good thing I'm going to New York. If I were staying here, I'd end up worrying so much, I'd be a basketcase by the time you guys came back."

"So you decided to go?" Becca asked.

"Yeah." Jenny shook her head. "It was silly to worry about it. I'm thirty-five years old. It might be awkward the first day or so, but they did make the overture, so at least one of them must be ready to hear what I have to say. I don't want to spend the rest of my life with our only contact being a couple of cards and letters a year."

"Good." Carol and Becca shared a glance. "We were hoping that's what you'd decide." Carol glanced at the wall clock. "Hey! It's six-o-one, and we are now officially on vacation."

"Why don't we all go to dinner together?" Jenny suggested. "We're all going to be out of town at different times, so this will be our last chance to get together until the holidays are over."

"Sure," Carol and Becca said simultaneously. Carol laughed. "Let me go grab my purse and then we'll lock up."

Homecoming

LaGuardia Airport was packed with holiday travelers, and Jenny sighed as she squeezed her way past yet another cluster of human congestion. Breathing a sigh of relief as she spotted the exit, she quickly made her way outside, hailing the first taxi driver she saw. The man hurried over and took her suitcase, deposited it in the trunk, and helped Jenny into the back seat.

"Nichols Park." She gave him the name of the upscale suburb her parents called home. "1312 Stamden." The cabbie nodded and touched the meter, then pulled out. Jenny relaxed back against the seat.

Her parents had offered to pick her up, but it was so much easier to take a cab. Especially with airport security so tight now. She tugged the book she was currently reading out of her purse, switched on the tiny book light she had purchased in the gift shop, and occupied herself with the story for the remainder of the hour-long drive home.

After she paid the cabbie and he had driven off, Jenny stood on the sidewalk, looking up at the house in the fading evening light. A four-inch layer of snow covered the front yard. She'd forgotten how beautiful the place could be in winter. A golden glow from the windows beckoned, and she lifted her suitcase and trekked up the steps carefully. The front door opened even before she had a chance to ring the doorbell.

"Jenny!" Meredith Dalton embraced her daughter warmly. "I'm so glad you decided to come."

"Me, too, Mom." Jenny hugged her tight.

"Well." Meredith pulled back after a moment. "Come in! Don't stand out there in the cold."

Jenny stepped into the foyer, greeting the man standing in the archway into the living room. "Hi, Dad."

Scott Dalton nodded stiffly. "Jenny."

They stood, staring at each other awkwardly.

"Scott." Meredith's tone was an admonishment. "Don't you have something to say?"

Jenny's father frowned. "I can't help it, Meredith. I guess I'm still a little angry."

"Scott, you promised not to --"

"It's okay, Mom," Jenny interrupted. "We might as well go ahead and get everything out in the open and get it dealt with, so we can enjoy the rest of the visit." Her mother pushed the front door shut as Jenny stepped forward and faced her father squarely.

"I'm sorry you feel like you wasted your money, Dad. But I tried to tell you what I really wanted, and you wouldn't listen." Jenny reached out and rested a hand on his arm. "And it wasn't really a waste. Nursing supported me very well while

I continued to study, and I'm grateful for that. But I love what I'm doing now, and I don't regret making the decision to change careers. I hope you can understand."

Her father's expression softened. "It's just -- did it *have* to be the entertainment business, Jen? You know how those people are."

She couldn't contain the deep, rich laugh that seemed to startle her father. "Dad, I think you have the wrong idea about how involved I am in the industry. I design and make period costumes for theatrical productions, S.C.A. enthusiasts, a few businesses that are themed to a particular time period. As a matter of fact, up until last week, we'd never landed a contract for a major Hollywood film." She put her arm around him. "I'm thirty-five years old, Dad. I'm not out partying and being propositioned -- I'm in my office or the sewing room, working my butt off to dress people I never even see."

Scott grinned sheepishly. "I guess I never really thought about it." He put his arm around her. "But am I allowed to hate the fact that you have to live on the other side of the continent in order to do this?"

"Mmmm...yeah, as long as you don't hate *me*."

Her father tightened his grip on her shoulders, holding her close. "Never, sweetie." He sighed. "What can I say? Your old man's a control freak, and it took me a while to absorb the fact that you weren't going to just up and move back and do what I wanted you to do."

Meredith stepped forward, tears in her eyes. "Oh, Scott." She reached up and cupped his face with her hand.

Jenny's father cleared his throat. "Okay, now. None of this weepy-weep stuff. Let's get Jenny situated, and then I'm taking you both out to dinner."

Caught

"Jenny? What do you think?"

Jenny stared at herself in the full-length mirror in her bedroom. The silver gown shimmered as she moved, accentuating the soft mounds of her breasts, glinting from the curve of her hips. She couldn't believe she could wear something like this and pull it off, but she had to admit, it suited her perfectly. Her mother had done an excellent job.

"I hope I wasn't too presumptuous." Meredith fluttered her hands nervously, smoothing out non-existent wrinkles in her own gown. "I just thought, from your letters, that you didn't really go to functions like this any more, and I was afraid you might not have anything to wear, and...oh, you're not angry, are you? Scott thought you might feel like we were treating you like a charity case, but parents should be able to buy gifts for their children, shouldn't they? And we've got seven years of gift-giving to catch up on, and --"

"Mom." Jenny met her mother's eyes in the mirror. "It's beautiful. And it doesn't feel like charity." She laughed. "I'm relieved, actually. I knew before I headed out here that we had all those parties to go to, and it never even occurred to me to shop for anything appropriate. I guess I was more preoccupied with how things were going to go between us. I'm just glad I don't have to wear a sack to Uncle Frank's tonight."

Meredith clapped her hands together. "So you like it?"

Jenny turned back to the mirror. "I *love* it."

"Good. And…well, I have to confess, there are a couple more dresses for you hidden away in my closet." Jenny raised her eyebrows. "Well, there's the dinner at the chairman's house next week, and Junie's annual Christmas party, and --"

She looked so worried that Jenny had to laugh again. "It's all right, Mom. I appreciate it; I really do. But don't buy any more, okay? If I don't have what I need, we can go shopping together, and I'll pay for it."

Meredith nodded. "Oh, hurry up. I can't wait to show you off!"

Jenny shook her head as she picked up the little silver handbag that went with the dress. "I swear, you're making me feel like a little kid again!" Her tone was chiding, but as they made their way downstairs, she was forced to admit to herself that she was actually enjoying being her parents' little girl again.

* * *

Three hours later, standing in a corner of her uncle's crowded living room, choking on smoke and perfume, she was having second thoughts. She had remembered hating these things, but over the years, her mind had glossed over exactly how out of place she felt among her family's friends and relatives. Despite her upbringing, she considered herself a simple girl, with simple tastes. She'd never been into the party rounds, the plastic surgery, the smoking. After the initial introductions, she'd found herself without anything to say to these people, hiding out in a secluded corner, as she had when she was young.

And it didn't help that she kept sensing that she was being watched. Several times, she'd had such an intense feeling of being observed that she'd almost felt...stalked. But when she scanned the room, there were no sudden turns of the head, no whispered conversations. It was probably just nerves. Maybe a little fresh air would help -- the room was stifling.

Jenny edged her way through the crowd to the French doors that let out onto the garden. They were partially opened, to help alleviate the heat created by the crush of people, so she slipped out onto the flagstone patio.

It was a clear, cold night. Moonlight bathed the garden with opal radiance, and Jenny found herself drawn to the fountain. She picked her way carefully down the steps, then walked over and stared at her reflection in the shimmering waters.

"Beautiful, isn't she?"

Jenny whirled as the voice spoke behind her. "What?"

"I said you're beautiful."

She stared into the piercing blue eyes of a man who appeared to be close to her own age. His hair was a little long -- sandy brown, tousled curls framing a deeply tanned face and a killer smile. He looked vaguely familiar. Jenny frowned. "Do I know you?"

His grin widened. "Yes." His eyes flickered toward something behind her. "You once promised to marry me."

Jenny laughed. "Oh, that's a good one. But I know that's not true, because I've never been proposed to."

"Oh, but you have." Another voice spoke from behind her, and she whirled again, losing her balance in the process. A strong, brown hand reached out to steady her, and then she was looking into an identical pair of bright blue eyes.

"But...you're..." Jenny turned, staring from one man to the other, virtual mirror images of each other. A forgotten memory began to stir, but a distracting heat invaded her arm where their flesh met, making it hard for her to concentrate. Where had she seen twins like this before?

The man holding her arm leaned toward her. "Run," he whispered.

Jenny pulled her arm from his grasp and backed away. What on earth were they doing? Somehow, they were between her and the house now. "W-What did you say?"

They both looked at her with eyes that were no longer bright and laughing, but dark and full of desire. "He said *run*."

Some primal instinct made her move just as they reached for her. Her heart raced as she stumbled past the fountain. She looked back, and they were coming. Slowly, but moving with a sleek power and animal grace that sent her heart leaping into her throat. Jenny kicked off her heels and raced down the path.

Why was this happening? She racked her brain, trying to bring back the faint memory that had stirred a moment ago. Where had she seen those beautiful eyes before?

Then it came back to her, and she was so startled that she stopped dead. Surely, they couldn't be the guys from the truck. As she stood there, that hot August afternoon replayed itself in her mind. Those compelling blue eyes, the smiles, the hair.

Shit. Jenny couldn't imagine that they would still remember her, yet alone recognize her. This had to be some kind of joke. Her heart began to race again, but this time it wasn't fear that pulsed in her veins, but desire. Jenny chided herself. She knew nothing about these two, except that they were obviously obsessive, to remember her this long. So why was she standing here, waiting for them?

Jenny made herself step off the path, behind the trunk of one of the large oaks that graced her uncle's property. Shivering, she closed her eyes, waiting for the sound of their footsteps. After they passed, she'd high-tail it back to the house and call the police.

Jenny almost screamed when hands closed around each of her arms.

"And now, we've finally caught you." The voice had a teasing quality to it, and Jenny opened her eyes. Her captors pressed close, the heat from their bodies chasing away her chill. "You aren't frightened, are you?"

Jenny swallowed. "Yes."

One of them reached up and traced the edge of her low neckline with a calloused finger. "But?"

Had there been a "but" in her tone? Jenny took a deep breath, intending to scream, but let it out as a sigh. Hell, yes. "But…" She searched for words that wouldn't make her sound like an idiot.

"But you do remember us." The finger outlining her dress slipped just beneath the edge of the fabric. The other man reached up and ran his hand through her loose hair, and the shiver that ran through her body had nothing to do with the cold.

"Yes." Jenny sighed.

"And?" The man caressing her hair was pressed up against her, his erection prodding her hip.

"I --" His mouth claimed hers, and Jenny moaned, meeting his thrusting tongue with her own.

The hand at her chest slid beneath the fabric, covering one breast. "Mmmm," a voice whispered in her ear. "I've been wanting to do this for seven years."

She couldn't believe she was allowing this to happen, but suddenly, dreams she had relegated to the darkest corners of her mind came to the surface. As much as she wanted to deny it, she remembered these two much better than she had initially let on. She'd dreamed about them, over and over just after her trip to California, then less frequently as the outrageous things she did in those dreams forced her to push them out of her mind.

Jenny leaned into the hand at her breast, deepening the kiss as hot fingers milked her nipple, bringing it to a taut, aching peak. "What's your name?" whispered the mouth against her lips.

"Jenny."

Two hands glided down her back. She was vaguely aware of a quiet rasping sound, and a sudden gust of cold air against her buttocks made her realize they had unzipped her dress. She knew she should protest, but the hands caressing her cheeks now were so warm, so gentle. She sighed and pushed the two men away from her. "Wait."

Jenny felt disembodied as she pushed the straps down her shoulders and let the dress fall to the ground. She was naked underneath -- it wasn't the kind of dress you could wear a bra with, and she hadn't wanted panty lines and never wore hose. "I-It's cold," she stuttered, suddenly shocked at her own actions.

They both stepped forward. "Let us keep you warm."

"W-Wait. What are your names?"

She could see slight differences between them now. One was leaner and seemed less serious, his hair just a tad lighter in the dappled moonlight. He moved, embracing her from behind, his hands caressing her abdomen just above the dark brown curls at her groin. "I'm Devlin." He nibbled at her ear, his hot breath sending spirals of pleasure down to the damp cavern between her legs. "But most people call me Dev."

The other one stepped forward, sliding one arm around her back, between her and the other, as he gazed down at her. "I'm Damien." He studied her seriously for a moment. "Are you sure about this?" he murmured.

Jenny shook her head. "No." The pleasant touch at her abdomen faltered, and she leaned into the man behind her, meeting Damien's eyes boldly at the same time. "But don't stop."

He smiled then, and it lit up his face. He held her gaze as he reached for her, his hand joining his brother's, both of them gliding down to tickle her bush. Jenny arched and sighed, allowing herself to forget everything but their touch.

Their fingers circled her clit, and she shifted one leg, wrapping it around Damien's thigh. He cocked an eyebrow, and she nodded. "Please."

"Who?" he whispered.

"Both of you."

Dev groaned and nipped her earlobe as their forefingers slid inside her. "God, Jenny. You're everything we imagined."

"And more," Damien insisted.

Jenny turned her head and kissed Devlin eagerly, hungrily, gasping as she felt the warmth that was Damien's mouth closing upon her breast. "Oh, God."

Dev backed up, drawing them with him until his back was supported by the huge oak. He let go of her briefly, and Damien's mouth claimed hers as she listened to the quiet sounds of Dev's pants being unzipped and pushed down past his burgeoning erection. Jenny moaned in disappointment as Damien broke away. "Turn around," he said.

She turned, and froze at the sight of Devlin's cock. She'd had her share of sexual encounters over the years, but Dev's shaft easily dwarfed every other man she'd ever experienced. The electric thrill that ran down her spine was part lust, part fear. Could she take him?

He must have sensed her anxiety, because he said, "Don't worry." His hands closed on her waist, and then he and Damien were raising her up. She lifted her knees and parted her legs, trembling as they lowered her toward his waiting staff.

Cold air wafted over the wetness between her thighs. Slowly, Devlin eased the tip of his cock into her. Jenny wrapped her arms around his neck. God, his cock was so *thick*.

Carefully, they let her weight bear her down. She whimpered with need. Her lips stretched painfully around him, but the discomfort only seemed to heighten her desire.

"Are you okay?" he whispered.

She nodded her head wordlessly, tightening her pussy around him. Dev groaned. "Let go," Jenny whispered. He hesitated for a moment, then nodded, loosening his hold. Damien let go and stepped back. She worked her legs around Devlin's waist, crossing her ankles just below his buttocks as he finally buried the last of his length inside her. "God, yes."

His hands were at her waist again, holding her steady while he began to pump his hips. "Yes, Devlin," Jenny sobbed. "Oh, yes!"

She felt Damien's hands on her cheeks, parting them, and then something warm and wet glided over her anus. She gasped, her pussy convulsing involuntarily. Dev chuckled. "I think she likes that, Damien."

"Do you, Jenny?" Damien purred. "Do you like me licking your ass?"

In the past, Jenny had always been too embarrassed to admit that she enjoyed anal play, but what they were doing to her felt too damn good. "Yes," she whispered urgently. "Oh, yes."

Damien's tongue flicked quickly back and forth over the now-throbbing pucker, the muscles in Jenny's pussy dancing with each stroke. Devlin groaned. "Oh, *hell*, yeah!" His rhythm increased, his powerful hips pumping rapidly, his huge cock plunging so deep that it almost hurt, and yet satisfying Jenny in a way she had never been satisfied before, so that she bit her lip to keep from crying out, afraid they would stop. It was torture, but it was exquisite torture.

"Oh, God." She trembled as her world narrowed to the hot core between her legs and the pulsing throb between her buttocks. When Damien's tongue disappeared, and the tip of a broad finger insinuated itself inside her, it was more than she could take. Wave after wave of pleasure slammed through her, and she arched, mouth open in a soundless scream of glee as Devlin's hot seed erupted inside her.

Damien stood and helped support her as she and Devlin trembled with their release. When they had both regained a modicum of control, Dev lifted her gently and set her on the ground. "Thank you," he said, his hands still holding her waist, looking her in the eye.

She looked away, not wanting him to see her desperation -- this sudden, rampant hunger that she had never felt before.

"Hey." His hand gently cupped her chin, turning her to face him. "You don't have anything to be ashamed of. This was beautiful."

"And it doesn't have to end." Damien's breath in her ear sent a surge of lust through Jenny's body that took her breath away.

"You don't understand," she said, meeting Dev's gaze. "I'm not ashamed."

He drew in a shaky breath at the look in her eye. "Oh, hell, Jenny. Don't look at me like that."

She didn't understand the sudden fear in his eyes. "What's wrong?"

His gaze flickered to Damien, and Jenny turned. "What is it?" *Please, God, don't let this be some kind of terrible joke.*

Damien's gaze seemed to drink in the sight of her, driving Jenny's anxiety away. Whatever else might be going on, this man definitely wanted her. And she wanted him. She stepped forward, trailing her fingers over the prominent bulge at his crotch. "You said it doesn't have to end."

Damien caught her fingers with his hand. "Not forever, but for tonight. They'll be missing you soon. And we need to get to know each other a little better, before --" He glanced at his brother -- they still hadn't said they were brothers, but only a fool would think they were anything but twins -- and didn't finish the sentence. He bent down and picked up Jenny's dress from the ground, brushing away the bits of snow clinging to its silver folds.

Jenny searched his face, and somehow sensed that he wasn't toying with her. For whatever reason, he was putting the brakes on, but this wasn't over. The smoldering gleam in his eyes told her that. She nodded, and when Damien held out the dress, holding it open so that she could step into it, she did so, drawing the straps up over her shoulders. She turned her back to him. "Could you zip me, please?"

She felt him grasp the pull, and then hesitate. Attached to the zipper were two long, fine silver chains, each tipped with a small, round crystal. It was one of the things that had made the dress feel so sexy to Jenny, because she could feel the chains swaying as she walked, the crystals occasionally brushing against the backs of her thighs. "Jenny?"

She knew instinctively what he wanted, and swallowed hard as she nodded without even looking at him. Devlin's eyes seemed to flash as he stepped forward, reaching behind her as she bent slightly, his strong hands parting her cheeks.

Damien pressed the first bead into her anus, and Jenny let out a small sound of pleasure. His touch lingered after he inserted the second bead, rolling the small globe back and forth between the tip of his finger and her aroused flesh. She pressed her hips back, moaning. Damien sighed and withdrew, patting her buttock gently. "Not now," he said. "But soon." He carefully pulled up the zipper and tucked the remaining lengths of silver in between the edge of the dress's low back and her skin. "We'd better get back."

Jenny nodded. Devlin restored himself to proper gentlemanly dress, and they walked at either side of her, their arms around her waist, as they escorted her back to the fountain. She slipped her feet back into her heels and smoothed her dress one last time.

"You'd better go in first," Damien suggested.

Jenny nodded. She longed to ask when she would see them again, but forced herself to remain silent. She wouldn't have them thinking she was some desperate, middle-aged, sex-starved spinster. Turning, she headed back to the house, head held high.

Once inside, she was shocked to find that the whole episode had only lasted about twenty minutes. It had seemed like an eternity. Jenny made her way over to the bar and asked for a margarita, on the rocks, no salt. The chains fastened to the zipper tugged at the tiny beads inside her as she walked, and she felt her nipples hardening. The bartender couldn't take his eyes off her breasts as he handed over her drink, and Jenny couldn't resist giving her chest a playful shake. He looked up, then grinned sheepishly. "Sorry."

"That's okay. I'm glad you like them." She turned away, smiling at his open-mouthed shock. Never in her life had she made such a statement before, but tonight, she felt again the way she had on that trip out to California. That same thrill she had experienced when she'd given Devlin and Damien a look at her breasts. Alive, and sexy, and free.

Jenny knew immediately when they had returned, their presence exerting an actual, physical pull on her, so that she knew not only that they were there, but exactly where they were at each and every moment. The feeling was so intense, it scared her.

Once again, as though sensing her anxiety, Damien managed to reassure her. They didn't even speak, but his gaze met hers, and something in his eyes calmed her. It occurred to her that she should be scared by *that*, as well, but somehow she couldn't muster up any concern. As she glanced over at him again, his gaze traveled over her body like a liquid caress, coming to rest on the swell of her butt. Jenny turned and walked over to another group, her hips swaying, the tiny beads shifting inside her, feeling his rapt gaze almost like a physical touch.

"Jenny!" She looked up to see her uncle walking toward her, with Dev and Damien in tow. "I want you to meet someone."

"This is my niece, Jenny Dalton." Frank waved a hand toward the brothers. "Jenny, I wanted you to meet Devlin and Damien Blake. Their father was a client, and a good friend of mine."

Jenny held out her hand, an electric tingle racing up her arm as she shook each of theirs. "It's nice to meet you."

"Their father passed away recently, and the boys are in town to check on his portfolio, get some of the estate issues taken care of. They're not from around here, so I thought you might like to give them an idea of what they should see while they're in New York." He winked. "I'd tell them myself, but you'd probably have a better idea what people their age might be interested in." With that, he smiled and walked away.

Jenny sighed. "Sorry about that. I guess he's decided to try and play matchmaker."

Dev grinned. "No problem."

Damien smiled, as well. "Now we have a perfectly good excuse to call you tomorrow."

Jenny's heart fluttered. "Are you? Going to call?"

His look was all the answer she needed, bringing a hot flush to her cheeks. "Join us for a fresh drink?"

She nodded, beckoning over a waiter and placing her now-warm margarita on his tray. "Thank you." Damien placed his hand on her lower back, guiding her over to the bar.

When they had their drinks in hand, Devlin led them to a quiet corner of the room, and the three of them stood, backs to the wall, watching the crowd. Damien's hand crept beneath her dress, his fingers catching up the silver chains. Jenny's pulse quickened, and she glanced at him from beneath her lashes.

A smile teased the corners of his lips, and he tugged gently on the chains, watching her face. She took a deep breath, locking gazes with him as he continued manipulating the delicate strands.

A spiral of need sprang up in Jenny, tightening with each subtle movement inside her. She found herself breathing quickly, as though she'd been running.

Dev stepped in front of her, facing them, shielding her from prying eyes. Jenny didn't even protest as she felt the zipper being drawn down. Felt Damien's determined fingers searching for her tight hole, then pushing inside, moving the beads deeper, guiding more of the two chains into the narrow canal. She closed her eyes as a ripple of pleasure shot through her body. "That's it," Devlin murmured. "Come for him, Jenny."

Damien began pulling one of the chains out, his finger swirling, wrapping it around the digit and stimulating her throbbing rim in the process. Jenny gasped. "That's it," Dev urged under his breath. "That's it, Jen. Come." Damien was pulling out the other chain now, his finger twirling rapidly. "Come *now!*" Jenny drew in a deep, gasping breath and stared into Devlin's eyes as the orgasm ripped through her, every nerve in her body urging her to cry out, to moan, to sigh, but she couldn't make a sound; people would hear. She reached out and grasped his hands, squeezing hard as the ecstasy went on and on, until she thought she was going to pass out.

"Breathe, Jenny." Damien spoke into her ear. Jenny let her breath out, and breathed in again. The orgasm finally crested and began to recede, leaving her shaking and weak-kneed. Damien pulled up her zipper, keeping the chains tucked inside her dress. "Good girl," he whispered in her ear, and she felt heat rising in her cheeks. How could she have let him do that to her in public?

Devlin's eyes were knowing, and Jenny tried to look away, but they held her, a deep blue sky that she was falling into, weightless. "We have to go now, Jenny," he murmured. "But we'll see you tomorrow."

She swallowed and nodded, not trusting herself to speak. Damien and Devlin made their way through the crowd, glancing at her over the sea of intervening bodies as they told her uncle goodbye, and then they were gone, and Jenny spent the rest of the night wondering if it had all been some strange waking dream, brought on by the press of people and her own feeling of displacement.

Heat

Jenny pulled the covers up over her head as someone knocked on the door again. "Jenny," her mother called. "There's a phone call for you."

She sat up in bed. "A call?" The events of the night before came rushing back, and she forced herself to breath slowly and deeply. "Okay, I'm up!" She picked up the extension on her bedside table. "Hello?"

There was a quiet click as Hannah, her mother's housekeeper, hung up. Her heart thrilled as Damien's deep voice came over the line. "Jenny?"

"Hi."

"Hi. How did you sleep?"

She started to say she had slept fine, but instead, found herself saying, "I didn't."

A soft laugh alerted her to the fact that Devlin was also on the line. "Why not?" he asked.

Jenny hesitated, but couldn't think of a single reason not to tell the truth. They both knew she wanted them; she'd made *that* perfectly clear the night before. There was no reason to play the coy, shy violet now -- they wouldn't believe it. "Because I was horny as hell, and nothing I did helped."

"Mmmm," Damien murmured. "I like the sound of that. Did you play with yourself last night, Jenny?"

Heat rose in her cheeks again. Damn him! Why did he keep doing this to her? She should hang up, let him know that he couldn't pull her chain whenever he wanted to. She winced at the unfortunate analogy. She *should* hang up on him. But she didn't. Instead, she said, "Yes."

"Will you show us?" Devlin asked. "Today. When we see you. Will you show us what you were doing?"

Jenny couldn't answer. Her voice wouldn't work.

"Please, Jenny. I want to *see*," Devlin whispered.

Her pussy wept. "Yes," she croaked. "I'll show you."

Devlin's long sigh was a gift. "I can't wait."

"Can we take you to lunch today, Jenny? Someplace quiet." The tone of Damien's voice held such promise that Jenny's pussy convulsed.

"Okay." She thought rapidly. "I know a place. What time?"

"When will the lunch crowd thin out?" he asked.

"Um, around two, I guess."

"And how long will it take us to get there?"

"About thirty minutes."

"Then we'll pick you up at one-thirty. Does that sound okay?"

Jenny nodded, then realized he couldn't hear that and said, "Yes."

"Good. We'll see you then."

Jenny hung up the phone and sat staring at it for several minutes as various parts of her body began to throb in anticipation. "I need a shower." Rising, she padded into the bathroom and turned on the water, making it as cold as she could stand it, and even then, she felt as though each drop should be turning to steam the moment it touched her skin.

* * *

They picked her up in the old blue pickup, grinning like fools as she clapped her hands in delight. "We thought it would be appropriate," Devlin said.

Jenny scooted in beside Damien, then Dev slid in and shut the door. "Where to?" Damien asked. Jenny gave him directions, and they pulled away from the sidewalk.

Dev turned toward her in the seat, the teasing light in his eye replaced with dark desire. "Show us," he said.

Jenny didn't hesitate. She pulled her blouse out of her skirt and slowly undid the buttons, keenly aware of both their gazes -- Damien's quick glances as he drove, Devlin's steady regard. She began rolling her nipples between her thumbs and forefingers, becoming more and more aroused as Dev's breathing quickened, his tongue darting out to moisten his lips as he watched. She drew one hand down along her belly, pulling up her short skirt, brushing her fingertips across the tight curls at her groin.

She could feel Damien's desire, as well; heard it in his rapid breathing, felt it in the quick, hot glances he cast her way. She drew up her legs, sitting cross-legged between them, resting her thighs against theirs as she fingered her clit, moaning softly. She looked at Devlin longingly, willing him to touch her. "No," he said, seeming to read her mind. "We want to watch *you* do it."

Jenny very deliberately slipped her forefinger inside her pussy, then just as deliberately pulled it out. She brought it to her mouth and engulfed the entire digit, sucking noisily as they watched, their breathing ragged and broken. She repeated the process with her middle finger, then with her ring finger, and still they wouldn't touch her.

Jenny arched against the seat. "Please," she begged.

"No," Damien insisted. "We want you to do it."

"But it won't work!" Jenny wailed. "I tried and tried last night, and nothing worked."

"Touch yourself, Jenny," Damien urged. "Show us what you did."

Frustrated, she plunged two fingers into her pussy. "This! All right? I fucked myself with two fingers, and when that didn't work, I --" She hesitated.

"What?" Dev asked. "What did you do?"

She shook her head.

"Do it, Jenny." Damien's voice left no room for argument.

Jenny brought her hand to her mouth and wet the entire length of her forefinger. Then she brought it down to her pussy. She thrust her middle finger and ring finger into her pussy, and hesitated again. "Do it," Damien said.

Jenny swallowed, then slid down a little in the seat to give herself better access. When she pushed the tip of her forefinger into her ass, Devlin drew in a sharp breath. "Oh, fuck!" He undid his pants with frantic fingers and began pumping his shaft as he watched.

Seeing the effect she was having on him sent a thrill of pleasure spiraling through her. She pushed the finger in deep, then pulled it out slowly. Dev's motions quickened.

Beside her, Damien took one hand from the wheel and unzipped his pants, as well, pulling out his cock. Jenny couldn't contain her gasp. He was even thicker than Dev, and at least two inches longer, and her pussy clenched at the thought of having that huge member buried inside her. She moaned, pushing her finger in and out of her anus more and more rapidly, finding her G-spot with the two fingers buried inside her pussy. "Oh, God," she gasped, as droplets appeared on the tips of both their cocks. "Oh, God!" Her pussy convulsed, and she was arching, pressing her thighs together tight around her wrist, as the orgasm rocketed through her. "Oh, yes!"

Dev's hand came up and tangled in her hair, drawing her head down to his cock just in time for her to take him in her mouth before his seed spilled. She drank greedily, her own body spasming as she came again. With a final shudder, he let go, and Jenny sat up, only to have Damien wrap his hand around the back of her head, guiding her down urgently.

His seed erupted so forcefully that she nearly choked, but she willed herself to swallow, drinking the thick, musky essence from a cock so big she could only take the crown of it into her mouth. In the back of her mind, she was amazed at the fact that he was still able to drive, but the pleasure of having his hot, pulsing flesh in her mouth drove the thought away. She kept drinking, awed at the amount of cum spurting into her mouth, wishing the hot flood were filling her pussy. Finally, he let go. "Jenny," he sighed.

She sat up, wiping her mouth. Damien grabbed her head again and kissed her, hard. "I have to fuck you," he whispered.

"Yes, please," she murmured. "Oh, please, yes."

"Tonight."

Jenny sat back abruptly. "Tonight?"

Damien nodded, fastening his pants as he drove, not even looking at the road, but guiding the car unerringly. One part of her brain realized she should wonder at that, but the only thought she had room for was the image of Damien's gigantic cock plunging into her pussy. "Promise?" she asked.

Damien kissed her again, plundering her mouth until her limbs seemed to melt. "Does that answer your question?" he whispered brokenly.

Jenny nodded mutely. "You'd better get dressed," he reminded her. "We're almost there."

As she pulled herself together physically, she tried to regain her wits mentally. What was it about these two? How could they make her want to do things so desperately, and not care who saw or what they thought of her? The questions were pushed aside as Damien pulled into the parking lot.

Once inside, Damien chose a table in a quiet corner, and the waiter took their drink orders. After he left, Damien leaned forward. "Tell us about yourself, Jenny."

Jenny shrugged. "There's nothing much to tell."

"What do you do?" Devlin asked.

"I'm a designer and seamstress for a company that produces historically accurate costumes for different time periods."

"You mean, for movies, that sort of thing?"

"Well, up until last week, it was for other things. Plays. People who are into the Society for Creative Anachronism. Do you know what that is?" Devlin and Damien both nodded. "And we have a couple of restaurants and hotels for clients. They're theme-oriented places, using period costumes as uniforms for their personnel."

Her escorts shared a glance. "So, what happened last week?"

Jenny smiled. "We finally got a movie contract. Well, a contract to do the costumes for a production company that's filming a movie. It's actually a pretty big deal. Not an indie filmmaker or anything. B&B Productions." Jenny felt silly, but she couldn't contain her excitement. She, Carol, and Becca had been working toward this goal from the beginning, and it was fantastic to finally feel like they were going to make it.

"That's great!" There was an underlying amusement in Devlin's tone that made Jenny wonder, but the waiter returned with their drinks, and they shifted their attention to the menu so they could place their orders.

After the waiter left, Damien asked, "Tell us about your life, say…seven years ago." He grinned and wiggled his eyebrows.

Jenny blushed. "I want you to know, that whole thing was an accident."

"There are no accidents," Damien said, seeming quite serious.

"No, really. It was hot, and my bra was sticking to me like a second skin. You guys were far enough back that I knew you couldn't see what I was doing, so I pulled it off. But then the wind caught it, and…well, you know."

Devlin grinned, raising his glass of tea for a mock toast. "Here's to accidents." Jenny smiled as she and Damien touched their glasses to his, but she noticed another odd glance passing between them. What was going on here?

Damien changed the subject, talking about his and Devlin's summers on their grandfather's land in Wyoming. Jenny found herself relaxing as she got to know them. Devlin was definitely a joker, relating raucous tales of teenage hijinks, quick to smile and always with a good-natured air about him. Damien was more serious, but not as though he were disturbed or sad. He simply looked at everything very deeply, refusing to dismiss anything as trivial. He was most passionate about his family's generations-long commitment to the environment. Jenny found herself liking them both more and more as they continued to talk over dinner, over dessert, and then over coffee, as they all seemed reluctant to bring the day to a close.

Finally, she sighed. "I hate to say this; I've had such a great time, but I have to get back. We're having dinner with one of my mother's friends tonight, and I'm afraid it's not something I can get out of."

"Of course." Damien motioned for the waiter and took care of the check.

Nestled between the two of them in the truck, Jenny felt warm and secure. The sleepless night caught up with her, and she fought to keep her eyes open.

Damien put his arm around her. "It's all right. Go ahead and close your eyes for a minute."

She stifled a yawn and leaned against him, meaning to rest her head on his shoulder for just a second. The next thing she knew, he and Devlin were shaking her gently awake.

"I'm sorry," she said, then smiled. "But it's your fault, you know."

Devlin laughed as he helped her out of the truck. "I'll tell you a secret. We didn't sleep last night, either."

Jenny shook her head, but Damien's expression convinced her it was true. Her breath caught in her throat as he bent his head, planting a brief, intensely passionate kiss on her lips. He stepped back, and Jenny looked at Devlin. He hesitated, glancing up and down the street. She realized that he was uncomfortable for *her* sake, thinking that she might be worried about the neighbors. She stepped up to him and kissed him long and lingeringly. When she finally pulled away, he held her, hands on her waist. "You're something else, Jenny Dalton."

She looked at them both. "There's something different about the two of you. Something special." She gave them both long, searching glances. "I hope...I hope this isn't a game." She didn't give either one of them the chance to respond, pushing past them to hurry up the stairs, waving goodbye from the porch before she disappeared inside.

Rendezvous

Jenny woke abruptly. She was burning up. Feverish. She'd been dreaming, but she couldn't remember what the dream was about, only that something had frightened her terribly. She sat up in bed. The heater was on, blowing hot air against her already heated skin. Slipping out of the bed, she walked over to the window. It had snowed heavily during their visit, and her mother's friend Wendy had insisted that Jenny and her parents bed down here for the night. The place was in the country, and the new-fallen snow glittered in the light of a bright moon floating in the now-cloudless, starlit sky. A flash of movement in the shadows beneath the trees caught her eye, then was gone.

Jenny picked up her slacks from the top of the dresser and stepped into them, then tugged on her sweater. She opened the bedroom door quietly and made her way to the kitchen. Stepping out onto the porch, she again glimpsed a flutter of movement from the corner of her eye. Oblivious to the cold, she stepped out into the yard, jogging quickly to the verge of a wooded hill behind the house.

A shaft of moonlight outlined a silvery tail as it disappeared between two trees. Though Jenny knew she should turn around and go back, she gave in to the compulsion to follow the grey shadow a little further. She'd gone only a few feet, finding it much darker beneath the trees than she'd expected, when a twig cracked behind her. She whirled around.

A massive silver wolf sat on its haunches, watching her with intelligent blue eyes. As she backed away, it stood yawning, baring fangs she would have sworn were the size of her hand. Then its muscles tensed, and Jenny's legs started moving even before her mind registered the fact that the wolf was going to attack.

She ran for her life, flowing in and out between the trees with a grace and speed she had never suspected she possessed. For a fleeting instant, she actually imagined she was going to be able to outrun the beast, and then she burst into a clearing, and there was another wolf.

Not quite as big as the one behind, but no less formidable to someone like her. She froze with fear. A crashing sound in the brush at her back warned her that the other wolf was getting close, but she couldn't move. She braced herself for the impact she knew was coming.

Leaves rustled behind her. Hot breath raised the hair on the back of her neck, and Jenny's legs buckled. The wolf before her stepped forward tentatively as she dropped to her knees. Stiff fur pricked through her pants as the wolf behind nudged her rear with a huge muzzle. Jenny clenched her fists, gasping as the beast in front of her also stepped forward and buried his snout in her crotch. Even more shocking was the heat that flooded her groin at their touch. What was wrong with her?

The smaller wolf sat back on his haunches, uttering a low growl that was almost like speech.

The animal behind quit nuzzling her rear and stepped around her, settling back on its haunches, as well. The two wolves stared at her, beautiful and terrible, moonlight reflecting from their brilliant blue eyes. Eyes that Jenny recognized, with dark depths that threatened to drown her.

And that's when she figured out what…no, *who* they were. She held out a hand, reaching for the larger wolf's chest, but hesitating just before she touched that glowing, silver-grey fur. "Damien?"

The wolf huffed and lowered its head. The beast licked her hand, its tongue rough and nearly as wide as her palm. Jenny shook her head, but she knew deep in her heart that she was right. She looked at the other wolf. "Devlin?"

The wolf cocked its head, baring its fangs in a frightening grin, tongue lolling from the side of its mouth. Jenny shook her head again. "What…what do you want from me?"

Damien huffed again, then opened his mouth and caught the edge of one fang in the sleeve of her sweater, pulling on it. Jenny's heart began to beat so fast and strong that she could almost hear it. Dev stood, nudging her cheek with a damp muzzle. Then they both sat back again. Waiting. The clearing was so silent, so still, that it seemed as though time itself had stopped.

Her brain whirled with impressions of the last two days. The almost supernatural way she had known where they were in a room, the times they seemed to be reading her mind, the size of certain parts of their anatomy, the way they always felt feverish to her. The fact that when they were around, the cold didn't affect her the way that it should. Even now. She looked down at herself, kneeling in a half-foot of snow, not even feeling it. Things that hadn't quite seemed right, but also weren't so wrong that she had worried that much about them. Could she accept this?

Hands shaking, she grasped the hem of her sweater and pulled it up over her head. She could feel their joy, a physical heat that washed over her in a palpable wave. Taking a deep breath, she pushed her slacks down past her hips and stepped out of them.

Jenny stood, letting their tongues bathe her -- licking, exploring, touching every part of her body save for the place she wanted it most. Finally, trembling with need, she grasped the ruffs of their necks, whispered in their ears. "Please. Take me." She threw her arms around Damien's neck. "You promised. Tonight."

His fur bristled, his nose quivering as he scented her arousal in the air. Jenny lay back in the snow, parting her legs, offering herself to him. He brought his head down, watching her with those incongruously human eyes as he lapped up her juices with his broad tongue. She spread her legs further, held them wide while Damien's tongue drank of her essence.

Devlin settled in the snow next to her, his breath hot on her chest. He opened his huge muzzle and covered her, kneading one captured breast between his tongue and the roof of his mouth. His eyes gleamed knowingly as Jenny sighed and arched into him. He flicked his tongue across her sensitive nipple, drawing out a cry of delight. The wuffling growl in the back of his throat was the echo of a dozen chuckles they'd had together in the short time she'd known him.

Damien's fur caressed her thighs, soft and silky as the golden strands she had run her fingers through earlier that day. Jenny moaned. She was on fire, burning with need. "Please, Damien."

He backed away, moving with exquisite grace and power to lie on one haunch beside her. He ducked his head and ran his tongue between his legs, and Jenny saw his huge erection and groaned in frustration.

She would have been hard-pressed to accommodate the cock he sported as a human. In his wolf form, it would be impossible.

Devlin left off his erotic torture of her breasts, nudging her shoulder. She raised up on her elbows, casting him a questioning glance. He nudged her again, more forcefully, and she sat up. "I don't understand." She glanced at Damien, who was still licking his cock.

Devlin nudged Jenny's shoulder again, then pressed his nose up against her butt. "You want me to...oh!" She swallowed. "But...he's too big. I can't."

Devlin huffed, baring his teeth, and nudged her again.

She turned, knowing now what they wanted, but scared. She pressed her hands into the hollow left by her shoulders, then paused, afraid to take the next step. There was no way she could take him. No way.

The sudden touch of Devlin's tongue on her lower back made her jump. He drew it down between the cheeks of her butt.

Her pussy throbbed in response, and she raised her ass just a little. Devlin's tongue probed eagerly, searching. Jenny's anus tingled, anticipating his touch, and she crossed her arms, dropping her shoulders down so that she could rest her head on her forearms. She spread her legs a bit, thrusting her ass high.

Devlin's thick tongue flexed, working its way between her cheeks. She cried out in delight as the rough, damp surface finally rasped against her tight opening.

Her face was turned toward Damien, and he raised his head. His gaze met hers -- intelligent blue eyes dark with lust. Jenny's pulse quickened. She glanced again at his massive, fur-covered cock.

Damien raised his head, and his howl reverberated through the night, so loud and deep a sound that Jenny felt the vibration in her teeth and bones. But her eyes were glued to his cock, and as she watched, it twitched, the furry sheath beginning to retract.

She gasped. A glistening red protrusion was revealed, lengthening rapidly until it was longer and thicker than his human cock, dripping with pre-ejaculate. Despite her concerns, Jenny felt herself overtaken by a wave of desire so powerful that she no longer thought of denying him.

Some deep part of her brain whispered that this was sick -- that she should run and never look back. But those were Damien's eyes. Watching her. Waiting.

"Yes," she whispered. "Please. Yes."

Devlin's tongue withdrew, and in one fluid movement, Damien straddled her, his great paws to either side of her elbows. His soft, furry underbelly tickled her back, and then he thrust.

She pushed herself up, arching as her pussy stretched, gasping at the searing heat of him. But then the pain faded, and she became aware of a deep throbbing that was unlike anything she had ever felt before. It took her a moment to realize that it wasn't her pussy throbbing. It was *him*. That long, thick member pulsed and undulated inside her. Flexing. Caressing her in a way no human cock ever could.

She wrapped her hands around Damien's forelegs, holding on as the first orgasm slammed through her. When it had passed, she waited for Damien to move, but he didn't. Her pussy responded to his cock's gentle pulsing, another climax building, but Jenny wanted more. Sobbing, she bucked against him. "Not this way," she choked out. "Fuck me, Damien. *Take me*."

Damien growled, and Jenny sensed that the fragile thread of his control had broken. He nipped her shoulder between two fangs as he withdrew, then plunged into her fiercely. "Yes!" She screamed as pleasure ripped through her yet again. "Oh, God, yes!"

Damien nipped her again, drawing blood, and Jenny gasped in sheer pleasure as his tongue lapped up her dark essence. Wave after wave of ecstasy crashed over her, and still she begged for more.

His thrusts became desperate, each one harder and quicker than the one before. She clenched her pussy around him and felt a ring of hot flesh swelling around the base of his cock, locking them together. "Yes," Jenny sobbed. She wanted him. Needed his hot seed loose inside her. Filling her. Quenching the fire in her belly.

Damien raised his head. Jenny's limbs quivered as her body spasmed in delight, her lover's fiery seed pouring into her like molten lava as a piercing howl rent the night.

* * *

Jenny woke in the guest bedroom. Her first thought was that it had all been a dream, but then she moved, and the soreness in her thighs and between her legs convinced her otherwise. When she tossed back the covers, she discovered that she was wearing her slacks and sweater. She had no idea how Devlin and Damien had managed to get her dressed and back in her room without being noticed. She didn't remember anything beyond that last, mind-shattering climax. Had she passed out? Or had one of them done something to make her sleep?

She walked stiffly to the bathroom and shucked her clothes. She still felt feverish, and she started a shower, keeping the temperature on the cool side. As she bathed, her hands began to shake. Abruptly, she sat down in the tub, tears spilling over.

What had she been thinking? Strangely enough, she could accept that Damien and Devlin were some kind of shape-shifters. Okay, fine. Admit it. Werewolves. What she couldn't accept was what she had allowed Damien to do to her in that form.

What would she say when she saw them again? How could the three of them have a normal conversation after *that?*

Then the pragmatist inside her kicked in, and she stood, washing the tears from her face. It was already done, and the only question remaining, really, was whether or not she would continue to see them.

And the reality was that she couldn't stand the thought of not seeing them again. Which seemed incredible, since she'd known them a sum total of about thirty-six hours. Was the mind-blowing sex that important to her?

But it wasn't just the sex. The twins were both incredibly easy to talk to, and the three of them shared many common interests. And already they seemed to cherish her, in a way no man had ever done before.

So. She definitely wanted to see them again. But they were going to have to talk about some things. Keep it strictly platonic for a little while.

Telling herself she was satisfied, she nodded and shut off the water. Stepping out of the tub, she dried off and searched out her underwear and bra, dressing again, quickly.

But for all that she told herself she was satisfied, there was a little voice inside Jenny's head reminding her that she didn't have much time. Only three and a half weeks before she went back to California. What would she do then? How could she allow herself to be in a situation where she might fall in love with someone -- *two* someones -- who lived on the other side of the continent?

Actually, that thought helped, because it put things into an entirely different perspective. There wasn't any reason why she had to take this whole thing so seriously. It wasn't like any of them had made any promises. She could continue to see these incredible brothers, enjoying both the friendship and the physical relationship while it lasted. She just wouldn't let herself fall in love with them.

Jenny tugged on her socks and shoes, and went out to breakfast with a much lighter heart.

The only problem was that damn persistent voice in her head, saying things she didn't want to hear.

Telling her that when it came to *not* falling in love, it was already far too late.

Fate

When Jenny heard Devlin's voice on the line three days later, it was like coming upon an oasis in the dessert.

"Dev!"

"Hi, Jenny." There was a long silence.

"I missed you," Jenny finally said.

Devlin drew in a sharp breath. "Really?"

"Yes. Why…why didn't you call? Sooner."

"Damien and I thought you might need…a little time. To…assimilate things."

"I don't need time, Dev. I need to see you. Both."

"Yeah?" His voice recovered some of its usual jovial tone. "You're not…you still want to see us?"

Jenny smiled. "Definitely."

"So, if we wanted to take you out to dinner tonight…?"

"What time are you picking me up, and how should I dress?"

Devlin was again silent for a long moment. When he spoke, his voice was thick with emotion. "You're incredible, Jen."

"You've said that before."

"I meant it."

"I know. That's one of the reasons I can't walk away from this."

Devlin laughed. When he spoke again, he sounded like his old self. "Seven o'clock. Something casual."

"I'll be ready."

Jenny could hardly restrain herself when they came to pick her up. She waited until they had climbed into the truck, then threw her arms around Devlin, hugging him tight. He hugged her back, smiling, planting a quick kiss on her lips. When she turned to Damien, he was staring at the road ahead. Jenny placed her hands on either cheek and turned him to face her. "Kiss me, Damien."

He released a pent-up breath and did just that, taking her mouth with a heat that threatened to melt her tongue and turn her lips to putty.

Jenny drew in a shaky breath as he pulled away. "Well, hello!"

Damien grinned sheepishly. Jenny rested her cheek on his shoulder for a minute, then sat up. "Let's go eat. I'm starving!"

When they were safely ensconced in a quiet booth at Jenny's favorite steak place, she decided they might as well get everything out into the open. She played with her straw nervously, wondering what to say first.

"I'm sorry." Damien's voice was gruff.

Jenny raised her eyebrows. "For what?"

"For...taking you that way. It was...I don't know. We should have talked first. I should have told you. What we were."

Jenny swirled her straw in her drink, watching the whirlpool diminish as she organized her thoughts. "It's okay, Damien." She looked up, meeting his gaze, not bothering to hide the desire she felt. "I wanted it. You didn't force me to do anything. As I recall, I even begged for it." Heat rushed to her cheeks, but she wouldn't look away. "I don't think there was a better way, really. I mean, I would have thought you were crazy, if you'd tried to tell me."

"You're being too generous."

Jenny leaned forward earnestly. "Not generous, Damien. Selfish. Trust me." She was seated between them, in a semicircular booth, and she reached out to take one of their hands in each of hers. "I want it, Damien. Devlin." She let go, slipping her hands between their legs, caressing the distinct bulge at each of their crotches. "All of it." She smiled wickedly as they shifted, spreading their legs as she explored, cupping their balls through the fabric. "The companionship. The conversation." She licked her lips, giving each of them a hungry glance. "The sex. I'll only be here three more weeks. I want to make the most of every minute."

They groaned simultaneously, the fabric of their pants straining. "God, Jen."

"Come on."

Jenny scooted up against Damien, forcing him to stand. Taking their hands, she led them toward the back of the restaurant. She tugged them into one of the bathrooms, locking the door behind her. They watched, bemused, as she tugged down her jeans and turned, bracing herself against the counter. "Oh, fuck!" In the mirror, she watched Devlin's fingers, trembling as he fumbled with his zipper.

"Let me help." Jenny turned and deftly released his cock, pushing his pants down past his hips. She ran her fingers over his hard length. "Oh, yes," she murmured. "I can't wait to have this inside me."

Dev groaned and grabbed her hips, turning her quickly. Damien had pulled down his pants, as well, and was now leaning against the counter, massaging his cock. Without a word, Jenny bent, taking Damien's ripe head in her mouth as Devlin's cock pushed between her swollen lips. "Oh, shit," Damien murmured, and then his hot seed was slaking her thirst, even as Dev thrust once, twice, three times, and then exploded inside her. She drank greedily, whimpering as her own orgasm rippled through her.

When their climaxes faded, Jenny stood, licking her lips. Damien groaned and moved forward, hugging her shoulders as Devlin wrapped his arms around her waist. "God, Jenny," Devlin murmured. "You drive us crazy."

She grinned impishly. "Then we're even, because you do the same to me."

They stood there, locked in a tender embrace, until Jenny said, "You know, we should probably be getting back."

Dev and Damien moved away reluctantly, pulling their pants up as Jenny tugged her jeans back over her hips. They washed their hands, then headed back to the table.

Their waiter raised his eyebrows as he witnessed their return, but said nothing. Jenny giggled as they slid back into the booth. Their food was waiting, and Damien reassured the waiter that they didn't need anything further. As the man walked away, Devlin slipped his hand between Jenny's legs, squeezing her crotch. "I'm still horny," he whispered in her ear.

She placed her hand over his, pressing into him. "Later," she promised. She glanced between them. "All night long, if you want." She looked down. "How-- however you want it."

Damien put his arm around her back, his hand slipping under her sweater to caress her breast. "You mean that?" he asked.

She wriggled. "Yes," she sighed. "Hell, yes."

She had never eaten a meal as quickly in her life as she did that one.

As the truck pulled out of the parking lot, Jenny shimmied out of her jeans and lay across the seat, resting her head in Dev's lap, drawing her legs up onto the seat between the two brothers. Devlin caressed her hair, then reached beneath her sweater, teasing her nipples into taut peaks. She watched Damien's stormy eyes stealing brief peeks at her pussy until he had the truck on the highway. Then he met her gaze and reached out, touching her wet lips. He inhaled deeply. "Mmmm. You're so ready."

She nodded, arching as Devlin pulled her sweater off over her head and bent to suck her swollen nipples. Damien slid two fingers inside her. She grasped Dev's hand, urging him to join his brother. She moaned as he obliged, their four fingers dancing inside her.

Jenny made an inarticulate sound of disappointment as Damien withdrew, but a moment later, his thumb was inside her. His fingers, covered with her juices, slid between her butt-cheeks, and she raised her hips, reaching down to hold them apart while his fingers sought her anus. His forefinger teased the tight pucker, flicking back and forth over it. Jenny moaned. He eased the tip past her rim, wiggling it gently. "Mmmm." Her pussy and anus both tightened.

"I like that reaction," Devlin murmured. "Do it again, Damien."

Damien slowly worked his finger deeper, massaging the tight canal as Jenny's breath came in ragged gasps, her pussy and anus contracting erratically as pulses of pleasure shot through her. "Mmmm. Oh, yes."

Damien's thumb withdrew, and Dev's fingers began to explore her pussy, delving deeper. Jenny shuddered as he located her G-spot. "Oh, you like that?" He grinned as she nodded vigorously, unable to trust her voice. A moment later, she cried out as Damien trapped the intervening flesh between his finger and his brother's.

"Oh, God," she sobbed. Damien's middle finger edged in past her tight rim. "Oh!"

Damien hesitated, looking at her in concern. "Should I stop?"

Jenny writhed. "Oh, God, no. Please don't stop."

Damien abruptly pulled off the road, the truck bouncing as he guided it along two ruts into the trees. He killed the engine and turned toward her. She watched as he reached out with his other hand, pressing her cheeks back, watching as he worked a second finger into her ass. She let go of her cheeks, putting one of her hands on Devlin's as she pulled his head down, rubbing the heel of his hand against her clit as she plumbed his mouth desperately.

Devlin reached out with his other hand, capturing her clit between two fingers and milking it as she whimpered and writhed. Every nerve in her body was singing, a tight core of heat gathering in her belly.

"Hurry, Damien, please!" she urged. "All the way." She reached down desperately, pulling her cheeks as far apart as she could.

Damien matched her urgency, forcing his fingers deep inside her. "Yes," she urged. "Oh, yes. Finger-fuck me. Both of you."

Their breath came in ragged gasps as they began plunging their fingers in and out. Jenny rose up on her elbows, watching Devlin's fingers glide rapidly between her glistening lips, Damien's hand twist and turn as he plumbed her ass. "Oh, God!" She bucked repeatedly, meeting them thrust for thrust, until the hot core inside her burst and her pussy and anus milked their fingers frantically. Devlin and Damien both raised their heads, howls ripping from their mouths.

Jenny lay panting after the orgasm faded. She rested her head in Devlin's lap, chuckling as she became aware of the huge bulge beneath her head. She sat up. "Where are we?"

"A back road off the highway, near the house you were visiting the other night." Damien looked out at the trees. "This is where Devlin and I came to change, that night." He turned to her. "We could smell you. Knew you were close."

"Do it." Jenny said. "Change. I want to see."

Damien took in a deep breath, then opened the driver's door. He stepped out, then turned back to her. Abruptly, he bent and drew his tongue over her crotch. "Damien," she whispered. His tongue invaded her pussy, his nose pressing against her clit. She sighed in delight. As Damien ate her hungrily, she raised her head, reaching for Dev's waist -- unfastening his pants, freeing his cock. She swept the tip of her tongue over his bulging head, tasting the drop of pre-ejaculate suspended there. Devlin growled, and she looked up. He arched, closing his eyes, and his shirt ripped as his chest expanded. He opened the passenger door abruptly and slipped from beneath her.

Another growl, this time at her crotch. Jenny looked down. As she watched, Damien's face broadened, his nose lengthening into a muzzle, fur sprouting from his skin. His tongue thickened and became rough, rasping against her labia as he drank her juices. Her pussy spasmed in excitement. Damien nuzzled her roughly, running his tongue between her cheeks, licking from her anus back up to her pussy. His hands, where they rested on the seat, seemed to spread out, becoming great, hairy paws tipped by five-inch claws that tore into the leather.

A howl sounded behind her. Damien raised his head and backed away. Jenny sat up, turning to discover Devlin, fully transformed, sitting on his haunches, muzzle raised to the sky.

Jenny stepped out of the truck and knelt between his forelegs, wrapping her hands around his furry cock. She stroked him, hard and fast. When the sheath began to move, the first hint of red flesh glimmering in the moonlight, she stood and turned, presenting herself to him, bracing against the truck seat.

The truck shivered as his broad paws pressed down on the running board. She could see Damien sitting just outside the other door, panting as he watched. And then heat invaded her once more, as Devlin plumbed her pussy with his slick, rippling cock, and she shuddered, losing herself in the feel of him as he plunged into her again and again, his breath hot on her back. Then she felt the knot swelling at the base of his penis, and shivered in anticipation of his release. His essence flowed, hot seed spilling into her. Jenny arched, pleasure sparking through her again and again as his cock pulsed within.

Slowly, the swelling abated and his member retracted. The truck shuddered as Dev's paws dropped heavily to the ground. Jenny shivered, closing her eyes and spreading her legs as his snout pressed between them, his warm tongue lapping at their mingled juices. She moaned, pressing into his touch, her pussy throbbing. Devlin gave her one last lick, then trotted around the truck.

Jenny followed. Devlin flattened an area of snow with his paws, then lay on his side, panting. Damien watched Jenny, blue eyes gleaming in the moonlight. She moved before him, and would have knelt and taken his cock between her hands, but he backed away, shaking his great head.

Puzzled, she reached out to him. "Damien, please. I want to have both of you inside me tonight." She heard Devlin move behind her, but she only had eyes for Damien.

Damien hesitated, nose quivering. Jenny felt the moisture between her legs, and knew he scented her arousal. "Please. I need to feel you." She took a step forward. "Ride me, Damien," she whispered huskily.

Jenny blinked as, without warning, Damien leapt. But suddenly, Devlin was there, standing between them, and Damien stopped short.

"Dev!"

Damien growled, a low, basso rumble that made Jenny's teeth ache. Devlin held his ground, facing Damien. His head was lowered as though in submission, but he snarled back at Damien.

Damien lunged, snapping at Devlin's neck, but the smaller wolf dodged away, then flowed back, keeping himself between her and his brother. Damien's eyes narrowed, and he snarled, baring his fangs.

"No." Jenny pushed past Devlin. "Don't do this." She turned her back to Damien, looking into Devlin's eyes. "I want this, Devlin. Why are you --"

Damien's paws hit her back, driving her to the ground, knocking the breath from her. She rolled over. Damien was straddling her, facing Devlin, the both of them snarling and snapping at each other. "D-Damien?" she stammered. She could hardly hear herself over the noise.

He must have heard, however, because he looked down at her, and his eyes widened. He stared for a moment, then whimpered, backing away. Devlin stepped forward, planting his paws to either side of her waist, still snapping at his brother.

Damien hung his head. He began to change -- his great bulk diminishing, skin replacing fur -- until he knelt before them. A man, one arm braced against the ground.

Dev subsided, backing away, reclining on the ground again, but with his head up -- alert, watching Damien closely. Jenny pushed herself into a sitting position. "Damien?"

He moved quickly, full of the same liquid grace she admired in the wolf. His strong hands grasped her arms, raising her to her feet. He wrapped her in his arms and held her close.

She caressed his head where it rested on her shoulder. "What's wrong? What just happened?"

Damien took her hands in his and settled to the ground alongside Devlin, drawing Jenny down with him. Dev curled around them.

"We have to talk," Damien said.

She nodded, eyes searching his face.

"Forget everything you think you know about weyrwolves," he said. The way he pronounced it was funny, not the way she'd always heard it. "We've been around for centuries, all over the world, and we're part of the land, in a way no other living creature is. Each weyr line is Bound to a particular tract of land. Bound to watch over it, to increase it if they can. But always to protect that land from those who would spoil it."

He leaned against Devlin's flank, beckoning Jenny into the crook of his arm, and she settled in beside him. She felt Damien's nose in her hair, heard him breathing in her scent. Then he sighed. "You have to make a decision, Jenny." He ran a hand through his hair. "If you were a normal female...but you're not."

"What are you talking about?"

"Do you remember what you told us when we met? The first time."

"You mean, when I said I'd marry you if you could catch me?" Jenny gazed up at the stars. "Is that what you're asking, Damien? For me to marry you?"

Damien grunted in frustration. "I'm not doing this very well. It's more complicated than that."

Devlin's head rested on his huge paws, his eyes half-lidded, but Jenny could tell he was listening very closely. She wondered what he thought about this proposal. Was he jealous?

"We're not human, Jenny. Don't think for a moment that we are, just because we resemble humans on the surface. We live by different rules." He rubbed a hand through his hair again. "Okay. Weyr bear two kinds of young. One is a breeding pair. A set of male twins who will be Bound to that weyr's land, and carry on when the alpha passes away.

"The other is a female. If a weyr female mates with a weyr male, all her offspring, of whichever sex, will be weyr. Able to shift, like we do.

"If a weyr female mates with a human, their children will appear normal. They won't be Bound unless they mate with another weyr. But the Blood still flows in their veins. They aren't able to shift, but they're healthier, stronger, more in tune with the pulse of the earth. Sometimes, they're aware of their difference. Sometimes, they're completely oblivious to it."

Jenny shifted restlessly. "What does this have to do with me, Damien?"

His arm tightened around her shoulder. "You're weyr, Jen."

"What?" She sat up and stared at him.

"You're weyr. The Blood runs in your veins."

She shook her head. "That can't be." But even as she denied it, she felt a stirring inside. "How can you know?"

Damien shrugged. "There's more than one sign. We can smell it on you, for one thing. And there's a…a pull. The Blood whispers, when you're near." He smiled. "We feel and hear so many things, Jen. Things that humans are blind to. I know a million things about you that you don't know yourself. Like the fact that you're ovulating right now."

Jenny stared. What an odd thing to choose to tell her. "I'm ovulating."

Damien nodded. "Yes." He noticed her expression and tried to explain. "That's why Dev and I have avoided having vaginal intercourse with you on the same night. Weyr reproduction is different from humans. Individually, our sperm can't impregnate you -- they're inert. But together, intermingled within your body, each acts as a catalyst for the other." He leaned forward. "And it wouldn't be a question of *whether* you would become pregnant, only what type of litter you would bear."

He started to say more, but Jenny cut in. "So, you're telling me that if I ever have sex with you both, that particular way, on the same night, I'll *definitely* get pregnant."

Damien nodded.

"What about using condoms?"

Devlin snorted, as Damien shook his head. Thinking back on their size, and the ferocity of their encounters, Jenny figured they were probably right. It wouldn't work.

"Well, that's all right. Dev was protecting me from getting pregnant. I can understand that." Even as she said it, she felt a deep foreboding. Damien was working his way up to something big, but she couldn't imagine what it could be. Devlin rubbed his cheek against her leg, looking up at her with compassionate eyes, as though he sensed her anxiety.

Damien's next words confirmed her thoughts. "Jen, it's not just that. Dev hasn't shifted. That's because he's still protecting you."

"From what? You?" She shook her head. "Quit beating around the bush, Damien. Just tell me what's going on."

"Dev and I want you. To make you ours. Forever."

Jenny's heart did a joyful flip, but she forced down the sudden elation. She barely knew these men, and they weren't even human. "This is happening fast, Damien. Can't we just keep seeing each other for a while? Get to know one another better, before we talk about making this kind of decision?"

"I wish we could." Damien sighed. "If you were fully human, it would be easier. But you're not. Weyr Blood has much of the beast in it, and the Blood in you speaks to us stronger each day. Devlin and I try to keep that part of us controlled, but it's very difficult. Especially since we've been looking for you for seven years.

"I meant it when I said there are no accidents. We were fated to meet, Jen. The three of us belong together." He took her in his arms again, burying his face in her hair. "We never forgot you. Your voice. Your scent. We walked into that party and knew instantly that you were there. And when we saw you in the garden, and realized for the first time that you were of the Blood..." She felt him tremble slightly. "We almost Bound you, then and there."

He drew back, looking into her eyes. "You have to understand. Devlin and I can Bind you to us whether you want it or not. And once made, this Bond is broken only by death. But we love you. We want it to be your choice. But the longer we see you, the harder it gets. Devlin was able to stop me tonight. He might not be able to next time. He might not even *want* to. That's what he's afraid of. That's why he hasn't Changed." Damien's gaze bore into hers, and the depth of the desire Jenny saw there sent a chill down her spine. "Because the danger hasn't passed."

"You're the alpha, aren't you?" she whispered. "That's why it's harder for you, isn't it?"

Damien nodded. "The urge to Bind you, Jen, it's --" He shuddered and turned his face away, as if to hide what she might see there.

Jenny felt a terrible fear building inside her -- not a fear of Damien, but of what he was trying to tell her. "What's the bottom line, Damien?" she asked softly.

His voice was hoarse when he answered. "If you're not willing to make this relationship a permanent one, we can't see you any more."

She swallowed the lump in her throat. "Ever?"

Damien's silence was her answer.

"When do you have to know?"

Jenny started shaking her head even before he said, "Tonight." He caught her face between his hands. His eyes were full of pain, but his tone was determined. "We can't take another chance. We love you. If Devlin and I ended up *forcing* the Bond on you, it would destroy us."

She looked down. Saw her nakedness and suddenly felt very vulnerable. "I'd better get dressed."

Damien let go reluctantly. Jenny stood and walked to the truck. While she was gathering her clothes, Damien reached behind the driver's seat and pulled out a fresh pair of jeans and a t-shirt and tugged them on. Jenny dressed, her mind racing, while Damien gathered his and Dev's torn clothes and stuffed them into a plastic bag.

How could she say yes? Her heart ached at the mere thought of turning them away, but how could she be sure this was love? She might have been dreaming about Devlin and Damien for seven years, but the reality was a whole new ball game. There were things stirring inside her, knowledge barely sensed over the years, and often repressed. The Blood was singing to her now, and she knew instinctively that the Bond was not just a different word the weyr used for marriage. The Bond was something much more complicated, an immense commitment and responsibility. Something so completely different from the plan she had envisioned for her life that she couldn't take it in. Couldn't accept it. Couldn't submit to it.

When she was dressed, she turned to face Damien. Devlin stood and shook himself, then padded over to sit beside his brother. Jenny had to swallow several times before she felt she could trust her voice not to betray her. "I'm sorry." She stared at a point past their heads, unable to look them in the eye. If they saw how hard this was for her, she wasn't sure what they might do. "I'm just…I'm just not ready for this."

Devlin's claws dug into the ground, but Damien only nodded. "Okay." His voice was neutral. Empty. "We'd better head back." He swung up into the truck.

Jenny walked to the passenger side, blinking back tears. "What about Devlin?"

The vehicle shifted as Devlin jumped up and sprawled in the pickup's bed.

Jenny climbed into the truck and shut the door.

The drive home felt like a wake. She felt a mixture of relief and dread as they pulled up in front of her parents' home. Damien shifted the truck into neutral, staring straight ahead. Jenny reached out to touch his arm, but drew back at the last moment. "I'm sorry."

"It's all right, Jenny." Damien's voice was raw with pain, and suddenly she wanted to beg him to Bind her. To promise him *anything*, if he would just make her his and Devlin's forever. And that, more than anything, convinced her that she had made the right decision. She was willing to lose herself in them, and every fiber of her being fought against that. She had not worked so hard to escape her father's cage, only to be trapped inside another.

Jenny opened the door and stepped out, shutting it carefully behind her. Damien shifted the truck into gear as soon as she stepped away, and she stood in the street, watching until their tail-lights disappeared in the darkness.

Barren

Five days later, Jenny sat in the kitchen drinking coffee, staring into space. Plagued by strange dreams, she had hardly slept the last few nights.

Her mother glided gracefully into the room. "Good morning, darling."

"Hi, Mom." For the thousandth time since Damien's revelations, Jenny thought how much her mother's grace resembled the fluid movements of a wolf. Caught that whiff of odd scent -- an earthy smell, like a newly turned field. And musky, like sex. A scent she'd never noticed before, but which now permeated the house and originated with her mother. She pushed these unwelcome observations away, staring into her coffee cup.

Meredith fixed her own cup of coffee and sat across from Jenny at the breakfast bar.

"Mom, I've decided to go back a little early.

Meredith regarded her evenly. "How early?"

"Tomorrow." Jenny looked away. "I guess I'm feeling homesick."

"You're afraid."

Jenny turned back, startled. "What?"

"They're Wolves." It wasn't a question.

Jenny shook her head. "I don't know what you're talking about."

Meredith's gaze didn't waver. "My senses may have dulled over the years, but I still know a Wolf when I see one. And I don't doubt that they've told you the Blood runs in your veins, as well. In fact, I'm sure of it. I've seen the way you're listening lately. You hear it now. The whisper in your Blood."

Tears sprang to Jenny's eyes. "Why didn't you tell me?"

"There didn't seem to be any reason to." She tilted her head, considering. "If we had lived on the farm, like your uncle, it would have been harder. But the city drowns the whisper. You never seemed to feel it, so I didn't say anything."

"Why wouldn't you want me to know?"

"You wouldn't have believed me. If you hadn't met Devlin and Damien, would you ever have noticed?" She shook her head. "There aren't that many of us. Chances were that you would never meet another. At least, more than in passing. I thought it would be easier if you didn't know."

"Dad's not..." Jenny raised her eyebrows.

"You know he isn't." Meredith stared into space for a moment. "I did meet some, once. Other than the ones in our weyr, I mean. They were quite a gorgeous pair -- thick black hair, dark eyes. From an Italian branch." She smiled. "It was a delicious diversion, but I didn't love them."

"Did they love you?"

Meredith laughed. "No. We parted quite amicably." Her expression grew serious. "But what about you?"

"What about me?" Jen shrugged. "I already made my decision."

Meredith took a sip of her coffee, then sighed. "You don't seem very happy with it."

"I'm just...ready to get back to work." Even to her ears, that sounded lame. "Sure, the sex is great, but I barely know them." Meredith's steady gaze seemed reproachful. "I *don't* love them," Jenny insisted.

Her mother stared at her for several long moments. Jenny tried to look away, but Meredith's dark eyes were like molasses, sucking her in. Meredith leaned over the counter. "Let me tell you what *I* think." Jenny drowned in those eyes. She felt as though her soul were being laid bare and found wanting. "I think you do. That's what scares you. You're afraid of giving yourself to someone, heart and soul. Someone you might do anything for. Like turning away from the life you've worked so hard to build in California." This pronouncement was so close to what Jenny's actual thoughts had been that it raised goosebumps on her flesh.

"Why are you doing this?" Jenny fought back tears, her voice breaking.

Meredith reached out and clutched Jenny's hands in hers, tears glittering in her own eyes. "When I married your father, I left my home, my family. Oh, we visit, but I no longer live the life. Everything is different. The Bond is still there, but the land is far away, and the city drowns its voice, every day. Even now, other Wolves ask why I was willing to give up everything that mattered, just to be with a human." Her hands tightened on Jenny's. "They don't understand that *nothing* mattered without him."

There it was. The root of Jenny's problem. Her feelings for Devlin and Damien made everything she'd done for the past thirteen years a waste. Nothing else mattered but them. And how could she accept that? How could she accept that doing double shifts in a job she hated to pay for a second college degree, pulling up her roots and moving to the other side of the country, working twenty-hour days for the last seven years trying to help Hartmann Designs become what she needed it to be -- how could she accept that it all meant nothing without them? She couldn't. She was thirty-five years old. Her life up to this point had to have *meant* something.

The tears finally spilled, and Meredith hurried around the bar. She held her, rocking her daughter like she had when Jenny was a child. "Shh. It's all right, baby. Everything will be all right."

Blessings

Jenny's parents drove her to the airport, even thought they couldn't come in to see her off. "Promise you'll come back soon for another visit," her dad gruffed.

"I will."

Jenny stared out the window during the entire flight, carefully keeping her mind blank. It was a relief to finally step through the door of her apartment. Here, she'd be safe. Surrounded by everything she'd worked for, she would be able to put Devlin and Damien from her mind.

She tossed her keys on the table and dropped her bag by the door. She checked the answering machine, smiling when she heard Becca singing "I'll be home for Christmas" very badly. Apparently, she had decided that her parents were aliens from another planet, her brother's kids were demons from hell, and she was coming back early. "You never did say when you would be back, so I wanted to let you know I'll be home on the twenty-second, if you're in town and want some company."

The message should have lifted her spirits, but instead left her feeling sad. It was a shame that Becca's visit home wasn't turning out so great, either.

Jenny checked her fax machine and found a copy of the B&B Productions contract waiting for her. "I know how you are," Carol had written across the cover sheet, "so I went ahead and faxed this over because I didn't want you calling me at midnight on New Year's Eve wanting me to bring it over *right now.*"

Carol knew her well. Jenny chuckled wryly, carrying the stack of papers into the bedroom with her. She set them on the dresser, intending to look them over after she changed. But once she was in her nightgown, she felt utterly exhausted and crawled into bed, praying for a dreamless sleep.

She didn't dream, but still woke the next day feeling sluggish and irritable. Trying to shake herself out of it, she went to the beach and wandered aimlessly for a couple of hours, one of only a few hardy souls out braving the misty rain. She went to the mall, picking up a couple of presents for Becca and Carol, and some small gifts for the seamstresses Hartmann regularly employed. She ate dinner out and returned to the apartment after nine o'clock, worn out.

For the next several days, this became her pattern. For the first time, her apartment felt like a cage. Her space no longer seemed warm and cozy. It was cluttered. Suffocating. So she wandered the beach, the mall, the boardwalks, keeping herself busy and active. Outside, the restless whisper in her veins grew stronger, but the sounds of the city made it easier to ignore. She came home so exhausted, she fell asleep the moment her head hit the pillow, and the dreams stayed away.

But the twenty-second dawned a sickly grey. Dark, ugly clouds dumped buckets of rain, flooding the streets. She pulled on some sweats and made hot chocolate. She considered calling Becca to see if she was home yet, but some part of her still wanted to be alone, so she curled up on the bed with a book.

The steady rhythm of the rain, the warm chocolate, and the slow pace of the story combined to make her eyelids heavy. Setting the book aside, she closed her eyes, meaning to rest for only a minute.

She dreamed of the ocean. Or rather, the beach. She was a million grains of sand, washed by gentle wavelets, warmed by the sun. Crabs and clams, seagulls and minnows -- she had a thousand constant companions. But the water ceased its gentle caress. Receding, it left her, baking in merciless heat. Her companions fled, leaving her to the grasshoppers and ants that now roamed her surface, but eventually even these left. She hardened, her surface shriveling, cracking in the white glare.

Every part of her was there. She was as whole as she'd been before the water went away -- even more so, because waves no longer carried tiny bits of her out into the ocean.

But nothing moved on her parched surface. Nothing stirred within her. She was empty. Dead.

Gasping, Jenny sat up in the bed abruptly, clutching at her sweat-soaked shirt. She stumbled into the kitchen and fixed a glass of ice water, drank it down, then poured another and carried it back into the bedroom.

The Blood was pounding in her veins. Desperate for a distraction, she grabbed the contract on the corner of her dresser. She never had gone over it. She sat down in a chair by the window and began leafing through the pages. Each and every clause had two sets of identical initials by it, albeit in very different handwriting: *D.B.* She idly flipped to the back page, looking for names to go with the letters.

Her head swam as two signatures leaped from the page.

Devlin and Damien Blake.

Blake and Blake.

B&B Productions.

Her hands shook as she dropped the papers in her lap. Had they known? Of course they had known -- she told them where she worked. Why hadn't they said anything?

Because she'd never see them, that's why. They owned the company, but probably had very little to do with its daily operations. She ran an unsteady hand through her hair. There was no reason to freak out. This didn't change anything.

But it did. She stared down at the lines below their signature. At Devlin and Damien's address in Wyoming.

She was as parched as the desert in her dream, and just as empty. Jenny hesitated only a moment more before folding that page and sticking it in her pocket. She pulled a jacket from her closet, grabbed her purse and keys, and headed out to buy a map.

* * *

When she reached the address on the contract, she discovered it was a real estate broker's office. She'd driven eight hours the day before, spent a sleepless night in a dingy motel, and driven ten hours more that day. She was cold, tired, and hungry. It was eight o'clock on Christmas Eve, and there wasn't a hotel in sight.

The only place open was a small diner on the main street. She slid into a booth and ordered coffee, then sat there, head in her hands, tears streaming down her face.

"What's wrong, honey?" Her waitress asked when she brought the coffee out. "You're not lost, are you?"

Jenny wiped away the tears and shook her head. "No. I was...I was trying to find Devlin and Damien Blake." She dug in her pocket and pulled out the crumpled page from the contract. "I have an address for them, but it turned out to be a real estate office."

Her waitress -- Jenny glanced at the nametag pinned to her chest -- Tara, nodded. "Yep. That's 'cause they live so far out. No proper address. All their mail goes to Glen. They pick it up once a week." She fiddled with her pen for a minute, staring. "You're not from around here."

Obviously, Jenny thought, but she just said, "No."

"We got some nice fresh snow for Christmas."

Jenny remained silent, wrapping her hands around the coffee cup for warmth.

"That jacket doesn't look too warm," Tara observed.

"It's not." The girl evidently wanted to strike up a friendship, but Jenny really just wanted to be left alone to wallow in her misery.

"I don't suppose you want to know how to get there..." Tara mused.

Jenny looked up in surprise. "You'd tell me?"

Tara shrugged. "I don't think some slip of a girl is going to be able to cause *them* any harm." The way she spoke, Jenny almost thought she might know what they were. "I'll tell you. You won't even be able to get in, unless they let you."

That sounded ominous, but Jenny decided to worry about it later. "Thank you. Thank you very much."

Tara smiled. "You just let me know how it all works out, okay?" She winked and pulled a page off her notepad. "It's a bit of a drive. Takes about two hours, but at night, with you not knowing the roads, it might take a while longer."

Jenny nodded. Tara bent down over the table, drawing out a map and explaining to Jenny where to go. Jenny finished the rest of her coffee, more for the warmth than for anything else, then got back in her car and headed out again.

At eleven o'clock, her car labored up a winding gravel road somewhere in the Absaioka Range. At least, that's what Tara had called it. Jenny's headlights hit something grey ahead, and she stopped, stepping out to look.

A seven-foot-high fence marched across the road. It was made of some kind of flexible metal mesh, drawn taut between steel posts set at five-foot intervals. Tara had loaned her a flashlight, and she turned it on now, finding that the fence threaded between the trees and meandered off into the distance. Jenny studied the gate. Three heavy chains secured it -- one each at the top and bottom, one in the middle. There was no intercom of any kind, or any cameras that she could see. So they wouldn't know she was here, because they weren't expecting her.

She studied the fence again. Another post ran across the top of each section, between the uprights. Sighing, she got back into the car and pulled up as close to the fence as she could. She killed the engine, clambered up onto the hood, and reached for that top bar, praying fervently that the fence wasn't electrified.

Her fingers didn't fry, so she pulled herself up, scrabbling with her foot until she got her leg over, then dropped to the ground on the other side.

There was at least three feet of snow on the ground and she shook her head as she slogged up the drive. She seemed to be making a habit of freezing her butt off in the snow for these two.

Except that she wasn't cold any more. As a matter of fact, she was extremely warm. Too warm. She stopped and tugged off the light jacket that had seemed so inadequate up to this point.

That was better. A stiff breeze cooled her fiery cheeks. Jenny opened her arms and raised her face to the sky, closing her eyes.

The ground beneath her feet seemed to pulse in time to her heartbeat. She opened her eyes and sat down, pulling off her shoes and socks. Standing, she buried her feet in the snow until she felt the hard earth beneath. Yes. She could hear it now, a rhythm that sang in time with her Blood.

She was on fire. She tugged off her sweatshirt, panting as the cold mountain air dried the sweat on her skin. *Damien*, she thought.

A sound traveled up through the bottom of her feet. The scrape of a claw against stone. It came from the northwest, and she turned in that direction. Abruptly, she was running. Flying between the trees like a hart, she opened herself to the song, letting the Blood guide her.

She ran into the center of a clearing, surrounded by great, tall trees the likes of which she had never before seen. Her feet refused to move, frozen in lush, green grass that couldn't possibly exist in these temperatures. A warm breeze caressed her face. She felt a surge of joy so strong it brought tears to her eyes. She had felt this way when she stepped back into her father's house a few weeks ago. It was like being welcomed home.

She enjoyed the serenity for a moment more, then grew anxious. She tried to feel Damien again, and couldn't. "Devlin," she whispered. The clearing was still and silent. Even the breeze had stilled. It was as though the earth itself were waiting. Waiting for something from her.

"I don't know what you want," she cried. "Please!" The words disappeared as soon as she spoke them, deadened by the still air.

She tried to move again, but the earth held her, silent and patient. "Please," she whispered. She dropped to her knees.

When she looked up, she noticed a stone slab, half-buried in the circle's center, that she hadn't seen before. Without thinking, she stood and stepped toward it. A warm tendril of air touched her cheek. She took another step, and another, until she stood before the stone slab.

There was a shallow depression in the center of the stone, from which a sliver of obsidian gave back the light of the moon. She reached for the sliver and picked it up carefully. A sudden image of blood, running in thick rivulets over the stone, made her drop it. Jenny knelt before the altar, resting her head against the cool stone. She was frightened, but more afraid of losing Devlin and Damien forever. "All right," she whispered. "If that's what it takes." She closed her eyes, shivering as the image of blood sprang to her mind again. "I love them."

She opened her eyes, and the grass, the trees, the stone were all gone. She was kneeling on a snow-dusted trail, staring at a circle of moonlight on the ground. She stood. She'd been tested. Had she passed?

She started walking, the fabric of her wet pants clinging to her flesh, seeming to drag with every step. Jenny stopped, removing the cumbersome garment. A shaft of moonlight dappled her form. She removed her bra and panties, as well, turning with her arms held out, allowing the moon's radiance to bathe her.

A twig cracked behind her, and she turned. Bright blue eyes regarded her steadily from beneath the trees. A branch creaked to her left. Another set of blue eyes studied her from the shadows.

"Catch me," Jenny whispered, then turned and ran.

Her Blood sang. She leapt through the trees like a forest sprite. Damien appeared in front of her, and she laughed, dancing away. Devlin pounced toward her from the right, and Jenny twisted between shadows. When she came again upon the clearing, she wasn't surprised. This time, the grass sprang beneath her feet, adding its own buoyancy to each step. She ran up to the altar and took up the dark blade. She hesitated for just a moment, feeling again a sharp tongue of fear, then lay back upon the cold stone.

Damien and Devlin bounded into the clearing, then stopped abruptly when they saw her. She sat up, cross-legged on the altar. She raised her hand. The Blood pounded in her head, and Jenny drew the obsidian blade along the thick, blue vein in the crook of her arm.

The blood flowed, dripping from her arm, pooling in the recess between her legs. Devlin and Damien walked forward slowly.

Devlin reached her first, putting his great forepaws onto the stone, looking her in the eye. Jenny swayed, feeling light-headed. Damien nudged her arm. She brought up her hand, gazing at the blade. Devlin looked up at the sky, baring his tender breast. She shook her head, but Damien's mouth closed lightly around her arm, tugging gently. Closing her eyes, Jenny slashed from left to right. Felt Devlin's essence dripping on her legs. She opened her eyes, breathing deeply to stave off the darkness that threatened to engulf her. Watched his life-blood join hers in the hollow.

Devlin stepped off the stone, and Damien took his place. Jenny's hand shook as she brought the blade to his skin. With a quick motion, she made the cut, and his blood flowed over her, as well, filling the shallow depression to the brim. Damien backed away, and the moonlight seemed to coalesce into a solid, brilliant shaft, hovering above the altar. Jenny looked up, and saw something she would never be able to describe -- a creature stunningly beautiful, yet incredibly ancient, compassionate and terrible, loving and vengeful.

The vision gestured and a soft pattering began, rich dark soil raining onto the stone, splashing into the hollow. A moment later, the dark fall stopped. A bright hand passed over the depression, and it disappeared, replaced by an earthenware bowl. The vision picked this up, offering it to Jenny. A voice filled the clearing, though they were words without sound, felt rather than heard. "What the Goddess has Bound, only Death may part."

Jenny reached out with trembling hands and grasped the bowl. She took a deep breath, then brought it to her lips.

The thick, rich liquid went down like honey, sweet and ripe. She drank until the bowl was empty, but when she rested it upon the bright hand, it was full once again. Devlin padded forward, and the bowl was held out to him.

Jenny lay back against the altar, savoring the Goddess's beauty while Devlin drank. Then he was finished and it was Damien's time. He stepped up, and as he drank, the Goddess's hand smoothed his fur in benediction.

And as he lapped the last drop from the bowl, the world spun. Jenny clutched the edges of the stone. She could feel everything. Her body was the earth. Every breeze caressed her skin, every tiny foot and claw found purchase in her soul. She felt the night creatures scurrying in the darkness around the clearing, drawn by the Goddess. Devlin flowed onto the altar. Jenny parted her legs, offering herself to him.

His rough tongue touched her, and she shook with ecstasy, her heightened senses feeling every tiny bump like a separate caress. He growled, and shifted, his hands spreading her wide, his tongue slipping inside her as she cried out in pleasure.

He moved, covering her body, taking her mouth with his, her essence a salty tang on his tongue. The Goddess hovered over them, watching. A million eyes watched, from out of the darkness, and Jenny didn't care. She pushed Devlin aside and down, rolling over to straddle him. His eyes clouded with need as she scooted back, running her tongue lightly over his bulging cock. She held him with one hand as she impaled herself, sighing with contentment as he filled her. Jenny melded herself to him, moving quickly, frantically. His breathing became ragged, his mouth jutting out, tiny hairs sprouting from his brow.

Devlin arched as she sat up, impaling herself on his cock, gasping at the sheer depth of the penetration. He pushed up, wrapping his arms around her waist, and looked at her. Half-human, half-wolf, his eyes searched her face, his lips drawn back from bright fangs gleaming in the moonlight. Jenny felt his heart beating fast and strong, its rhythm matching hers. "Yes," she whispered. "Mark me. I am yours." His teeth pierced her shoulder, and the heat in her core flamed into incandescence as Devlin's seed and her blood flowed, joining them. Making them One. Feeding the flames of desire until the pleasure was more than she could bear, and she raised her head and howled at the night.

Jenny shivered as the feeling passed, Devlin's warm flow slowing inside her. Reluctantly, she eased herself off of him. "Thank you," he whispered, and cupped her cheek lovingly, his kiss on her lips soft as a rose.

"I love you," she said, and he held her tight. "Don't ever let go," she whispered.

"I won't." And he released her, moving from the altar, but she felt him deep inside, his grasp on her heart a tangible, living presence.

Jenny's already racing heartbeat quickened as Damien approached. He seemed more majestic than ever, a lord in his element, and she marveled at the idea that she would be the one to have his heart, for all time. He placed his forepaws on the slab, and his magnificent shaft gleamed in the moonlight. She looked at him from beneath her eyelashes and turned, lowering her head to the slab, pushing her butt high, parting her legs so that she presented her dripping sex to him. She felt a tiny prick as the tip of a claw touched the hollow of her back, then glided between her cheeks to tickle the tight pucker there, the tip sliding in as Jenny moaned.

She reached back and held her cheeks wide, and he slid the claw, smooth as glass, in and out, until Jenny gasped and let go, her muscles clenching tight around him as pleasure danced in her core.

When it had passed, he drew his tongue between her legs, then placed his great paws to either side of her. He pressed himself against her, and damp fur tickled her pussy. She gasped, looking over her shoulder at him, as he slowly, very slowly, worked the tip of his fur-covered sheath between her lips.

Jenny clung to the altar, her pussy stretching, the pain of his entry only speeding the rapid tattoo of pleasure thrumming through her veins. He stopped when she drew in her breath with a sharp hiss.

He melded his body to hers, his soft underbelly tight against her back, his huge muzzle hanging over her shoulder. His hot breath gusted in her ear, and a spiral of pleasure twisted in her belly. Her pussy tightened, and he drew in a deep breath, his throat rumbling. The tip of his sheath expanded, and then Jenny felt his cock, slick and hot, growing inside her.

She started to pump her hips, but Damien nipped her lightly on the shoulder, and she subsided. She moaned as his flesh filled her, his flexible member undulating, sending hot streaks of pleasure throbbing through her pussy. She felt him meet resistance as his cock extended to its full length, filling her completely, and then it moved, and she couldn't think any more.

His cock moved. Not his hips, but his cock, extending and retracting inside her. Slowly at first, as Jenny whimpered with pleasure, only able to keep still because Damien nipped at her shoulder every time she moved. Then faster, plunging in and out, and Jenny uttered sharp cries of delight as the short, coarse hairs that covered his sheath pricked her pussy with each penetration, sending delicious shivers of sensation through her.

Damien's breathing changed, exciting her. Jenny's pussy clenched and unclenched in time to his shallow, rapid panting. "Yours," she whispered. "Yours, forever."

Damien raised his head, loosing a deafening howl, and then his fangs pierced her.

"Yes. Oh, Damien, yes!" His great mouth closed on her shoulder, gently, as he licked and suckled.

She screamed his name as she came, over and over, Damien's cock hammering in and out so rapidly, it was like nothing she'd ever felt before, creating a heat that drove her again and again over the brink, each climax building before the previous one faded. Higher and higher he prodded her, until the base of his cock expanded, and he froze. His hot essence poured into her. The world seemed to explode, and Jenny felt as though she were floating in a sea of stars.

When she came to, the only light was the pearly evanescence of the moon. The Goddess's manifestation was gone, though Jenny could still sense her presence in this sacred place. Devlin and Damien lay beside her on the altar, their flesh warm against hers. She moved and they stirred, Dev sighing in his sleep. Damien's eyes opened. Jenny smiled.

"You came back," Damien said.

She nodded.

"I'm glad."

"There are no accidents," she whispered. "The three of us were meant to be."

"I know." His eyes gleamed in the dark. "I've always known."

"You can't stay in California," Dev murmured in her ear. "It's too far. Now that the Binding is complete, you can't live away from the land."

"I know," Jenny said. He rose up, leaning on one hand as he studied her face in the moonlight. "It's all right. I have no regrets." Her mother's words echoed in her head. She grasped his hand and brought it to her lips, kissing his palm. "I had nothing. Now I have you."

Their hands caressed her body, worshipping her in the light of the moon. Desire rose in her belly, that fiery heat that only they could ignite. She sat up, engulfing Devlin's cock with her eager mouth as her fingers closed around Damien's rock-hard shaft. She laved Devlin with her tongue, getting him good and wet. She took his hand and guided his fingers into her pussy, coating them with her warm juices. Then she shocked him by parting her cheeks. She licked his cock as she murmured against him, "Stretch me, Devlin. I want to take you. Help me be ready." His cock jumped. "Mmmm. Do you want that?" she whispered.

His finger plunged inside her ass -- quickly, eagerly. Jenny wriggled her hips, meeting him thrust for thrust, sucking greedily as he worked her rim in ever-widening circles. He thrust in a second finger, plunging it in and out -- once, twice, three times -- while the other finger continued to circle. Jenny brought her thighs together, clenching her ass tight as she climaxed, her throbbing anus clutching his fingers over and over. Damien's eyes glittered as he watched, his hands stroking her thighs. "That's it, baby. We love to watch you come."

Moaning, she moved, forcing Devlin to withdraw his fingers. She squatted over him, facing his feet, her cheeks spread wide. "Oh, damn," Dev murmured. Damien reached out and held Devlin's cock upright as Jenny lowered herself. She hesitated, his thick head barely inside her, already stretching her to the point of pain. Damien slipped a finger into her pussy, wetting it with her juices. He worked it just past her rim, massaging her as she began to inch down, little by little, determined to take as much of Devlin as physically possible. Damien's ministrations eased the pain. In fact, his subtle movements were such an erotic counterpoint that Jenny froze, caught in the throes of yet another orgasm. "Oh, hell!" Devlin gasped as she tightened around him. "Oh, yeah!"

The climax only made her more eager to take him. She reamed her pussy, then coated Devlin's shaft with her juices. Reaching out, she tugged Damien, urging him to come around, between Dev's legs. She brought his hands to her shoulders, reached behind her, and guided Dev's hands to her waist. "Help me," she coaxed them urgently.

Damien applied gentle pressure to her shoulders as Devlin held her waist tight, beginning to thrust shallowly, then more urgently as the tight orifice stretched to accommodate him. "Damien!" Jenny cried.

He knew what she wanted and straddled Devlin's legs, thrusting his own quivering cock into her pussy as Devlin penetrated her ass. "Oh, Goddess," she whispered. "Yes." Damien pressed harder, using his hands on her shoulders to steady his own thrusts, helping to bury Devlin deeper in the process. "Yes. Yes!"

Her eager cries shattered any semblance of control the brothers had. They pounded into her, and she cried out in triumph as Devlin buried his cock completely. "Yes, yes," she sobbed. "Take me. Please. Both of you."

Damien's hands joined Dev's at her waist, holding her immobile as they both gave one last, mighty thrust. The rings at the base of their cocks began to swell, and Jenny gasped as Devlin's stretched her ass painfully. But then their cocks met inside her, and the pain was forgotten as they trapped her tender flesh between them, the pulse of their release driving her into a bucking, frenzied climax as the three of them became One, in body as well as soul.

As their joint ecstasy faded, Devlin sat up, wrapping his arms around her waist, resting his cheek against her back. Damien's arms encircled her shoulders, her head resting in the crook of his neck. They held one another for a long time, Jenny shuddering with brief mini-climaxes as she felt their cocks shrinking within her.

Finally, they lay on the altar once more, Jenny ensconced between them, warm despite the cold night air, comfortable despite the rigid slab beneath them. Damien spoke of his plans for the future. He was determined to make their relationship official as soon as the justice of the peace opened on Monday. His words began to slur as he spoke of ways she might still work for Carol. "You can still design here," he murmured.

Jenny nodded. "And I can sew the prototypes, and ship them to Carol. She can oversee the duplication."

"And you can travel, Jen," Devlin pointed out. "This isn't a cage. You just can't stay away from the land for extended periods of time."

She shook her head. "I can't stay away from *you* for extended periods of time."

Dev smiled sleepily. Jenny listened as his and Damien's breathing slowed, watched their faces soften in sleep. She looked up at the stars and thanked the Goddess for bringing them to her.

She hardly needed a civil ceremony to know that Damien and Devlin belonged to her, now and forever. They were already married in the eyes of the Goddess, who had showered her with double blessings on this most sacred of nights.

Jenny sighed in contentment. Twice wed.

She chuckled wickedly. Twice sexed.

She rested a hand on her tummy, already sensing the two lives that stirred within her womb.

Twice blessed.

Rachel Bo

Rachel Bo is an award-winning author currently published in several genres. On the weekends, she works as a Clinical Laboratory Scientist. During the week, Rachel writes and rides herd on her handsome husband, two wonderful daughters, a rabbit, a snake and several remarkably hardy goldfish.

Feel free to look for Rachel on the Internet at http://webpages.charter.net/rachelbo/ or e-mail her at rachbo03@yahoo.com

CHRISTMAS NOIR

Barbara Karmazin

Chapter One

It was a plain manila envelope. There was no return address.

Shannon licked her suddenly dry lips. Every piece of mail that came to her house was automatically scanned by her security system for explosives, drugs, poisons, DNA, and infectious bacteria. There was no reason for her to be suspicious or feel afraid.

Her name and address had been hand-printed on the envelope in large block letters.

Shannon opened the envelope and upended it. Twenty holo-photographs spilled out onto her coffee table, shimmering 3D reproductions faithful to the last detail. Twenty perfect images of Meredith.

The first image showed Meredith lying on her back upon a white fur rug with her arms stretched over her head. A bright fire blazed merrily in the fireplace behind her. Mistletoe hung on the mantelpiece. Long blond hair fanned out behind her head. Her cerulean blue eyes glowed with love and laughter. A faint blush highlighted her pale skin. Gentle shadows caressed

Meredith's sweet, uplifted breasts, pert nipples, the lush curve of her hips, and the silky soft curls nestled at the base of her erect cock.

The rest of the images were horror personified, a grotesque, blood-splattered rape of Merry's slashed, twisted, disemboweled body. She lay perfectly centered in a pool of congealed blood. Fear had distorted her face into a mask of agony.

Oh, god! Not Merry!

She'd looked so happy yesterday evening when she called on the vidphone and said she was going out on a date.

Shannon's heart pounded against her chest. Tears spilled down her face. *Poor, beautiful Merry. She never had a chance.*

A single sheet of plain white paper lay beside the images. Two words in solid block printing filled the center of that paper. YOU'RE NEXT.

Whoever sent this envelope knew exactly how her security system scanned all incoming mail deliveries.

Shannon swiped at the tears that kept blurring her sight. She focused on the security monitor images playing across the opposite wall. No windows in her house. Too much of a security risk. Snow blanketed the ground, transforming the city streets into a winter night's fairytale with glittering icicles dangling from trees and shrubbery.

A picket line of angry men and women walked past the sealed gate entrance to her home. Snowflakes whirled around their tightly wrapped coats and scarves. They'd trampled the snow into an ugly gray slush under their booted feet. They remained the mandatory ten-meter distance from the gate.

Their holographic signs flashed biblical verses from Genesis about God creating man in his image.

Shannon raked her hands through her hair. "God created man in his own image. In God's image, he created him; male and female, he created them."

Of course, the protestors took those verses out of context.

In her mind, when she read those words, it meant God was a hermaphrodite. How else could both man and woman be created in God's image, unless he had the attributes of both sexes?

To the men and women on that picket line, Shannon, Meredith, and all the hermaphrodites who chose to live within this enclave were abominations. Gaining equal protection under the law for herms had been only the first step in a long, gradual campaign for acceptance in normal, everyday society. Should she retreat from New York City and establish a new enclave in one of the orbital habitats?

Shannon shook her head. Retreating would only encourage this murderer.

She'd been one of the lucky ones, born into wealth with loving parents who'd refused to have her altered at birth. About one in every five thousand children was born with ambiguous genitals. In 2062, for a city the size of New York, that came out to ten thousand intersexed people.

Unfortunately, too many of those children were surgically altered at birth to reflect either a female or male sexual identity. Those herms not surgically altered often faced sexual abuse from their families, and many became prostitutes because of this abuse. Getting the equal rights amendment for intersexed people passed in the World Congress meeting was only the first step in her legal battle for herself and others like her.

It didn't matter if she had full-scan vidcams cleverly disguised in simple trims and moldings around all her buildings, and privacy screens activated at all windows. It didn't matter if there were motion pads at every access, palm and DNA ID locks, and top-of-the-line alarm droids.

Meredith had used the exact same security setup for her apartment, and now she was dead.

During the last decade, technology wizards had transformed image creation into an esoteric art form on the web. What if someone had faked those images and sent them in an attempt to panic her?

She couldn't stick her head in the sand and hope the images from this envelope were fakes. "Computer."

"Yes, Ms. MacNal?"

"Connect me to the police department in full audio and visual mode. I have a murder to report."

* * *

Detective Tannamae Jones arched her eyebrows at her partner, Fergus DeSoto, while their aircar circled the building. The parking protocol was programmed into the computer controls. All she'd had to do was state the name of the street and building and let it find the best parking space available. "Pretty high-class digs here. The only herms I knew when I grew up in Vietnam were prosts."

DeSoto stretched his arms over his head and flashed her one of his sexy grins. Six-five and all muscle, half Scottish and half Puerto Rican, with dark red hair and gorgeous caramel brown skin, he could turn her body into pure raging hormones with just one look. The midnight-blue casual shirt and slacks he wore accented his build without binding. It was the perfect combination of style and comfort. "The times, they are a-changing, *mi carina*. Herms have equal rights now."

She shrugged. Yes, the times had changed. A hundred years ago, her great-grandparents had fought on opposite sides. Now, *she* existed. Half African-American and half Vietnamese.

The aircar settled down on the rooftop beside six more police cars. Tannamae and Fergus exited and strode across the tarmac. Puddles of half-melted slush and snow splashed against their boots. A uniformed officer -- a tall, broad-shouldered woman with dirty-blond hair -- stood guard at the emergency exit access door. The holopic ID on her uniform pocket read "Officer Browning."

Officer Browning lifted a portable scanner and aimed it at Fergus and Tannamae. Two quick blips from the device confirmed their IDs. She tapped the golden metal button of the comlink clipped to her left earlobe and spoke. "Detectives DeSoto and Jones have arrived."

Tannamae pulled a pair of surgical gloves over her hands, slipped shoe gloves over her boots, and waited for Fergus to don his regulation crime scene duds. "Where is the victim?"

Browning jerked her thumb at the door. "Penthouse apartment. This gives you direct access through the kitchen."

The short staircase took them past a basic security cam setup to a solid titanium-alloy door wedged open with a chair. Two droids whirred back and forth on cushioned track feet, scanning for fingerprints, DNA, hair, fibers, and other evidence.

White ceramic-tiled floor and gleaming silver countertops greeted them. Two plates of uneaten food and two full wine glasses rested on the teakwood table between matching chairs. Two candles had burned out long ago.

Fergus went first and eased open the living room door. They stepped inside. The smell of blood and feces hit her first. Blood splatters on the wall, sofa, and floor detailed a violent struggle. The techs had already sprayed fluorescent markers on the blood. Every drop glowed bright red.

Two more uniforms and four techs waited outside the open door of an adjoining bedroom.

Tannamae and Fergus circled the living room without stepping in the blood, then entered the bedroom.

The victim had been positioned in the middle of the blood-drenched bed with her intestines draped over her legs and her amputated cock jammed into her open mouth. The murderer had posed her with sliced-off breasts in her cupped hands.

One of the techs stepped forward, a short, blond man wearing full surgical suit and half facemask. "The scene's already been recorded. We got all the angles and did the trajectory layouts and splatter analysis. The coroner has already declared her dead and is waiting for you to release the body for autopsy."

Tannamae sighed and exchanged a weary stare with Fergus. It didn't matter how many times the techs had recorded the scene or how well they'd gathered evidence, nothing beat actual physical observation by the detectives on duty. "Everyone vacate the area," she said. "We need to be alone now. After we finish making our own recordings and observations, we'll call you on the comlink to remove the body."

Chapter Two

Shannon landed her aircar on the rooftop of the Herm Foundation office building. She scowled at the security vidcam images on her dashboard showing yet another group of picketers at the ground floor public entrance. Droid guard units patrolled the pedwalks and kept them away from any physical contact with her employees. With only two more days until Christmas, they should have more pleasant plans for their holidays than wasting their time waving signs and shouting ugly slogans.

A blizzard was predicted for this afternoon. The extra misery factor of trudging through the storm should dampen their enthusiasm. She grinned at the thought of them stumbling half-frozen through the snowdrifts.

Shannon exited the aircar. The anti-theft alarm system automatically went live when she locked the door. She strode across the rooftop. A fat snowflake landed on her cheek and melted in a warm trickle. She lifted her face to the sky and spun around in a circle. *Yes!* Let the snow come and drive away the protestors.

Finally she stopped, went to the private elevator entrance, and placed her hand on the ID panel. It glowed under her hand and the door slid open. Merry had looked so happy in the first image. How long had she experienced the joy of feeling loved and cherished by another, even if it was a lie?

The elevator slowed to a stop. The door opened and Shannon entered her office. She tossed her coat on the couch, went to the desk, reduced the exterior vidcam images of the picketers to one small corner of the wall screen, and pulled up Meredith's job schedule for the week. Two red flags glowed on emails from the Social Service departments at Memorial Hospital and City Hospital. Merry's basic administrative duties and files could be divided among her co-workers, for now.

Shannon opened the emails. Parent consultation interviews were scheduled at nine and ten tomorrow morning. Both mothers had gone into labor this morning and the ultrasounds had already confirmed the ambiguous sex of their babies. Too late to schedule another worker to take those interviews.

She would have to conduct those interviews and see if she could convince the parents to move into the hermaphrodite-housing enclave. Young herms growing up within a community of well-adjusted adult hermaphrodites limited the potential psychological damage of their sexual identities.

She clicked on the office interior communications system and programmed it to send a full audio and visual transmission to every employee in the building. Green lights flashing across the top of the screen signaled that her programming had taken effect.

She folded her hands in her lap and gazed into the vidcam's lens. "I'm sure you've all seen and heard this morning's top news story. Meredith Jackson was brutally murdered yesterday."

Her employees, men, women, and herms, black, white, Hispanic, Asian, and mixed-raced, stopped in mid-motion at their desks and turned to their computer screens. Their shocked faces gazed back at her in overlapping images from the full-sized wall screen like the images from an insect's multiple eyes.

Her mouth felt dry and raw, as if she'd swallowed ashes. She sucked in a deep breath and willed herself to remain calm. "When the police conduct their interviews of Meredith's friends and co-workers, it is vitally important that everyone cooperates fully with their investigation of her murder. Because I have no idea when her body will be released for cremation, I am holding a special memorial service two days from now, on Christmas Eve."

Her breath hitched, forcing her to take a gulp of air. Shannon unwound her fingers and rested her hands on the desk. She must present a calm and dignified appearance in front of her employees. The treacherous tears streaming down her face weren't helping matters any. "I'll send a memo around the office with specific details of this memorial."

She blinked away her tears, and murmured, "End transmission," then slapped her hand on the cut-off switch.

Shannon activated the employee handbook file on the computer and inserted the appropriate codes for paid bereavement leave and counseling services for all employees. She stopped to check the memo over one last time. What had she missed?

Two red arrows flashed again on the organizational chart indicating Merry's liaison appointments. How could she forget that very important detail? She needed to create another memo opening Merry's job position for new applicants.

Later. She'd do that after the holidays. The office would be shut down from Christmas Eve through New Year's Day anyway.

The memory of Merry's happy face in that first image flashed across Shannon's mind again. Was she going to die without ever experiencing love? She wasn't picky. All she wanted was to love and to be loved. You'd think being a herm and having the capabilities to love either sex would make it easier instead of harder to find someone to love.

She'd kept her distance from Merry just like she did with all of her employees because she didn't want to be sued for sexual harassment. *Damn it! It wasn't fair!* She had enormous wealth from her parents' computer stocks and even more income generated from the orbital habitats they'd built. She'd spent her entire life striving to help all herms. And in the end, she sat alone in her office, too afraid to risk losing her heart to another.

I'm sick and tired of being lonely! Sick of using sex toys to satisfy myself. I want someone to love.

Shannon hit the send key for the bereavement leave memo and shut down the computer.

I wish I had someone I could trust never to betray me. Someone to love me forever. The way Mom and Dad loved each other.

The security link chimed. She activated it. "Is there a problem?"

Rolf Danner's familiar face appeared on the viewscreen. Standing six-and-a-half-feet tall, with strawberry blond hair and piercing blue eyes, he reminded her of a Viking prince instead of a modern-day security operative. He leaned forward and studied her face with an intent stare. "I just wanted to know if there's any way I can help you. Meredith's death must have been a total shock."

Shannon shook her head. She dared not trust him or anyone Merry knew. Not now. Not after what had happened. Why was he making friendly overtures to her now, after two years on her staff? He'd always kept his distance before. "I'm fine. I've already contacted the police. I expect you to cooperate with them fully."

He nodded. "Just remember. If you need me, call me. Anytime, day or night, and I'll be there for you."

* * *

Fergus paused the monitor screen, sat back in his chair, and quirked an eyebrow at his partner. Tannamae's hair flowed past her neck in a cascade of soft black spirals. Spirals he loved to twist around his finger whenever he kissed her. "So far, we have fifty-six regular contacts in the victim's email. The basic security scans eliminated forty-nine as valid suspects. As for the other seven contacts, guess who was the most recent?"

"Shannon MacNal?"

"Of course."

Tannamae shook her head and sent her curls bouncing again. "It doesn't make sense. Why would she contact the police and report a murder if she was the one who did it? Why would she murder another herm after working so hard all her life to obtain equal rights and legal protections for them?"

She had a point there. He shrugged. "Murder doesn't have to make sense. Maybe they were lovers at one time and Ms. MacNal got jealous when a new lover came on the scene. Maybe she reported the murder in order to throw us off the scent. What I want to know is who shut down the victim's security system so that there's no audio or visual records available of her death."

Tannamae pursed her lips. "Five minutes after Ms. MacNal's email, the victim's entire security system went offline. Are the two events linked, and if so, how did Ms. MacNal accomplish this?"

She scowled. Her dark eyes went even darker with her thoughts. "This is the fifth hermaphrodite murder in the last two years. As far as we know, Ms. MacNal had no contact with the other four victims."

Fergus tapped his fingers on the side of his keyboard and shook his head. "Depending on how skilled the murderer is with computer security programs, he or she could have inserted a piggyback code into Ms. MacNal's email system. That would have triggered a direct link between her email and the victim's security going off grid." He pulled the keyboard up and tapped in another request.

"What are you looking at now?" Tannamae asked.

"I'm wondering how many other incidents occurred in the victim's security links. I'm wondering if the victim was in the habit of shutting down her system in order to accommodate a secret lover. Then, I'm going to see if we can match up any of her contacts with system shutdowns."

He tapped his fingers on the keyboard again. "I'm running a third-level security background search on Ms. MacNal. We might as well, just to be on the safe side."

Tannamae booted up her computer. "While you're doing that, I'm going to take another look at the other victims' reports and autopsies."

Almost four hours later, their suspect list had been pared down to three possibilities.

The interoffice comlink went green.

Fergus exchanged an annoyed look with Tannamae. "This better be good. I hate interrupting an investigation for stupid meetings." He flicked open the link.

Their district captain's bald-headed visage glared at them from the monitor screen. "Detectives Desoto and Jones, report to my office now for a private meeting on your newest case."

* * *

Shannon gritted her teeth, paced back and forth, and counted to ten. Her hands were clenched so tight that her fingernails cut into her palms, but it was either that or pull her hair out in sheer frustration. Besides, turning around and assaulting two police detectives would only make the situation worse, not better, for her. "This is crazy! You can't do this to me."

The male detective, Fergus Desoto, spoke in slow, reasonable tones. His voice had a lovely Spanish lilt that sent every nerve ending on her body into super tingle. "We don't like this any more than you do. It's orders. We don't have any other choice. It's either this or put you into protective custody."

Shannon whirled around. "Protective custody? You'd put me in jail? I'm not the murderer. Shouldn't you be focusing your energies on capturing whoever's killing herms instead of harassing me?"

The female detective, Tannamae Jones, had soft brown skin, almond-shaped eyes, and loose, black curls that gave her an exotic, almost magical appearance. Five-six was the minimum height for police officers. She must have barely squeaked by that requirement. Standing above her, Shannon felt like a clumsy elephant in her six-foot-tall frame.

Fergus splayed his hand across the small of Tannamae's back and guided her to the other side of the table. She tilted her head to the side, flashed a seductive smile at him while he pulled out a chair for her. When she sat down, he moved behind her chair and rested his hand upon her shoulder.

Shannon sucked in a deep breath. Her throat ached. Detectives Tannamae Jones and Fergus DeSoto were more than just partners. They were lovers. Why couldn't she have someone give her little touches and looks like that?

Tannamae held up her hand. She had short, clean nails and delicate wrists. Plus, she worked out regularly; Shannon was sure of that because the muscles in her arms were whipcord-hard. "We're not harassing you. It's your choice. You know the law mandates protective custody for potential victims of domestic violence. You qualify because of the threatening note you received with the holopic images of the latest victim. Either accept that we're moving in with you until this case is solved, or accept protective custody in a more secure establishment."

Shannon bit back a weary sigh. They were right. That particular law was an offshoot from domestic violence cases where the police hadn't protected potential victims to the fullest extent possible. Even though this murder didn't appear to be a domestic violence case, they couldn't be sure and had to abide by the letter of the law. She didn't have any other choice but to let them move in with her until the murderer was captured or killed. "All right. You can stay. I'll tell the house droid to put clean sheets in the spare bedroom."

Tannamae shook her head. "One of us must remain within three feet of you at all times. Would you be more comfortable having a man or a woman bunked down in your bedroom with you?"

Shannon stopped, crossed her arms under her breasts, and took her time looking them over from head to toe. Good. A blush darkened both detectives' faces now. Served them right for doing this to her. If she called their bluff, would they back off and give her a semblance of privacy? What the hell? She might as well stick it to them deep and dirty. "It doesn't matter who sleeps in my bed. I'm a herm, a shemale with breasts and a penis. Both sexes turn me on."

She placed her hands on her hips and smiled a slow, seductive smile. "I'm going to take a shower now. Do you want to watch?"

Chapter Three

The sound of water splashing in the shower came out loud and clear past the half-open door. Standing outside the bathroom was a compromise that gave Shannon a semblance of privacy while satisfying the letter of the law that said a police officer or detective must remain in the same room as the potential victim. Tannamae leaned against the wall and rubbed her arms. A nice, hot shower would help her relax, too. "Shannon did a great job of goading us with her remarks. How are we going to resolve this fiasco?"

Fergus lifted his arms and stretched himself with the unconscious ease of a wild animal. A tigerish glint gleamed in his whiskey-amber colored eyes. Per departmental regulations, he kept his dark red hair in a military buzz cut. The café-au-lait skin he'd inherited from his Puerto Rican father always reminded her of a surfer's tan. He flashed a wicked grin and said, "We could always flip a coin."

And what would that prove? Nothing, really. If she won the toss, she'd spend a sleepless night totally aware of her proximity to Shannon. And if Fergus won the toss, she'd still lose sleep. Not that she didn't trust her man. No, it wasn't that. She just didn't feel comfortable with the thought of him sleeping in the same bed with Shannon.

Fergus grinned, strolled over to Tannamae, and traced her mouth with his fingertip. "What's the matter, *mi corazón?*" He leaned in for a long, slow kiss that curled her toes and made her want to rip his pants and shirt off so she could savor every inch of him.

She managed to pull away from that kiss without groaning in frustration and glared at him. "The last thing we need right now is to get ourselves all hot and bothered and then not be able to do anything about it. I don't like the coin toss idea. The only logical way to solve this without causing any problems is to have both of us sleep in the bedroom with her."

"That sounds like a fabulous solution." Shannon's sultry murmur behind Tanny raised goosebumps on her arms. "I've always wanted to try a ménage."

Tanny sighed, schooled her face into a bland mask, and turned around. She'd be pissed, too, if she had to allow strangers to invade her personal space like they were invading Shannon's.

Shannon leaned in the wide-open doorway, very properly clad in a long-sleeved, white cotton pajama top and pants. Tall, broad-shouldered, and small-breasted, she looked strong enough to hold her own against most assailants. Her brown hair swirled in wet waves around her face and neck, leaving damp patches on her shoulders. The front of her loose-fitting pants failed to completely conceal the small bulge of her sex. Pale peach glitter polish added a disconcerting and very feminine gleam to her fingernails and toenails. "For my own peace of mind, I recommend pajamas for both of you. That would be less tempting all around."

Shannon grinned and arched sardonic eyebrows at them. "You did remember to bring pajamas, didn't you?"

Tanny bit her lip and did her best not to react.

Fergus cleared his throat. A slight flush darkened his cheeks. He pulled his gaze away from the front of Shannon's pants up to her face. "I forgot to bring any with me."

Shannon's grin widened even further. "I'll gladly lend you a pair of mine." She let her gaze travel over Fergus in a smoldering and lingering assessment of his physique. "How tall are you?"

"Six-five."

"They might be bit snug on you. I'm only six foot." Shannon pursed her lips and a speculative gleam deepened within her light blue eyes. "As for your partner?"

Tannamae gritted her teeth. After they solved this case, she had every intention of ripping a few departmental heads off. In the meantime, they were just going to have to make the best of a very awkward situation. "I need to borrow a pair of pajamas, too."

Shannon took her time looking Tanny over from head to toe, tsked, and shook her head. "If you roll up the arms and legs, I have another pair that should fit you very nicely. It's such a shame. As much as I would enjoy it, I suppose it's against the rules for you to sleep in the nude with me."

She spun on her heel, padded barefooted across the thick hunter green carpet to a sturdy dark cherry wood bureau, and opened the top drawer.

* * *

No matter how much Fergus soaped and scrubbed his body, it didn't change the fact that he had a raging hard-on.

Shannon's sultry-voiced insinuations had kept his mind in the gutter all night long. Plus, the sexy way she kept staring at him and then Tanny made him remember that in addition to her pussy and breasts, Shannon had a cock she wanted to use on both of them.

Slow and easy, he stroked the slippery, soaped length of his cock. He closed his eyes and considered the possibilities. How would it feel if he started out with Tanny sandwiched between him and Shannon? Or would Shannon prefer to be in the middle while he and Tanny played with the startling blend of soft, womanly breasts on her chest and the small penis sticking up from the wiry curls and folds of her pussy lips?

What was that word she'd used to describe herself? Shemale? Yeah, that was the perfect word for her. Hermaphrodite sounded like something from a medical textbook. But shemale -- that word rolled off your tongue just right. One thing for sure, having both male and female sexual parts gave Shannon a very special advantage whenever she made love. As a shemale, Shannon knew how it felt as a woman and as a man. Because of this dual perspective, she probably knew exactly how to satisfy both sexes.

Fergus switched the shower to steam pulse and let it sluice across his skin. Stabs of needle-sharp spray teased his balls and cock. He groaned under his breath, tightened his grip, and stroked faster. The tender skin at the head of his cock swelled and throbbed on the cusp of release. Had Shannon jacked herself off, too, while she showered?

What about Tanny? Was she as interested in Shannon as he was? Had she aimed the shower spray directly onto her pussy and let it tease her to orgasm?

How would it feel to pump his cock into Tanny's pussy while Shannon pressed her breasts against his back and thrust into his ass? Come to think of it, it would probably feel a lot more natural than a woman wearing a strap-on cock trying to give him a new experience. Or would Tanny prefer to have Shannon take care of her ass while he handled her pussy and felt Shannon's shemale sex rubbing against his larger male cock inside Tanny?

He pictured himself humping both of them, one after the other, and every nerve in his body centered on the friction of his hands slipping and sliding up and down his cock. His come spilled out in long splats against the shower curtain.

Fergus collapsed against the wet, tiled wall and shook his head to get rid of the ringing sound in his ears. Then he bent over and snagged the washcloth from where it lay on the floor of the tub.

That was one hell of fucking mess he'd left on the curtain. Talk about leaving incriminating evidence behind. Tanny would nail him to the wall if she found out he'd been jacking himself off in the shower. He was here to solve a series of brutal murders and bring a criminal to justice, not waste his skills and experience as a homicide detective by thinking and acting like a horny teenager with no self-control.

If Shannon became the next victim because he couldn't keep his mind on his job, he'd kill himself rather than live with that shame. He and Tanny were the best detectives in the division. No way in hell was he going to ruin her career along with his just because they had to remain celibate for the duration of this investigation.

* * *

Shannon reset the views on her bedroom wallscreen. Staring at the exterior street views was a lot less tempting than watching Tannamae sitting in front of the mirror combing out her wet hair. As for Fergus, wisps of steam were trickling out from the bottom of the closed bathroom door. He was taking a very long time in there, most likely because he had to jack off just like she had when she took her shower.

Yep. Tonight was going to be another long one. Instead of torturing herself with the fact that she was going to spend the night with a hunky man and a beautiful woman who were here only because it was their job, maybe she should take a sleeping pill to knock herself out. Trying to push their buttons and annoy them with her sexual quips had backfired and made her hornier than ever.

Snow fell in fat flakes and had already piled up in thick drifts on the streets and sidewalks. Large and small droid plows and snowblowers whirred back and forth trying to keep up with Mother Nature's latest onslaught.

A quick stab of her finger opened a link to the weather channel at the bottom of the screen. The latest prediction was eight to ten inches of snow by midnight. The City Air Patrol Squad had posted severe restrictions with heavy fines and citations for private aircar traffic. The only aircars allowed out between the hours of ten p.m. and eight a.m. were ambulances and other emergency vehicles.

"Where did you hide the controls for your hairdryer?" Tannamae's soft-voiced question sent a tingle of carnal anticipation straight to Shannon's groin.

Shannon turned around and managed a casual stroll across the room. It was probably safer to just tell her where the hairdryer was instead of moving closer, but she couldn't stop herself. She rested her hand on Tannamae's shoulder, then tapped at the buttons cleverly hidden within the roses carved around the mirror frame. "This one is for the hairdryer and styling droid, Ms. Jones. This one starts up the hair-dye droid. You can ask it to do a complete dye job, frosts, or just the tips of your hair. That one's for the manicure droid. It has a full selection of styles and colors for your nails."

Tannamae tilted her head back, patted Shannon's hand on her shoulder, and smiled. With the arms and legs rolled up on the oversized pajamas, Tanny looked like a kid playing dress-up. But there was nothing childish about the tantalizing glimpse of her full breasts where the top gaped open. "Thank you. Call me Tanny, please. Every time you say Ms. Jones, I find myself looking around for my mom."

Shannon's knees wobbled under her. This wasn't working at all. Tanny was turning the tables on her. She better snag another chair soon before she fell over and made a complete idiot of herself. "Sure."

She carefully moved her hand and twisted a strand of Tanny's soft hair around her finger. "You have lovely hair. It's so thick and curly. Would you like to dye the tips with silver and gold glitter for the holidays?"

The bathroom door flew open. Shannon spun around in her chair with a guilty blush on her face. She snorted and bit back a laugh at the sight of Fergus stuffed into a pair of her pajamas. The arms and legs were way too short. Instead of hanging loose around Fergus's hips, her pants outlined his crotch in explicit and damp detail. He'd also given up on trying to button the top. Dark hair furred his chest and arrowed down past his taut stomach.

And for a final touch, the holster, stun gun, force cuffs, and shield he carried in his hands added a very wicked flavor to his attire. Shannon grinned and refrained from making comments about bondage, in deference to Fergus's embarrassed scowl.

His voice had a decidedly peeved tone to it. "While the two of you finish your discussion of hair colors, I'm going to grab a set of sweats from my gear. I can't sleep in these things."

This was true. Pajamas were supposed to be loose and comfortable, not tight and constricting. Of course, this didn't stop her from admiring the delectable view of those light cotton pants clinging to the curves of his tight-muscled ass when he exited the room.

Chapter Four

His old pair of sweatpants and sweatshirt with its sleeves torn off felt way better than those tight pajamas. The only reason he'd even put them on was because the blasted house droids had snagged his discarded clothes in order to clean them. He should have hung his clothes on the wall hook instead of leaving them on the floor, but he hadn't expected that kind of efficiency programmed into the housecleaning system. The only things the droids didn't cart away were his weapon belt, stun gun, force cuffs, and badge.

It was either wear the pajamas or walk out with a towel draped around his hips like a porno model. Not that it made any difference. The damned things were so tight, they'd clung to him like a second skin. He might as well have strutted around stark naked with a bright red arrow flashing above his groin. At least the ones Tanny wore were loose enough to conceal her weapon belt.

On the other hand, this gave him the opportunity to explore the rest of the house from top to bottom. He didn't care how extensive the security system was, walking through the layout himself would give him an advantage if anyone disarmed it and tried to sneak past his guard.

Aside from the fact that he felt properly armed now with his weapon belt around his waist, the self-imposed tour of the house had also given him the time to figure out what to do about their ridiculous sleeping arrangement. He opened the bedroom door and stepped inside.

Tanny and Shannon had cleared off the coffee table in front of the fireplace so they could play a game of 3D chess. They sat cross-legged on oversized cushions in their matching pajamas. But the pajamas were the only things that matched. Ebony and ivory, Tanny with her dark skin and petite build, Shannon with her pale skin and tall, broad-shouldered build; they were a study in contrasts.

Fergus stopped in mid-stride and took a second look at the flames roaring behind them. "Is that a real fire?"

Shannon uncoiled her long legs and rose to her feet. She peered at the fire for a few moments, selected a small log from the woodbin, nudged it into the fire with a pair of tongs, and waited until it took before she turned around. "Yes, it's real. I don't like fakes."

Tanny stood up. Shannon moved sideways and replaced the tongs in their stand. Then she crossed her arms and murmured, "Come a little closer, honey. I can handle you."

Fergus stopped and stared. Shannon's body language didn't mesh with her provocative attitude and words. If she really wanted Tanny, she'd hold her arms out instead of crossed protectively over herself. She was trying to fake them out so they wouldn't approach her too closely. Why? What was she hiding from them?

Later. One thing at a time. Fergus jerked his thumb at the small desk in the corner. "Do you maintain a decent uplink in your bedroom for your comp system?"

The puzzlement that flickered across Shannon's face was the first normal expression he'd seen from her thus far. "Of course I do. Why do you ask?"

Fergus crossed the room and seated himself at the desk. The chair was a marvel of ergonomic efficiency with black leather padded seat and smooth ball bearings in its wheeled feet. As for the desk, it looked like an antique rolltop, with real cherry wood instead of a molded plastic reproduction. The keyboard, sofscreen, voice, and uplink panels were top-of-the-line models. He placed his detective's shield in the uplink slot. The system clicked and whirred for a few seconds, then accepted his police security access with a soft chirp. "The best way for us to protect you is to guard you in shifts. I'm going to stay awake and work online during my shift. When I'm ready to sleep, I'll wake Tanny and she can take the next shift."

Shannon strode to the desk and leaned on the edge. Angry tension held her body tight and hard. "You overrode my house computer. Why?"

He swiveled the chair around and faced her. "You're under protective custody per domestic violence parameters. In order to achieve that, NYPD security protocols will replace yours for the duration of our stay."

She backed away and crossed her arms. "I see."

Tanny came over and leaned against the side of his chair. He felt the soft flesh of her breast pressing into his arm beneath the thin fabric of her pajamas.

"How well did you know the victim?" Tanny asked, her voice deceptively soft, yet hard as steel.

Shannon swung her head around. There was a definite wrecking-ball effect to that sudden movement. She stood totally still and stared at them for one long moment. Finally, she blinked, then turned, walked to the bed, and seated herself on the edge. A soft sigh gusted from her parted lips. Two bright spots of red stood out against the light skin stretched across her high cheekbones. "You probably already know how many times I called Merry just to talk."

Shannon sat with her back perfectly straight and folded her hands in her lap. All the hard-edged sexuality she'd been projecting at them for the last couple of hours had vanished into a hesitant vulnerability.

Tanny tightened her fingers around Fergus's arm. It was his turn now. Good cop, bad cop. Hell, it didn't make any difference which side he took. Tanny would switch from one to the other without thinking. Instead of following a preset scenario, he would just go with the flow. And now that Shannon was finally relaxing and letting him see her true personality, what he wanted to do was take her in his arms and comfort her obvious distress over her friend's brutal murder.

Shannon looked away. Firelight flickered across her face and softened the strong lines of her body. "I wanted to be close to her, but she already had a lover. I don't know who her lover was. I don't even know if her lover was a man, a woman, or another shemale like me." She lifted her chin and glared at them. "I didn't kill Merry. Why would I contact the police if I killed her?"

Fergus cleared his throat. "You had the motivation and the means, but..."

Hope blazed in her eyes. "But what?"

Tanny spoke next. "You were at a board meeting when Merry was murdered."

Fergus explained the rest. "We've documented your whereabouts during the time of death for the other four murders. We know you're not the killer."

The shock on Shannon's face also helped confirm her innocence. "Four other murders?" She croaked out the words in a strangled voice.

Fergus rubbed his chin with his thumb and forefinger. "The only common link between all the murders is that all victims were hermaphrodites. Merry is the only one you had any contact with."

Shannon frowned. "What does that mean?"

Fergus shrugged. Giving her a little information should keep her off-balance and hopefully more willing to cooperate with their investigation. "We don't know. One theory says the other murders were practice murders, all leading up to you."

Comprehension splashed Shannon's pale skin with a vivid blush. "Because I'm the one who has all the money. I'm the one who's in the news every day with my campaign for equal rights for all herms."

Tanny nodded. "So, now that you know we have a serial murderer to find, we'd appreciate it if you stopped all your sexual teasing and let us do our job."

Shannon's mouth dropped open. Then she shut her mouth and grinned. It was the first natural smile she'd given and it looked even better on her than her faked leers. "When did you figure out I was bluffing?"

Tanny chuckled. "That was easy. It happened when I let you look down my shirt and you didn't follow through by making a move on me."

Shannon shook her head. "Damn, you're good. Now what?"

Fergus smiled. "Now you tell us everything you know about Merry. Tell us who her friends were, and give a list of your friends and acquaintances so we can question everyone. Then we also need to know every detail you can give us about your daily routine and Merry's."

* * *

Tannamae removed her belt, stun gun, and shield. She placed them on the dresser beside the bed, reset the alarm implant on her wrist to awaken her in four hours, then lifted the sheet and crawled onto her side of the bed. One thing for sure, the intensive grilling they'd given Shannon had apparently exhausted her. She was already sound asleep on her side of the bed with the pillow bunched under her head and the sheet pulled over her back and shoulder to her chin.

The routine of getting into bed was both disconcertingly familiar and off kilter. Tannamae had to keep reminding herself that it wasn't Fergus on the other side of the bed. That she couldn't just roll over, snuggle against his long, lean warmth, comb her fingers through the springy curls on his stomach, and find the solid flesh of his cock waiting for her.

He was sitting at the desk, studying data on the sofscreen while the flickering flames from the fireplace behind him painted the wall and ceiling with surrealistic shadow shapes. They had a serial killer to stop. Tonight's session with Shannon had given them a long list of possibilities -- possibilities they needed to weed out one by one while they sorted out the truth.

Flames splashed shadows on the wall and painted Fergus's hair with dark red highlights, giving him the look of angel and devil all mixed together. Fire and brimstone, clouds and shadows. Smoky old bars. Bright holographic neon lights flashing above bored faces looking for a night of pleasure in a stranger's arms. Ice-cold beer and a shot of brandy. Santa Claus bringing presents down the chimney. Was making love the devil's candy or the whispered echo of an angel's touch? What happened when a fallen angel learned how to fly again? What did you do when you felt hungry for all the things you couldn't change?

* * *

The persistent buzz against her wrist woke her. Tannamae untangled her arms and legs from the twisted sheets and rolled out of bed. Fergus was slumped over the desk, his head propped on his arms, the data on the sofscreen scrolling past unseen.

She placed her hands on his shoulders. He uncoiled himself from the chair, took her into his arms, and gave her a long, satisfying kiss. It was like coming home all over again in the strong ease of his embrace.

Finally, they pulled apart. Tannamae touched his lips with her fingers and whispered, "Go to sleep, honey. I'll take the next shift."

Chapter Five

Baby Jamie nestled in the curve of Shannon's arm, like one of the dolls she used to have. A doll with cobalt blue eyes and a fragile head covered with thick brown curls. Except no doll, no matter how cleverly made, could create the warm, solid weight and baby-powder smell of a newborn infant wiggling against her grip. Jamie's pale blue blanket with pink bunny rabbits embroidered along the edges added a bright touch to the hospital nursery with its row upon row of incubators and babies.

Fergus smiled, reached past Shannon's arm, and let Jamie latch onto his finger with one tiny hand. "He's a strong little bugger." A confused frown creased Fergus's brow. "Uh. Jamie *is* a he, isn't he?"

Shannon turned to the medical data chart glowing on the sofscreen embedded in Jamie's incubator. "Jamie has adrenogenital syndrome."

"Adrenogenital syndrome?" He snorted. "Break it down into layman's terms, please."

"She has the XX chromosomes and internal organs of a female, but the external genitals of a male. Her labia is fused and she has a small penis but no testicles."

Fergus's eyes widened with surprise. "Whoa!" He swiped his hands through his hair. "How common is this?"

Shannon carefully returned the infant to the incubator. Fergus was a homicide detective. Not a stereotypical entertainment holovid star stomping around with a weapon belt and shield. He obviously had a keen intellect hidden beneath his macho exterior, an intellect geared to analyzing facts and evidence and putting the pieces together to solve crimes. "It occurs in one out of every five thousand births. Because of routine DNA testing, we're able to diagnose them during the pregnancy instead of at puberty when the child's secondary sex characteristics appear."

Tanny moved closer. "I'd be very confused if I were Jamie's parents. Are they going to raise Jamie as a boy or a girl?"

Shannon bit back her automatic sigh of annoyance at this question. Instead of looking at children as unique individuals with their own minds and souls, many parents made the mistake of seeing their children as extensions of themselves. They'd try to mold their children to fit their dreams, instead of letting their children find their own dreams. "That decision is best left to Jamie when Jamie reaches the age of consent. Many choose to identify themselves by their genotype rather than their external genitalia."

Fergus nodded. "What happens if the parents want to raise Jamie on their own?"

"Per the equal rights amendment for intersexed people, they must agree to monitoring by the Herm Foundation to ensure proper education and support for Jamie's upbringing."

Shannon sighed and stroked the sleeping infant's feather-soft cheek. "Merry, the herm whose murder you're investigating, had adrenogenital syndrome just like Jamie."

Fergus lifted his head. Angry sparks flared in the depths his dark eyes. "Some investigation we're doing right now."

Shannon jerked her chin at the exit sign. "You can walk away and investigate any time you want. I'm not exactly thrilled to have you around, either."

He winced and gave her an apologetic smile. "I shouldn't have snapped at you like that. I'm sorry."

Shannon sucked in a deep breath, exhaled, and managed a brief nod at his apology. She turned and went to the next incubator marked for her attention, and reached inside to pick up a baby with straight blond hair. She peered at the chart glowing on that incubator's monitor. "This is Theo. He has the exact opposite condition from Jamie, called Swyer's syndrome. This syndrome occurs in one in every twenty thousand births. Theo has the male sex chromosomes, but his external organs are female. He has a vagina, uterus, and enlarged clitoris. He has neither ovaries nor testes. Theo can get pregnant via in-vitro fertilization, if he chooses."

A dark blush spread across Fergus's olive-skinned face, almost matching the color of his mahogany-brown hair. At the same time, avid curiosity gleamed in his eyes. He gestured at Shannon with an awkward wave of his hand. "What about you?"

Despite his curiosity, he still found the topic of her ambiguous sexual state embarrassing. Shannon couldn't resist the temptation to flash him a sultry grin. "My condition is very rare. The frequency is one in every eighty-three thousand births. I have Ova-testis or true hermaphroditism. My genotype is XX. I have both ovarian and testicular tissue, a half-uterus, breasts, a vagina, and a functional penis. I could get pregnant and possibly carry a child to term. My sperm count is low, but there is a slight possibility that I could father children, if I chose."

Tanny tilted her head to the side. A deep frown etched her brow. "Now I understand why you always refer to yourself as she instead of he. Even though you have a fully functional penis, you have the genotype of a woman."

Fergus cleared his throat and asked, "Are what you, Jamie, and Theo have the only kinds of hermaphrodites?"

A great weariness filled Shannon's heart. The baby in her arms suddenly felt like he weighed fifty pounds. She carefully returned Theo to the incubator. "No. Turner's syndrome has the XO genotype where there isn't any Y chromosome at all. Klinefelter's syndrome is the XXY genotype. Then there are various mosaic genotypes where a few chromosomes are XX and the rest are XXY all mingled together in the same person."

Shannon turned around and waved her hand at the rest of the incubators. "On the other end of the scale, there's a rare hormonal disorder called Kallmann's syndrome. This syndrome causes a hormonal deficiency. The person fails to go through normal puberty and remains sexually underdeveloped and infertile."

She arched her eyebrows at Tanny and Fergus. "I call it the Peter Pan syndrome because they never grow old. Who knows? Maybe Kallmann's syndrome is behind the old legends about the fairy folk not growing old like the rest of humanity."

Tanny snapped her fingers. "I saw a vid about a little boy who had the exact opposite problem. He was only seven years old and looked like an old man."

Shannon nodded. "That's progeria, an extremely rare genetic disease that accelerates the aging process. Progeria affects one in four million children. Most of them don't live beyond their early teenage years, though one or two have lived to their early twenties."

Fergus grimaced. His gaze turned somber. "That's horrible."

Shannon sighed. Christmas was just around the corner. They should be feeling happy and ready to celebrate, not sad and depressed. "Last, but not least, of the more uncommon genetic variations are the XXX and the XYY genotypes."

"XXX and XYY genotypes?" Fergus arched his eyebrows.

Shannon turned and led them to the exit. Rattling off all these statistics made her feel like she was auditioning for a position as an educational holovid teacher. "The XXX variation or super female occurs in one in every five thousand births. The physical manifestations of triple-X are larger than average breasts with wider spaced nipples, a narrow, wasp waist, wider hips than average, and a height of usually more than six feet. By most standards, triple-X females are quite attractive, proving that a genetic/chromosomal abnormality need not be considered a deformity. However, learning disabilities or developmental delays are not uncommon."

"What about the XYY variation?" Tanny asked.

Shannon strolled past a pair of droid orderlies wheeling medi-carts through the corridor. She led Fergus and Tanny past the nurses' station, where six nurses sat at a wall of monitor screens and data ports, and to the social services office. Her first parent liaison appointment was scheduled this morning. "This condition affects males who have an extra Y chromosome. Their physical characteristics are often indistinguishable from a normal male, though it is not uncommon for them to appear even more masculine. They have low, wide waists; narrow hips; broad, flat chest; wide shoulders; high hairlines; prevalent facial and body hair; and extra-large testicles."

"Aren't they also more violent and prone to criminal behaviors because of the extra Y chromosome?" Fergus asked.

Shannon stopped at the door for the social services office. "There's no scientific evidence to justify that belief."

She placed her hand on the ID panel. It glowed under her touch, verified her DNA as the authorized representative for today, and the door slid open. A huge mahogany desk dominated the room. A single vase of red roses adorned the corner of the desk and a sofscreen glowed in the center. Three black, cushioned swivel chairs were lined up behind the desk. Four more chairs and a black, cushioned sofa took up the space on the clients' side. A side door in the right-hand wall provided a separate entrance for the clients. White floor-length curtains adorned the window viewscreen in the left-hand wall.

She stepped inside and gestured at Tanny and Fergus to take the two extra seats behind the desk. The door slid shut and locked itself behind them.

Tanny seated herself. Tailored hunter green slacks and tunic clung to the lush curves of her hips and breasts and contrasted very nicely with her white scarf and café-au-lait skin. The matching bag slung over her shoulder contained her stun gun, shield, and force cuffs. She'd confined her raven-black hair in a sleek bun. Silver studs flashed at her earlobes. She wore her computer access and security link pads as wristbands. The control studs on the dark leather glinted under the fluorescent office lighting.

Fergus snagged a chair, leaving the middle one vacant for Shannon. He leaned back and crossed his long, lean legs at the ankles. No business suit for him today. He'd chosen faded jeans, a plain white T-shirt, and a loose jean jacket that gave him easy access to his holstered stun pistol. The snug-fitting jeans emphasized a very masculine bulge at his crotch.

All this talking about the different genetic and genital variations had made Shannon excruciatingly aware of Tanny's womanly appeal and Fergus's blatant masculinity. She smothered a sigh. No way in hell would they be interested in her. She'd never have lovers. Choosing a loose, supple indigo pantsuit with a long jacket this morning had been a very wise move. It did an excellent job of concealing her hard nipples and erect cock.

* * *

When Mr. and Mrs. Nordstrom entered the social services office, Shannon gestured at them to take either the chairs positioned in front of the desk or the couch. Mr. Nordstrom managed an aristocratic sneer while he sank into his chair. His somber, pinstriped gray business suit was perfectly tailored. Diamonds glinted on his wristbands.

As for Mrs. Nordstrom, she strutted into the room and tossed her sable coat onto the couch, then sat with her legs crossed at just the right angle to slide the hem of her little black dress up to her perky little ass. Translucent spike heels, artfully styled hair tipped with silver and blue sparkles, and an expensive emerald necklace and matching earrings completed her standard "trophy wife" ensemble.

Shannon frowned and requested the stats for Mr. and Mrs. Nordstrom on her desk screen. She couldn't picture this woman giving birth to any child, let alone one as strong and healthy and beautiful as little Jamie. Oh, of course. That explained it. They'd transferred the fetus from Mrs. Nordstrom's womb into a surrogate mother at one week's gestation. Mrs. Nordstrom had no intention of ruining her size-three figure and augmented breasts with the ravages of pregnancy and breastfeeding.

DNA tests at one week's gestation pinpointed the XX chromosome but not the adrenogenital syndrome. By the time they'd found out Jamie's intersex status through ultrasound, the fetus was at the six-month stage. Because abortion after the first trimester had been ruled illegal in 2021, they couldn't go that route and terminate the pregnancy.

Shannon folded her hands together and stretched her mouth into her best professional smile. "Have you come to a decision regarding Jamie's future upbringing?"

Mr. Nordstrom studied Shannon with a cold, reptilian stare that made her skin crawl. He transferred his gaze to Tanny and Fergus and curled his lip into a contemptuous sneer. "Are all of you freaks, or just one of you?"

Fergus leaned back in his chair and laced his fingers behind his neck. That move opened his jean jacket and revealed his holstered stun gun and detective's shield. "The only freaks I see in this room are sitting on the other side of the desk."

Mr. Nordstrom's face turned red. He jumped to his feet with an incoherent roar, lunged forward, knocked the vase aside, and slammed his hands onto the desktop. The vase shattered, spilling water and roses across the tiled floor. A small panel beneath the window viewscreen slid open. A servobot rolled out and used a suction-tipped hose to vacuum the crumpled flowers, broken pieces of glass, and puddled water.

"That's right." Fergus deepened his voice into a purring growl of anticipation. "Go ahead. I'd love to arrest you for assault on a police officer."

Mr. Nordstrom swallowed, sucked in a deep breath, and exhaled very slowly. He backed away and returned to his seat. When he spoke, his voice had the flat, empty intonations of a computer-generated greeting. "We have decided to waive our parental rights and give the infant up to the custody of the Herm Foundation for adoption."

"Thank you," Shannon murmured. She printed out the required documents and focused on keeping her hands from shaking. The last time she'd looked at the Herm Foundation's waiting list for adoptive parents, they had fifteen couples and four triples, all of which had stable, long-term cohabitation contracts. As for explaining to Jamie when she grew old enough to understand why her parents had given her away, the child psychologists on staff would be the best people to handle that task.

* * *

After the Nordstroms' hasty exit, Fergus prowled around the office. He stopped at the window viewscreen and cycled through the available selections. The animated images ranged from the typical Earth wilderness scenes to recent images of the lunar, Mars, and Jovian Moon colonies. He reset it to a panoramic display of Saturn spinning against the star-strewn splendor of deep space and turned around. "That was interesting. Are all the parents that hostile?"

Shannon sat like a statue behind the desk, cold and distant, without expression on her face. Her brows drew down in concentration over her narrowed eyes. Dark lashes curved above her creamy skin. Two dark red blotches followed the line of her high cheekbones like rouge, except he already knew she used no cosmetics. "Each interview is different. Many parents do agree to raise their children according to the equal rights laws for hermaphrodites."

She straightened her shoulders and shot him a steadfast stare. "Nowadays, when the majority of hermaphrodites reach the age of consent, they decide not to have their genitals surgically altered and mutilated."

Tanny shot a glare at him, too. Then she reached out and covered Shannon's hand with hers. Shannon gasped, looked Tanny over from head to toe, and murmured in a husky whisper, "Watch out. I bite."

Tanny threw her head back and chuckled. The smooth café-au-lait skin of her throat gleamed like burnished gold above the cool green of her tunic top. The pose thrust her full breasts against the soft fabric. "I like that. But then you'd have to be very strong-willed to put up with this bullshit, wouldn't you?"

Bzzzzzzzzzzz. The entry buzzer at the office door warned them that the next scheduled appointment stood outside.

Fergus crossed the room in three strides and hitched his hip onto the corner of the desk previously occupied by the vase of roses. Shannon composed her face into a professional mask and arched her eyebrows. "Are you sure you want to be on that side of the desk?"

He grinned. "Don't worry. My bite is worse than my bark."

Her mouth twitched. She smoothed it back into a bland smile. "Of course." She pressed a button to unlock the client entry door.

This time it was a young couple barely old enough to vote. They crept inside, holding hands, white-knuckled and somber. The guy was skinny and blond. The girl looked like she might be Hispanic, with light-brown hair and olive complexion.

Shannon gestured at them to sit.

They sat.

The guy straightened his shoulders and stuck his bony chest out like a bantam rooster getting ready for his first time in a back-alley cockfight. "We're not going to let you take Theo away from us."

The girl nodded. "That's right. We know our legal rights. You can't take my baby away from me without proof of abuse."

Shannon propped her elbows on the desk and rested her chin on her folded hands. Her mouth relaxed into a gentle smile. "We're not going to take your baby away from you. We're offering you a place where you can raise Theo in a safe environment, free from harassment."

Chapter Six

Shannon stepped behind the screen in her sub-basement private gymnasium and peeled her business suit off with short, angry tugs. She grabbed the white cotton shirt from the hook and slipped it over her shoulders. Soft cotton rubbed against her heated skin and swollen nipples. She belted the kilt around her hips. The pleated fabric hung to her knees in the only type of skirt she'd ever wear. No underclothing, of course. Stockings with garters and brogues completed the traditional attire for her bi-weekly sword-training session.

Her sexual tease game with Fergus and Tanny had backfired. Now, with every little gesture, every look, she kept thinking they actually liked her and saw her as a person instead of a grotesque aberration of humanity.

When Fergus defended her with his sarcastic response to Mr. Nordstrom's cruel words, her heart had melted into a puddle of pure happiness. Then when Tanny reached over and gave her hand a sympathetic squeeze after the Nordstroms left the office, Shannon almost exploded with the need to turn and kiss her sweet lips.

They didn't really care about her. To them, she was a freak. She must remain strong. They'd only hurt her, the same way she'd been hurt so many times before when all she wanted was to love. And be loved in return.

She'd let her guard down in the nursery, touching babies she'd never be able to have and hold as her own.

Tanny and Fergus stood at the table where the broadsword waited for Shannon's usage. His mouth slightly agape with awe, Fergus touched the blade with a reverent fingertip. "Holy shit! This ain't no toy. It's got to be at least three feet long."

Tanny touched the hilt and looked up with a shy smile that cut through Shannon's heart like a needle-sharp dirk. "It looks just like the one hanging over the fireplace in your living room, except that one has gemstones."

Shannon strolled across the room. Her cock swayed under the kilt with the motion of her long-legged stride. "The one over the fireplace is a family heirloom. This one is a reproduction. It's pure tempered steel, hand-hammered for three days over an antique forge. The Society for Creative Anachronism requires authentic reproductions for their combat simulations. That's why I wear a kilt during my practice sessions. It keeps me from feeling uncomfortable when I wear it during the events."

As soon as she said that, both detectives' gazes went straight to her crotch and then moved just as quickly away. They didn't have to say anything. She knew exactly what they were thinking about her non-existent undergarments.

Fergus coughed and cleared his throat. "Ah, yes. I guess it would take some getting used to if you aren't in the habit of wearing a kilt every day."

Tanny gave her a look of startled comprehension. "You have the muscle to handle this kind of sword?"

The memory of her father swinging the MacNal sword one-handed in a full circle above his head flashed into her mind. "The strength to wield a broadsword is bred into my heritage. The double groove in the center of the blade is often misrepresented as a 'blood groove'. It's called a fuller groove and it serves to lighten the sword, making it easier to swing while maintaining the structural integrity of the blade. The basket hilt keeps my hand from slipping off in the heat of battle."

She gestured at the practice mats. "Would you like to join me in stretching first, then try a practice bout afterwards?"

Fergus gave her a sheepish grin and held up his hands in surrender. "I know diddly-squat about sword-fighting. You'd probably cut my head off with the first swing."

* * *

The automated juice bar was fully stocked. All Tanny had to do was name her poison and the computerized bar whirred into action to create a frothy concoction. She sipped at a banana-orange cream with sprinkles of cinnamon and arched her eyebrow at Fergus. He tasted his whipped pineapple-coconut blend and winked at her. "Better watch out. This kind of service is very seductive." He rotated his stool sideways so he had a good view of the workout area.

Shannon faced an android representation of a red-haired Scottish clansman. She held the enormous broadsword with the grace and strength of a man. Side-on to her opponent in the classic dueler's stance, Shannon kept her sword arm bent with the blade ready and her back arm raised with open hand to show there was no hidden dagger in reserve.

"She's an interesting combination of opposites, isn't she?" Fergus murmured. "One second, she's all woman, the next, she's a typical man. Have you noticed how she blows hot and cold around us?"

Tanny savored another icy sip from her frosted glass. "I don't blame her. I'd probably be the same way. I'd always be afraid of letting my guard down around strangers. I'd always be wondering if they thought I was a freak instead of another human being with physical and emotional needs."

"*En garde.*" Two blades met with a whisper of contact.

A sidestep. A quick beat of the blades. Shannon's kilt swirled around her muscled legs. She'd plaited her wavy brown hair into a braid. A lunge and then a counter-lunge brought the blades together in a screeching duel along their deadly lengths. Both swords held fast at the hilts for a split second. Shannon and her droid opponent broke, stepped back and circled each other, looking for another opening.

"She's good." Fergus rubbed his chin and narrowed his gaze. "She won't be an easy victim, and she would probably defeat the usual attacker."

"Why didn't you take her up on her offer of a practice bout?"

Fergus twisted his mouth into a rueful grin. "I really don't know a damn thing about sword-fighting. What I'd like to do is ask her to train me, but…"

"You can't. Not while she's in danger from this serial killer. We've got to focus on our job first."

"Right."

"How about after we've caught the killer. Then what?"

The blades clashed together again. The sound echoed through Tanny's teeth as if a tuning fork had been laid against them. Shannon swung aside with a flare of her kilt that exposed the top of her thigh and buttock.

Fergus knit his brow together in a worried frown. "You wouldn't mind?"

Tanny sucked in her breath and released it slowly.

There! He didn't actually say it out loud. But yes, the unspoken question was there. Fergus was interested in Shannon not just as a teacher in sword-fighting, but also in other areas. The one thing she always cherished about their relationship was the fact that they never lied to each other about anything. Trust was such a precious commodity nowadays, and so far, he'd never given her reason not to trust him.

"I like her, too. A lot."

Fergus swiveled his head around and locked gazes with her. "You do?"

Tanny took another sip from her glass and licked the foam from her lips. Fergus's gaze followed her tongue with the hungry fascination of a cat tracking a mouse. Warmth pooled in her pussy, and she crossed her legs against the sudden thought of letting him fuck her standing up like he had two days ago. Was it only two days ago? It seemed like forever. "Whatever we do, we have to wait until after this case is solved. You know the rules against fraternization while on duty."

The smoldering heat in his eyes flared into a searing look that curled her toes. He nodded. "Of course. What's on the itinerary for tomorrow?"

Tanny breathed out a sigh of relief and lifted her glass in salute to Fergus. He returned her grin and they drank together. Having it out in the open like this felt so much better than the both of them playing mind games and trying to pretend they weren't interested in Shannon. They were adults, not high school kids who didn't know what they wanted.

Steel against steel. Human versus droid. A steady beat of blade upon blade clanging together like cymbals and throwing sparks in the air

Tanny accessed the computerized link on her wristband. "Herm Foundation is closed for Christmas vacation, starting tomorrow, until the day after New Year's. The only thing on the schedule for tomorrow is Meredith's memorial service."

"Right. The memorial service will give us the perfect opportunity to scope out the crowd for possible suspects."

Chapter Seven

Shannon accessed the house computer and studied the kitchen inventory. It was just about non-existent. Two bottles of apple juice, one bottle of orange juice, one container of chocolate milk, two bananas, one tomato, a dozen eggs, and a half loaf of raisin bread. The well-stocked droid coffee and cappuccino bar was her one indulgence. She wasn't used to having company. Hell, she wasn't used to having *anyone* stay with her for longer than a couple of hours, let alone sleep over.

She turned around. Fergus slouched against the counter beside the droid coffee dispenser. He pulled out two whipped mocha cappuccinos, handed one to Tanny, and arched an eyebrow at Shannon. "What's your poison?"

"French vanilla, please."

He nodded and reset the controls for her order. A few seconds later, a cup dropped out of the slot, filled with steaming hot liquid and topped with a large dollop of whipped cream.

Shannon pulled up the shopping menu on the main comp control pad. "You have a choice of Vietnamese, Szechwan, Japanese, Thai, Italian, Tex-Mex, Hindu, Algerian, or Turkish."

Fergus widened his eyes and peered at the counter space for yet another droid input pad. "You maintain an auto-chef here, too?"

What would he say if she told him she actually knew how to cook? "No. Most times I order out."

Tanny grinned, smacked her lips, and rubbed her stomach. "I vote for Italian. I'll take a tossed salad with raspberry vinaigrette dressing, eggplant parmesan, angel hair pasta with sauce, and garlic bread. And for dessert, I'd like lemon cheesecake."

Shannon cocked her head at Fergus.

He shrugged. "I'll have the same, but make it a double order. I'm a growing boy and I need to keep up my strength."

Shannon selected an identical order for herself, and hesitated. Even though, technically speaking, they were on duty as her police guards, ordering a full-course meal like this made it feel like she was hosting a romantic dinner date. Hmmm. She might as well go all out and tell the robo-butler to set the dining room table with candles, formal tablecloth, napkins, dishes, and wine glasses. "This restaurant has an extensive selection of wines. Any particular preference?"

Fergus snorted. "I usually drink whiskey or brandy. Whatever wine you pick is fine with me."

Shannon bit her lip over the selection, requested four bottles of Merlot and one of Pinot Noir, and hit send. If nothing else, the wine should relax her enough to sleep without dreams.

* * *

Maybe she should do this more often. Maybe after this was over, after they'd captured whoever had killed Meredith, she could invite Fergus and Tanny over for a special celebratory dinner and they'd become friends.

A backless, wide-legged, green velvet pantsuit swished with every step Shannon took. Cool air caressed her spine. The one-carat diamond pinned to the high-necked collar matched the diamond studs at her earlobes.

Tanny stood at the bottom of the staircase. A sleeveless scarlet velvet sheath clung to her curves like a second skin. The thigh-high slit gave the perfect exposure to the smooth length of her leg. Diamond dangles at her earlobes cast miniature rainbows against her brown skin. She flashed a shy smile at Shannon. Gloss on the lush contours of her lips gave them a just-been-kissed wet look. "Thanks for loaning me these earrings. They're beautiful."

Fergus descended the staircase clad in black slacks and shirt with silver studs in his earlobes and at the cuffs of his shirt. No tie. He'd left two buttons open at the top, giving a teasing glimpse of dark curls furring his chest.

Tanny grinned and strolled to him with an easy sway of her hips. They linked arms.

Shannon turned and led the way into the dining room. The sudden intake of breath she heard when Fergus saw the backless state of her pantsuit was very gratifying.

The double pocket doors for the dining room slid apart at her approach. Spirals of votive candles glowed in the chandelier hanging above the massive table. A single candelabra flickered in front of three place settings. The brilliant white synthsilk tablecloth dripped lace down to the burnished hardwood floor. Embroidered vines and flowers decorated the tapestry cushions on the Georgian reproduction chairs. An oversized fireplace took up the entire back wall. The flames cast dancing shadows on the ceiling.

Shannon took her seat at the head of the table. Fergus and Tanny took the other two chairs positioned on either side in an intimate seating plan. Robo-maids swooped around the table, pouring wine and depositing steaming platters of food, bowls of tossed salad, and crispy slices of garlic bread.

Fergus took his first bite of the entrée. His eyes went black with pleasure. He uttered a soft gasp under his breath. Would his eyes darken like that during the first fragile moment when his cock slid inside his lover? How loud would his cries get when he climaxed?

Shannon lifted her cut-crystal wine glass. Red and violet fragments of refracted light drifted across her hand. "To a joyous holiday season."

Fergus and Tanny lifted their glasses and drank the toast with her.

The robo-butler stopped in front of the fireplace, spun around, and announced. "Incoming call. Priority-level personal from Angus and Kathleen MacNal."

Shannon suppressed a groan. Her mom and dad must have ESP. Why else would they call in the middle of her private dinner for three? Should she excuse herself and take the call in the library?

Too late.

The robo-butler's program had all calls from her parents listed on the auto-accept list. It extruded a holovidphone projector arm and pointed to the empty space between the table and the fireplace. Two 3D images appeared in mid-air, floating six inches above the floor. They'd paid for the normal-sized projections rather than the inexpensive eighth-sized ones.

Her father, Angus, had his black hair tied back in a neat ponytail. Grey at his temples added an elegant air to his rugged face. He wore a pair of casual jeans and a soft, white cotton shirt.

Her mother, Kate, wore her usual rumpled lab coat over faded jeans. A black headband held thick auburn curls away from her face. Freckles dusted her nose and cheeks.

Both of her parents worked hard on their orbital Ark. They'd retired from the business and spent their time recreating extinct and endangered animal and plant species from frozen DNA samples. Just setting up the natural habitats for each species required extensive gene-splicing and ongoing monitoring.

Her mom and dad exchanged startled glances at the sight of Shannon eating a formal dinner with two strangers. Then they smiled, linked hands, and walked around the table, taking their time scrutinizing Fergus and Tanny with obvious approval.

Kate tucked a wayward curl behind her ear and said, "Please introduce us to your new friends, Shann."

Shannon managed to return her wine glass to the table without spilling a drop. The avid delight on her parents' faces meant only one thing. They envisioned their only child and heir becoming part of a happily married triple and producing a horde of grandchildren. "Mom, Dad, my friends are Detectives Fergus DeSoto and Tannamae Jones."

Shannon almost jumped out of her chair when Fergus and Tanny reached out from either side of the table and covered her hands with theirs. Did that mean they were going to let her parents assume they were her lovers, rather than cause them to worry with the real reason for their presence in her home?

Fergus said, "We're very happy to meet you, Mr. and Mrs. MacNal."

Her parents' smiles widened into ecstatic grins. Her father nodded his head but he kept his voice clipped and businesslike. "My apologies for interrupting your dinner like this. We hadn't expected Shann to have company." He turned to Shannon. "We'll be coming down to see you on New Year's Day. Can your friends be there for our visit?"

Fergus and Tanny both gave Shannon's hands an extra squeeze. Did that mean yes or no? She gulped and said, "I'm not sure if they'll be able to make it on such short notice. I hope so."

Her mom blew a kiss at her. "Goodbye, sweetheart. We'll see you on New Year's Day."

Their images shimmered and disappeared.

* * *

Shannon gathered her neatly folded pajamas from the foot of the bed and jerked her chin at the bathroom door. "I'll take the first shower, if you don't mind."

Fergus swiped his hand through his hair and exchanged a smoldering look with Tanny. "That's fine. No problemo. We don't mind, do we?"

"That's all right," Tanny said in a husky murmur. "We can wait."

Fergus held up his hand. "Let me check out the room first." Then he strolled inside the bathroom, peered inside the linen closet, and pulled the shower curtain aside to make sure no one was hiding there waiting to attack her. He exited the room and gestured at her to enter.

Shannon ground her teeth and carefully placed her necklace and earrings in the jewelry box. She hustled past him but left the door open so he could continue to monitor her safety. With an abrupt flick of her wrist, she tossed the pajamas on the toilet seat, then glanced over her shoulder. Tanny and Fergus had already turned their backs to give her a modicum of privacy.

She peeled off her pantsuit and underwear and dumped them in the laundry chute. Two thick towels hung on the wall beside the tub. Hot water, plenty of hot water, was what she needed to ease the sexual tension coiled in her body. She turned the dial to a hot and pulsating mist and pulled the curtain shut. Steam billowed past her ankles to her waist and then over her head and past the top of the curtain.

No lingering this time. Just soap her body and get the hell out before she went crazy from thinking about having both Fergus and Tanny shower with her.

She stood under the water and let it sluice over her and remove the soapsuds. Shampoo next. This time, she took a little longer letting the water rinse her hair clean. She reached for the conditioner. There wasn't any. Fergus must have emptied it last night and discarded the empty bottle in the trash for her. No big deal. She had another bottle by the sink.

Shannon twitched the curtain to the side, leaned out, grabbed the new bottle, and stopped.

Tanny stood in the doorway with her eyes closed. Fergus knelt in front of her. The top of Tanny's dress had been pulled down and the hem yanked up so that the fabric was now tucked in a thick roll at her waist. Her large nipples were dark chocolate tips upon the creamy caramel skin of her small, perky breasts. The areolas were wet and swollen from sucking. Shannon caught a glimpse of the sable curls on Tanny's pussy, trimmed to a narrow strip, just before Fergus moved his head lower.

He splayed his hands across the top of her thighs. When he fastened his mouth upon her pussy, Tanny sighed and tightened her grip on his hair.

Shannon carefully placed the bottle of conditioner on the side of the tub. She pulled the curtain back and left it open a crack, just enough to see them without them seeing her. This was nothing like any of the porno vids she watched when she jacked herself off. The men and women in the porno vids made exaggerated faces and their loud moans always sounded so fake and crude.

None of the women in the vids had ever uttered the soft mewls that escaped from Tanny's half-open mouth while she rubbed her pussy against Fergus's mouth in fierce demand. The muscles in her thighs bunched with her eager thrusts.

Fergus unzipped his pants and released his cock. It sprang out into his hand. He was uncircumcised. The foreskin slid back under his fingers and exposed the bulbous, blood-engorged head. He stroked his hand up and down the length of his cock with a slow, steady motion.

The tightness in her throat made her shake. It became an itch in her breasts, then her cock, and a hot wetness in her pussy.

Shannon wrapped her right hand around her cock and duplicated his movements. Would he like to stroke her while she stroked him?

Water splashed into the ceramic tub and gurgled down the drain. Steam billowed against the ceiling and fogged the mirror above the sink.

She pictured the three of them lying in bed together with her in the middle. She reached for Tanny. They shared a kiss while Fergus pressed his cock against Shannon's ass. He moved his hands between them and played with their breasts.

Shannon visualized Tanny sighing with pleasure and opening her legs for Shannon's erect cock.

Shannon moved her left hand from her breasts. She feathered her fingers down her belly, past her cock. She imagined the feel of Fergus's strong, muscled body lying behind her while he parted her wet pussy lips with his fingers from the rear. Then she inserted two fingers into her pussy.

It would never happen.

But that didn't stop her from imagining it.

In her mind's eye, she mounted Tanny at the exact same moment Fergus penetrated her with his cock. She imagined the tender joy of being able to leave her heart and body open and vulnerable to both of them.

Shannon's cock jerked within her stroking fingers. The image of Tanny shaking and crying out in pleasure while Fergus rode both of them to a shattering climax filled her mind. Her cum spurted out in a long, shuddering release of sensation.

Shannon sagged against the wall. Her legs shook under her. She felt as weak as a baby, unable to walk or move.

Finally, she opened her eyes, opened her hand around her cock, and pulled her fingers from her pussy.

The shower continued to spray water and steam into the tub. The curtain remained cracked open just enough for her to see Tanny and Fergus pulling their clothing together again.

Crumpled wrinkles marked the scarlet velvet of Tanny's dress.

Shannon picked up the hair conditioner bottle, squeezed out a generous dollop, and raked it through her snarled, wet hair with both hands. The tangles smoothed out and strands of loosened hair clung to her fingers like spider webs. She stepped back under the shower and let the steaming hot water rinse her hair and body clean from conditioner, soap, and sex.

Coming after watching Fergus and Tanny was so much more intense than any orgasm she'd ever felt before. Much better than she'd ever felt after watching a porno vid. Was she a voyeur? Would she freeze up if her fantasy became reality?

Shannon shrugged and turned the shower off. No use thinking about a fantasy that would never happen anyway. She squeezed the excess water from her hair. Now that the three of them had released their sexual frustrations, tonight should be a little more restful.

One night at a time. That was the best they could do for now.

Chapter Eight

Shannon staggered into the kitchen after Fergus. The aroma of freshly brewed coffee filled the air. Tanny stood at the counter slicing thick hunks of crusty French bread, hot and fresh from the oven. Butter, cream cheese, honey, grape jelly, apple jelly, and orange marmalade waited on the table.

Tanny stopped cutting bread. She picked up a steaming mug of coffee and turned around with it cradled between her hands. The handle was chipped and the phrase "Save a horse, ride a cowboy" had been inscribed on it in a lopsided red script.

Shannon almost stumbled under the impact of Tanny's open smile. *Stop reacting like a lovesick fool!* she warned her heart. *That smile didn't mean a damn thing. She's just being friendly.*

A faint blush flared on Tanny's face. She gestured at the table. "I took the liberty of ordering a brunch from French Twist's. Do you mind?"

Shannon clung to the back of a chair and caught her breath. *Keep the conversation simple. Don't overdo the platitudes.* "Oh, no. This is great! French Twist has an excellent breakfast menu. Thank you." *Gah! That was terrible! Now she sounded like a teenager in the throes of her first crush!*

Fergus grinned at Shannon. "Good morning. I like your coffee cup collection. You must have spent years at estate auctions snagging all the good ones."

He grabbed three ragged hunks of bread from the countertop, then sat at the table and buttered them. The words inscribed on his mug said "Ask me no questions and I'll tell you no lies." He stirred generous helpings of cream and sugar into his coffee.

The way Fergus was acting, it felt like the three of them had been living together for months instead of only two days. Shannon picked out a mug that said, "Hit Shappens!" and filled it to the brim with black coffee.

She'd chosen black slacks and a heavy black sweater to wear for the memorial service. Fergus and Tanny wore black pants and shirts, too. All they needed now were matching sunglasses to complete their look of a covert-ops team getting ready to go out on assignment.

Fergus shook his head and grumbled. "I don't like it."

Shannon licked her lips and stared at him over the rim of her mug. The memory of Fergus on his knees, jacking off while he ate Tanny's pussy, flashed into her mind. She placed the mug on the table and managed to sit without knocking anything over with her shaky hands. Now was not the time to be thinking about sex. "What don't you like?"

He pointed at the data stream scrolling across his wrist screen. "I don't like the setup for the security at the Herm Foundation Chapel. It's too risky for you. Anyone can walk in whenever they want during the memorial. The building comp system has no weapons-scanning capabilities. There's no security vidcams or audio recordings, either."

Shannon sucked in a deep breath and focused her attention on slathering apple jelly onto a warm chunk of bread. Fergus didn't have any personal feelings about her. Worrying about her safety meant he was just doing his job. "That's because everyone is scanned at the Enclave's main entrance before they enter. Only private residences like mine have the secondary, deep-scan set-up." She steeled her heart against the thought that he actually cared for her. "Besides, from what you've told me, this killer prefers to work one-on-one inside the victim's home, not at public locations."

Fergus scowled. "None of the other victims were under police protection at the time of their deaths. The fact that we're with you twenty-four hours a day could force the killer into changing his plan of attack."

Tanny leaned back in her chair and narrowed her gaze. Her dark lashes curved against her café-au-lait skin. "I'd rather force the killer out into the open than play cat-and-mouse games for days and weeks at a time."

Shannon looked away. She didn't blame them for wanting to leave. Hell, she'd be just as anxious to end this charade if she were in their shoes. Judging by what she'd seen last night, staying here with her was putting a serious cramp in their love life. The sooner they captured the murderer, the sooner they could leave and resume their usual routine of love and laughter. And the sooner she could return to her normal life of celebrating the holidays alone in an empty house.

* * *

Tanny hunched her shoulders under her thick coat. Her breath puffed out in a white cloud in front of her face. At least it wasn't as cold outside as it had been yesterday. Unfortunately, the moderate increase in temperature meant more snow. Thick clouds smothered the city and turned the sky to the color of dull pewter. Even though it was morning, it felt like late afternoon under the dark clouds. Fat, wet snowflakes fell in a steady monotony. The city had declared a snow emergency thirty minutes ago. The only vehicles allowed out on the streets and in the sky were police, fire, and EMS.

Tanny took the rear-guard position behind Shannon while Fergus led them on a two-block hike to the chapel. They trudged single file in each other's footsteps along the path Fergus broke for them on the snow-covered sidewalk. The chapel with its stained glass windows loomed in silent gloom at the bottom of the hill. Signs, trees, mailboxes, and parked groundcars wore fluffy caps of new-fallen snow.

More mourners trudged on the sidewalk in front of them. Their coats swung back and forth as they struggled to keep their feet inside the narrow path carved through the snow.

Shannon had remained very quiet and distant last night and this morning. Was it because she was thinking about today's memorial service? Was it because her parents were coming down for New Year's Eve under the mistaken belief that they were Shannon's lovers? Or was it because Shannon had seen them stealing a few moments of pleasure while she'd showered?

They should have kept better control of themselves. Even if Shannon hadn't seen them, if she decided to review her house security records prior to auto-erase at the end of the week, she'd be able to see in explicit detail how they'd made love to each other while she'd showered. What would she do then? File a complaint? Or confront them with the recording?

A steady stream of mourners trickled through the chapel's doorway behind them. Tanny stomped the snow from her boots onto the rubber mats placed in the lobby. Droid cleaners whizzed back and forth, sucking up the melted slush. She ran a quick scan of the faces in the lobby and matched them to the list of names on her wrist computer. All family, friends, and co-workers so far; any one of them could be Merry's killer.

They moved into the next room. The funeral director, a gaunt-looking man with his dark hair slicked back and tied at the nape of his neck in a sedate ponytail, greeted Shannon with a relieved smile and hurriedly brought them down the aisle to the front pew. Instead of a coffin, a two-foot-high cenotaph, engraved with Meredith's image and dates of birth and death, had been placed in the front of the room. But there would be no release of Meredith's body until after the murders had been solved. No burial, no cremation, and no closure until then.

The heavy aromas of the floral arrangements piled around the bronze cenotaph permeated the air. Tanny took shallow breaths through her mouth instead of her nose. Going into a sneezing fit would not be appropriate behavior at a memorial service.

A man and woman, both thin and worried-looking with their blond hair liberally streaked with gray, stood beside the cenotaph. Per the discreet ID badges clipped to their dark business tunics, they were Meredith's parents. They'd chosen to play a series of holovid images of their child from babyhood, childhood, and teenaged years all the way through more recent images of her dancing and laughing her way through life.

A simple yet poignant piano piece played in the background. It sounded familiar. Where had she heard that song before? Tanny accessed her link and requested more information. A few seconds later, the answer appeared on her wrist screen. It was Tchaikovsky's *Sleeping Beauty Waltz*. She shook her head at the parents' choice of requiem music. No prince would ever arrive to awaken their child from her dark slumber.

Her wrist screen changed to code red. A private message from Fergus, via the security band, scrolled across it. "Last pew, second man on right. He's not listed under friends, family, or co-worker. Still searching for possible cross-references for him under security protocols."

Oh, shit! Tanny checked her stun gun and shifted sideways in the pew so she could view the suspect.

* * *

The service itself was mercifully brief. Meredith's parents lit candles in front of the bronze plaque. Her mom stood and thanked everyone for coming here today to celebrate and remember the happy and courageous moments of her child's life. Then the mourners filed up the center aisle to hug the parents and whisper a few words of comfort.

Fergus shifted sideways in the pew and kept the suspect in sight. Dammit! Whoever was in charge of Herm Foundation Security had screwed up royally letting him inside the chapel. According to the data dump he'd received from police records, the suspect's name was Günter Snell. He was a member of the Anti-Herm League and one of the more prominent protestors picketing Shannon's corporation. His arrest record for disorderly conduct, assault, and weapons charges was long enough to stretch from Earth to the moon.

It didn't matter if Shannon's security ran a basic scan for conventional weapons on every person who came in through the main entrance of their gated community. With the kind of rap sheet this guy had, he probably knew how to turn common, everyday items like shoelaces into weapons.

Cool down. One thing at a time.

Rolf Danner, Shannon's security chief, stood beside the lobby doorway, his face schooled to a blank mask while he surveyed the room. The rest of the security team had been positioned as five ushers keeping the crowd moving smoothly past the victim's parents.

Fergus buzzed Tanny via their wrist computer link while he tapped the comlink clipped to his earlobe and murmured, "Code nine. Pew six. Right two."

Rolf Danner's frigid gaze flickered toward Fergus in silent acknowledgement of the warning. Then the security chief turned his gaze to the suspect and reached inside his jacket for his stun gun. The ushers spun around, reached inside their jackets, and started moving in on the suspect from five different directions.

A muffled series of booms echoed in the air. The ground rippled and tilted under Fergus's feet. The lights flickered and went out. The only light in the room came from the two memorial service candles.

A split-second of total silence reigned.

The soft classical music playing in the background had stopped in mid-note as if someone had pulled a plug on it.

Fergus jumped to his feet and turned around. The suspect had already vacated his seat.

A man shouted, "What the hell was that?"

A running shadow darted up the aisle.

A woman screamed, "He cut me! He has a knife!"

More figures jumped to their feet. Confused shouts and panicked cries filled the air.

Time went into slow motion for Fergus. Despite all the confusion and action going on around him, he felt like he had all the time in the world to react. Judging by the explosion, this was a two-pronged attack. A bomb timed to disable the power grid gave the attacker the element of surprise.

He pulled out his stun gun, shoved a shouting man aside, and maintained his position. Günter Snell would have to go through him before he'd get to Shannon.

There! A raised arm with a transparent knife shining within the fisted hand.

Fergus fired his stun gun.

Twin arcs of crackling blue light spilled from the tip of his gun and stabbed into the attacker's chest. The knife glowed red.

More screams filled the air. Panicked figures jammed the exits.

The attacker stumbled.

Fergus fired a second time. Again, twin arcs of blue stabbed into the man's chest and he crumpled to the floor.

The knife shattered into fragments.

Plas-glass!

That explained how Günter had managed to sneak his weapon past the scan at the gate. A plas-glass knife wouldn't trigger a security alarm. Shannon's solid weight leaned into him from the rear. Fergus braced himself. No way was he going to let her move past him into danger. She whispered in his ear. "Is it safe to move now?"

Chapter Nine

When the lights went out, Shannon jumped up, wrapped her arms around Fergus's waist, and clung to him as her anchor against terror. Leaning against him, feeling his warm solidity under her arms, felt wonderful. She felt safe and secure, like a child in her father's embrace. He didn't push her away. He braced himself in front of her and handled the attacker. When she whispered in his ear, "Is it safe to move now?" her cock rose of its own accord against his hard-muscled ass. Instead of jerking away from that contact, he patted her arm, turned his head to the side, and brushed her cheek with his lips. "It's over now, *querida*. You're safe."

Now that Fergus had unwound her arms from his waist so he could cuff his prisoner, the entire incident felt unreal and anticlimactic, like a second-rate crime vid. All the aggravation of having Fergus and Tanny staying with her for two days straight and sleeping in her bedroom for *what?* A distant explosion, a temporary power failure, and a silly, knife-waving man who Fergus handled with two shots from his stun gun. End of story.

On the one hand, she was relieved to know Merry's murderer was caught and would now have to pay for his crimes. Unfortunately, it also meant Fergus and Tanny would no longer be staying with her. She'd be alone again for the holidays. Tears flooded her eyes. Shannon sat with a sudden thump in the pew and wiped away the treacherous tears with the back of her hand.

Finally, the generator kicked in and restored electricity to the chapel. Pale yellow emergency lights glowed in the ceiling above the windows and doors.

Shannon turned to Tanny and curved her mouth into a sardonic smile. "It's over. You have a murderer to book. Don't worry about your clothes. You can stop by tomorrow morning and get them if you want."

Tanny's eyes went black. A flush darkened her cheeks. She shook her head. "It's not over. Not yet. We still need to interrogate him and see if we can link him to all the murder sites. After that, there are a few things Fergus and I want to discuss with you. Okay?"

Shannon's heart flipped over in her chest. Did that mean they wanted to continue to see her afterwards as a friend? Or, maybe even as their lover?

"Everyone, please return to your seats," Fergus shouted from the front of the room. He waved his arms in the air and pointed at the unconscious man, his hands and feet cuffed, lying at Fergus's feet. "The attacker has been subdued. We've contacted a team of investigators to gather evidence, and they will need to question all witnesses before we can release you to go home."

A man shouted from the rear of the room. "What about the power failure? How long will it take to correct?"

Fergus shrugged. "Another team of investigators is going to the site of the explosion to assess and repair the damages. I will keep you informed of their progress in restoring power to this section of the city."

"Ms. MacNal?"

Shannon twisted her head around and stared at Rolf Danner, her security chief. He had his long blond hair tied back into a loose ponytail. A hard black vest protected his broad chest. He smiled. "It's over now. You're safe."

She nodded.

"It's Christmas Eve."

She nodded a second time. *Why the hell was he standing there telling her things she already knew? Yes, it was over, and yes, it was Christmas Eve. Why wasn't he busy doing his job and taking care of crowd control like the rest of the security personnel here?*

"I know this is very short notice." He stared at her as if she was the only person in the room. "But I was wondering if you would allow me to stop over at your house tonight with a Christmas gift and…if maybe you'd accept an invitation to go out for dinner with me."

Shannon blinked. *A date! He was asking her out on date!*

"I have to go now," Tanny murmured behind her. "Talk to you later." Then she squeezed past Shannon and joined Fergus at the front of the room.

Rolf winked at her. "What do you say? Is it a yes or a no?"

What the hell? It *was* Christmas Eve. He was only asking her out on a dinner date. Why should she have to be alone tonight of all nights? Even though she felt nothing when she looked at him, maybe that would change after she spent a few hours getting to know him.

She gestured at the people settling down in the pews and managed a belated smile. "This may take a while, but I think I'll be free tonight."

Rolf grabbed her hand and raised it to his mouth, brushing his lips across her skin. "Great! I'll be at your front door at six o'clock tonight."

* * *

Fergus swore his eyes were going to be permanently crossed. He grimaced at the taste of the stale, vending-machine coffee in his mouth, completed the last section of a detailed incident report, and sent it to the main database.

They'd revived Günter under the care of a physician. When they read him his rights and the charges against him, they did a full holographic/audio recording of their actions in the presence of his appointed attorney. The crime scene technicians had gathered, labeled, and collated the evidence and done onsite full holographic recordings of witness testimony.

You'd think that would be enough. Oh, no. Now, he and Tanny had to complete five separate detailed reports for each stage of the arrest and evidence-gathering procedure. Plus, it was Christmas Eve. The station was deserted, with only a skeleton staff on duty and ninety percent of the staff using either vacation or sick leave days.

He slouched on his tailbone and tilted his chair back until it was balanced on two legs. He raked his hands through his hair. The cheap plastic chair creaked under his weight. You'd think he'd learn not to do it after he tipped back too far last month and split the back of his scalp open on a desk corner. That cut required six stitches and three weeks' worth of teasing from the rest of the station about him trying to get workman's compensation for on-the-job injury.

On the other side of the cubicle, Tanny slapped the send button on her deskcomp and flashed him a sympathetic smile. "I finished my reports. Now I've asked the system to pull up the data on Günter's so-called alibis for the rest of the murders."

He pursed his lips. "Send me a copy, too. I don't like the way he kept insisting he didn't know a damn thing about the other murders."

She glanced at her screen. "It's coming in now." She keyed in a command to reroute the information to his screen.

He cleared his screen and waited for the new data. It showed up in a double-column format meticulously listing dates and times for each murder, with mini-holographic vids of Günter zealously waving anti-hermaphrodite signs on picket lines.

"Oh, shit!" Fergus jumped to his feet and slammed his hands down on the desk. His chair flew sideways and crashed into the cubicle wall. "Fuck!"

Tanny jumped to her feet, pulled out her stun gun, and checked the settings. "Fucking right. Günter's not the killer. The killer's still out there and we've left Shannon unprotected."

The look she shot Fergus wasn't good. "You know what happened right after the attack at the memorial service."

"What happened?"

"Rolf Danner asked Shannon out for a dinner date tonight and she accepted."

"Danner! That dickhead!"

"Yes."

"Fuck!"

Fergus grabbed his phone and dialed Shannon's number. The phone rang and an automated recording said, "Due to the high volume of calls at this time, all lines are currently busy. Please try again later to place your call."

He tossed the phone aside. "Fuck! Everyone and his uncle is trying to contact each other on account of the snow emergency, and they're jamming up the cell phone broadcasts. And with the power failure, her computer's down and we can't contact her via email."

He cleared his screen and requested the police transport grid. "Snowmobile! The SWAT team has snowmobiles and battering rams. We'll never make it through this storm in a groundcar or aircar."

The grid for the parking garage popped up on his screen. One snowmobile remained. He keyed in a requisition and tapped his fingers while the request went through.

Green light!

He glanced at the time. 5:30 p.m. "What time did Rolf say he was going to pick Shannon up for this so-called dinner date?"

"I don't know. I didn't stay around long enough to hear what time they set for the date. All I know is that she accepted."

"Let's go!"

Shannon might get pissed off at them for going along as chaperones, but it was better to be safe than sorry. And if Rolf *was* the killer, they damn well better get there before he did.

Chapter Ten

Fergus ran to the equipment locker, inserted his hand in the ID panel, and pulled out a double set of gear for himself and Tanny. Gloves, computerized helmets linked to the snowmobile's sensors and guidance modules, full body armor, boots, and stun rifles. Images of Merry's mutilated body flashed into his mind.

He swallowed the taste of bile in his mouth, shook his head, and focused on fastening each section of his armor shut. *Don't think about the hours you wasted booking Günter. Don't think about Shannon getting killed.* They would make it in time. Shannon wasn't Merry. Even though Rolf was her security chief, she still wouldn't trust him enough to get close to her right away. Shannon kept herself distant from everyone because she didn't want to get hurt.

Tanny donned her body armor with short, angry jerks and slaps. She yanked her boots on and jammed her hands into her gloves. Her mouth and jaw were tight with frustrated anger. "Damn! Damn! Damn! I should have figured it out sooner.

What the fuck was I thinking? Merry trusted her killer. No way in hell would she have let a certified nutcase like Günter Snell into her apartment, let alone posed nude for him."

Fergus handed Tanny a stun rifle.

He saw Shannon, broadsword in hand, step sideways and avoid her android partner's blow during her practice bout. Her kilt flipped up and revealed a tantalizing glimpse of her buttocks. He saw Shannon's laughing eyes when she lifted her wine glass to drink a toast during their dinner the night before. "It's all right, *querida*. I made the same mistake. Let's go."

He turned and led the way out to the elevator and the underground parking garage. Tanny's steps echoed his in the empty, white-walled corridor. Fully armored, with the helmet under one arm and heavy-duty stun rifle swinging in his other hand, he felt like he was running in slow motion to the elevator while every second ticked mercilessly away to oblivion.

The lift doors opened in front of him. He charged inside, waited for Tanny to brace herself beside him, and yelled his voice commands at the computerized control panel. "Parking garage, second sub-level."

The floor jerked under them in swift and sudden descent. When the elevator finally stopped and the doors flew open, Tanny charged out beside him and matched him stride for stride into the shadowed bowels of the garage. They raced past a line of armored groundcars and turned the corner.

A service droid hovered beside the two-man snowmobile. Tanny climbed into the rear seat. Fergus inserted his hand into the glowing red hole of the droid's access panel. Five seconds later the aperture changed from red to green, confirming his

ID as an authorized user of the vehicle, and spat the keycard into his hand.

He climbed into the driver's seat and inserted the keycard. The electric engine started up immediately and the dashboard lit up in a brilliant blue backlight with white print and a GPS map of the city. He flipped the seatbelt switch. Safety webbing extruded and fastened him to his seat. The little figure on the dashboard indicating Tanny in the passenger seat showed safety webbing deployed around her, as well. As an extra safety precaution, both seats turned into auto-eject capsules during an accident.

Clutch in the handlebars, brake pad and gas pad under his right foot, GPS map grid on the dash, and a bright yellow button for reverse. So far the controls looked identical to what he was used to on his motorcycle. No problemo. He punched Shannon's address into the map search grid. Six routes popped up on the screen. The longest and safest route took the legal streets. The shortest route cut straight across the river and went through Central Park. He selected the shortest one, of course.

Tanny's angry voice came over the helmet speaker. "How the hell is Rolf going to get to Shannon's house with the current restrictions on transportation? Let alone take her somewhere for dinner?"

Fergus guided the snowmobile to the exit. The huge double door rose into the ceiling at their approach and thick gusts of wind-driven snow roared over them. The snowmobile surged into the night upon the pre-selected course with blazing headlights that barely lit their way through the wild storm. "He's the security chief, remember? He can commandeer any suitable vehicle from the Herm Foundation garage. Plus, he doesn't have to go as far 'cause he lives in the Enclave just like she does. As for where he's taking her, he's not taking her anywhere. He'll kill her if we don't get there in time."

* * *

Shannon stood in front of her closet. Should she wear a dress or a pantsuit? Maybe it wasn't such a good idea after all to have accepted a date on such short notice. And where the hell was he going to take her, anyway? With the snow emergency and the temporary power failure for this section, there weren't any restaurants open.

Wait a minute. Rolf's apartment within the Herm Foundation Enclave was only three blocks away from hers. He was probably planning to walk here and then walk her to his place for a private dinner. If she called him now and canceled their date, then all she had to look forward to was a long, lonely night sitting in front of her fireplace.

She pulled a high-necked, long-sleeved, scarlet velvet shirt and black velvet slacks from the rack. A pair of sturdy black boots, a long, black opera cape, hat, scarf, and gloves would be enough for her to walk with him to his apartment. But then again, Rolf was chief of security; he could commandeer one of the Foundation's snowmobiles if he wanted to drive rather than walk her through the storm.

Shannon slipped on the shirt and slacks and studied the effect in the closet's full-length mirror. Not bad; the outfit was simple yet sexy. The pants were loose enough to hide any bulge in front, and the shirt clung just enough to hint at her breasts without being tacky. She selected a pair of diamond studs for her ears and brushed her dark brown hair out into a soft tangle of curls that hung down to the middle of her back.

She stopped in mid-brush, frowning, then tapped the brush against her chin. The one thing that didn't make any sense to her was how and why Merry had trusted an obvious hate-monger like Günter Snell. Where had she met him? Working like she did with the public, wouldn't she have at least done a routine background check on the man when he first contacted her? How had he convinced her to go out with him, let alone pose nude for him like she did before he killed her?

He must be one hell of an actor to have hidden his hatred so completely when he first contacted Merry. When they revived Günter from the stun gun and carried him out of the memorial service, he'd turned his head and stared at Shannon with such a look of sheer rage that it had seared through her like liquid nitrogen.

* * *

Heated seats, heated handgrips, sonar-ranging warning system, self-adjusting rear treads, and auto-defrost helmets and windshield gave them maximum comfort, traction, and visibility. Fergus watched the route unfold on the dashboard map and used the sonar ranging capabilities to avoid impact with obstructions thrown into their way by the wind.

If it weren't for the fact that they were on a life-or-death mission, he'd be enjoying himself. Especially when they hit the river and zoomed along so fast above the ice that it felt like they were flying. The wind screamed while it drove thick, wet gusts of snow at them in blinding fury.

With the siren blaring and warning lights flashing red and blue, they hit Central Park at full speed and sped down the twists and turns of the terrain like Olympic racers. One block away from the Herm Enclave, he radioed a full police override and warning to the gated entrance and zipped in without stopping. From the gate, he had only three more blocks to traverse in a straight line.

Last, but not least, he deployed the titanium alloy ram from the snowmobile's nose and aimed the vehicle dead-center for Shannon's front door.

* * *

Just like every other residence within the gated community, a small generator built into her house had kicked in with the temporary power failure. Of course, without the link to the city power grid, Shannon could only power up the minimum components in her security system. The house was under manual lockdown rather than electronic lockdown. The front doorbell rang promptly at 6 p.m. Security cameras weren't online yet.

Shannon tossed her cloak over her arm and walked down the hallway to the front lobby. Her soft-soled leather boots made no sound on the smooth tiled floor. Now that Rolf had finally arrived to pick her up, she didn't really feel like going out with him. What would he say if she told him she'd changed her mind?

The doorbell rang again. She stopped and took a look through the peephole.

Yes. It was Rolf. He stood on the landing and carried a bouquet of long-stemmed red roses. Where in the hell had he been able to buy roses in the middle of a blizzard and power failure? Snowflakes feathered his hair and trickled moisture down his face. A large, two-seater snowmobile waited in the middle of her sidewalk.

She unlocked the door and opened it.

Rolf immediately shouldered his way inside and kicked the door shut behind him. "Thanks." He stomped the snow from his boots and thrust the roses at her in a classic lunge.

Shannon sidestepped the lunge without even thinking it through. As she sidestepped the blow, the holographic roses disappeared, revealing the deadly blade he'd aimed at her.

She whipped her cloak over the blade in trained reaction to its danger, spun on her heel, and ran for her life. Did she have the time to reach the broadsword hanging over her fireplace before he cut her down in cold blood?

Don't stop. Don't look back. Just run down the hall, through the living room, straight to the fireplace.

She jumped, grabbing the sword and spinning around in mid-air to land facing her opponent with three feet of solid steel ready to block his blow. Their blades clanged with an ugly screech that shattered the deadly silence. A parry, then a dodge knocked his blade aside. The flames hissed behind Shannon. She whirled to the side with a panther-like speed trained into her from many long years of practice bouts with her droid and tournament competition bouts at the SCA faires.

He tried to force her against the couch. She parried his blows with a resounding clash that went straight through her teeth and bones, and refused to give ground.

Pattern after pattern she blocked. Not thinking, just reacting. Fast and furious. Sweat ran down her face. Her shirt and pants clung and flared against her body as she turned and fought and fought again.

His gaze shifted. He changed pattern on the next step. She made the instinctive move. Her blade swung around and sliced his hand off at the wrist.

Blood spurted up in her face. His sword toppled to the floor with his hand still clenched around the hilt.

He lifted the spurting stump of his hand and opened his mouth to scream.

But she didn't hear his scream. The horrific sound of a massive object crashing and ripping through her front door drowned it out.

Chapter Eleven

Fergus pulled Shannon into his lap and hugged her close. "It's all right, *querida.*" She shivered uncontrollably.

Diablo! The sight of her standing tall and straight with that sword in her hand while she disarmed Rolf was seared into his mind forever. She was magnificent! Strong and beautiful! A unique and perfect combination of male and female within her mind, body, and spirit.

Shannon tucked her legs up and curved her body in a desperate need for his comforting touch. Tears spilled past her long, dark eyelashes, and she made a sound halfway between a sob and a gasp. Her soft breasts pressed against him. He automatically ran his gaze down her body, making sure she wasn't injured, and his gaze caught at the small bulge of her cock in her pants. A detail he wouldn't have noticed before he'd met her.

And the funny thing was, he couldn't think of Shannon in any other way than who she was now. Imagining her without a cock was like imagining himself without one. It felt *wrong.* Utterly wrong and bizarre.

He shifted his position under the solid, muscular weight of her body and stroked her trembling arms. "We're here now, *mi corazón.* You're safe. It's over."

Blood pooled on the floor around Rolf's severed hand and the machete. Shannon had laid her broadsword upon the coffee table when Rolf had crashed to the floor after they'd stunned him. More bright splashes of blood had sprayed over Shannon's clothes, the wall, and the floor.

Tanny had grabbed the emergency medical kit from the snowmobile. She was on her knees beside Rolf, applying a tourniquet to his arm with quiet efficiency. She sprayed the bloody stump with disinfectant, then stood and carefully transferred his severed hand to an ice-filled medical storage bin. Tanny contacted the police medical service with her vidphone and gave them terse and precise directions. The criminal evidence technicians had already been contacted. They would be arriving momentarily.

Shannon took a long, shuddering breath and wiped the tears from her face with the back of her hand. A blush stained her cheeks. She struggled to untangle herself from his embrace. "I'm a mess. I shouldn't be sitting on your lap like this. I was only trying to stop him, not hurt him."

Tanny stood over them. She tilted Shannon's chin up with her hand and brushed a tear away with her finger. "It's okay. You did what you had to do, and now that it's over, you're experiencing the delayed reaction of shock and horror. Don't be afraid to accept the comfort you need right now."

She gestured at the vid over the mantelpiece. "The power came on while you were fighting. We'll be able to transfer a solid database and document everything for the criminal investigation."

Shannon pushed against Fergus with desperate strength. He sighed and let her go.

She staggered to her feet and straightened her shirt and pants in an automatic gesture. "I'm okay now." She sucked in a shaky breath and gestured at Rolf. "Go ahead. I mustn't keep you from doing your job."

Sirens wailed in the distance. It sounded like both teams, investigative and medical, would arrive at the same time.

Fergus stood and shot a pleading look at Tanny. She was so much better at talking than he was.

Tanny nodded at him, then stepped forward and rested her hand on Shannon's arm. "Tomorrow, we'll be back. Okay?"

Shannon shot them a confused stare. The sound of footsteps in the hallway alerted her to the imminent arrival of the investigative and medical technicians. She straightened her shoulders, tightened her mouth in sudden decision, and spoke in a crisp, no-nonsense voice. "I understand. You don't have to stay here anymore. I'll pack your clothes and have them ready for you to pick up tomorrow."

Fergus lifted his hand and then dropped it. *Later.* After the investigation was completed and they were no longer on duty would be a much better time for them to talk.

* * *

Shannon walked through her empty house. The storm had ended. It was ten in the morning already. Sixteen hours had passed since Rolf attacked her, and it all felt so unreal and distant, like a strange dream. Her house droid had already repaired her damaged front door and cleaned up the debris. She had to reprogram the droid to seal off the living room in order to preserve the crime scene intact, as evidence for the investigators.

They'd taken her clothing away as part of that evidence.

And her sword.

The clothes she didn't mind. Hell, she never wanted to wear them again after what happened. In fact, as soon as she'd torn them off, she went into the shower and scrubbed herself raw, getting rid of the horrid feel of dried blood on her skin.

But the sword was a family heirloom. She wanted it returned to its rightful place above the mantelpiece as soon as possible.

Christmas Day and she was alone again. No laughter, no one talking, drinking coffee, and eating breakfast with her. Her bed remained empty. Fergus and Tanny no longer took turns lying beside her in slumber, comfortable in her presence.

Shannon entered the kitchen, ordered the droid to prepare fresh coffee. She went to the refrigerator, pulled out the remains of yesterday's brunch, and set it out on the table.

Fergus had the habit of gulping his coffee and taking greedy bites of his bread, leaving a smear of butter on his lips. Tanny ate and drank with delicate, quick bites and sips. She always waited until after she ate to sit down and comb the sleep tangles from her long, black hair. And her caramel-colored skin always glowed with a soft heat after she woke up.

Shannon selected the mug she'd used the day before and filled it to the brim with steaming-hot coffee. The mug was one thing that still remained the same.

The only reason Fergus had held her in his lap after the attack was because she'd gone into shock and needed the simple comfort of his touch. Nothing more. Nothing less. If she tried to read anything more than that into the way he'd held her and murmured words of comfort and endearment, she'd be setting herself up to be hurt.

Querida was the Spanish word for dear. It didn't mean he cared for her. The same thing when he called her *mi corazón*. He wasn't really calling her his heart. He didn't mean it as an endearment. They were just words said to make her feel better and get over the shock.

Just because Tanny had wiped a tear from her face with her finger didn't mean she cared, either. She was just doing her job. Taking care of Shannon, making sure she was all right. The same way Tanny took the time to make sure Rolf wouldn't bleed to death while they waited for the rest of the crime scene technicians and medics to arrive.

Shannon tore a piece of bread from the loaf and buttered it with short, angry strokes.

Dammit! It hurt! The house felt so *empty* without them!

It didn't matter before. True, she wanted love. But she hadn't missed what she'd never known.

She hadn't known how good it'd feel having them around her at all hours of the night and day. She never knew before how solitary her lifestyle had been.

Maybe she should get a dog. That might help keep her mind occupied and fill the house up with the presence of a living being again. Not one of those pedigreed dogs. She'd contact the Humane Society tomorrow. They'd have plenty of unwanted dogs who needed good homes.

Fergus and Tanny never did say when they'd be stopping over. Probably later this afternoon after they'd had a chance to rest. They probably spent most of the night writing reports and listing evidence from last night's events.

Plenty of time left to pack their clothes.

* * *

The storm had ended at 2 a.m. Now, at eleven in the morning, the city permitted aircar travel with one safety restriction. All aircars must remain on auto-pilot, with no deviations from the programmed course. The deep snow was considered too high-risk for manual piloting and landing.

Fergus entered Shannon's address into the aircar's comp system. Then he raked his hands through his hair for the fiftieth time. "Do I look all right?"

Tanny patted his knee. "You look fine. Just relax."

The stubby aircar taxied to the end of the ramp and lifted off with its wings extended and copter blades whirring.

All too soon, they arrived on Shannon's rooftop. Her house droids had melted every scrap from the landing pad. The bright sunlight flashing from the snow almost blinded him. Fergus unfastened his seatbelt and climbed out. He clutched a bottle of Coquito to his chest with his gloved hands and waited for Tanny with his heart in his throat. A cold, crisp wind blowing across the roof whipped tears from his eyes.

Shannon's surprised voice boomed from the speaker set into the rooftop entrance panel. "I'll be right up! I wasn't expecting you to get here until later this afternoon."

About fifteen seconds later, a buzzer sounded. The light above the entrance glowed green and the door slid open.

Shannon looked gorgeous. She wore a thin, white cotton top and a pair of gray sweatpants. Her whiskey-colored hair fell over her shoulders in loose waves. The bright sunlight showed a faint dusting of freckles across her nose and cheeks.

He let Tanny step inside first, then followed and immediately handed Shannon the bottle. "*Feliz Navidad*," he said with all the élan of a teenager on his first date. "This is called *Coquito*. My father makes it every year for the holidays. It's a mixture of coconut cream, rum, and cinnamon."

The elevator hummed and moved under their feet, bringing them from the roof to the first-floor lobby. Shannon fingered the silver ribbon and bow tied around the bottle. A slight flush darkened her cheeks. "Thank you." She looked away. The feathered screen of her lashes hid her eyes from him. "I didn't get your clothes packed yet."

The elevator stopped and the doors slid open. Shannon stepped out, holding the bottle in front of her like a shield. "You can wait in the library. It won't take long. Fifteen minutes at the most for me to bring down your clothes."

Fergus exchanged a startled glance with Tanny.

Diablo! After all they'd been through together, Shannon was acting as if they were total strangers.

Fergus shrugged his coat off and tossed it onto the bench against the wall. He stepped forward and covered Shannon's hands with his.

Bad move. Now the damned bottle was in the way.

Shannon tried to free herself. "Let go, please."

He blurted out, "Not before I say what I came here to say."

Shannon glared at him. That slight flush had deepened into two bright red spots on her cheekbones. "Go ahead. Say whatever it is you have to say."

He ground his teeth and shook his head. "Let go of the bottle first. It's in my way."

"I can't let go of the bottle until you let go of my hands."

Tanny's throaty chuckle broke the deadlock. She reached between them and carefully seized the bottle at the bottom. "On the count of three, both of you let go. Okay."

Shannon nodded. "Okay."

"*Uno, dos, tres!*"

Fergus lifted his hands and hurriedly moved them to Shannon's waist. Shannon relinquished the bottle. Tanny placed the bottle beside the vase of poinsettias on the little end table against the wall.

Shannon placed her hands on Fergus's chest and gave him a gentle push. "Let go of me, please."

He tightened his grip on her waist and shook his head. Shannon was so stubborn and proud, she made his heart ache just looking at her. "No. Not yet. I want to kiss you first."

"K-Kiss me?" She shifted her gaze to Tanny and then back to him. "What about Tanny?"

Tanny's carnal murmur sent a rush of blood straight to Fergus's groin and rapidly rising cock. "After he finishes kissing you, it's my turn."

Shannon's eyes darkened. Her body relaxed under his hands, from stubborn tension to a hesitant sensuality. She wrapped her hands around his neck. Her fingers teased his hair.

She moistened her parted lips with the tip of her tongue and moved closer. "Like this?" Her soft breasts flattened against his chest and the hard bulge of her cock nudged him.

He moved one hand up to the back of her head, cupped her ass with his other hand, and pulled her close. The feel of her arousal against him was driving him crazy with anticipation. He bent his head and kissed her, long and hard and greedily. Shannon opened her mouth, sighed, and kissed him back just as greedily. At the same time, she tightened her arms around his neck and ground her hips against him, matching him thrust for thrust.

Dios! Dry-humping Shannon like this was driving him crazy. He wanted to feel her, every inch of her sweet, strong, passionate body against him.

They ended their kiss with reluctant groans. He stepped back with his heart hammering against his chest.

Tanny nudged him aside with her hip and wrapped her arms around Shannon's neck. "My turn."

Shannon's grin was carnality personified. She cupped Tanny's breast with one hand and her ass with her other hand.

Tanny arched her back and pulled Shannon's head down to hers.

Por dios! Watching the both of them kiss and hump each other was even worse torture for Fergus. All the blood in his body went to his groin. His balls and cock felt like they were going to explode. It took all of his self-control not to unzip his pants right then and there.

This time, Shannon ended the kiss. She crooked her finger at him to join their embrace. "Come on. I want to finish this in my bedroom."

Chapter Twelve

Shannon climbed the staircase with Tanny, their arms entwined around each other's waists. Tanny rested her head in the hollow beneath Shannon's shoulder and she fit perfectly. Not too tall and not too short.

Fergus walked beside Shannon, holding his hand at the small of her back. With that intimate and simple touch, he claimed both her and Tanny as his lovers.

She wanted to pinch herself and prove once and for all that this wasn't a dream. In a few moments, she was going to enjoy the best Christmas Day of her life. This was far better than any sexual fantasy she'd ever imagined. Two experienced and sexy partners, man and woman, both ready and eager to show her the infinite possibilities of making love to them.

They stopped at her bedroom door. Fergus opened the door and ushered them inside. Shannon's heart stuttered. She kicked off her sneakers, removed her socks, and then sat on the edge of the bed. Sweat drenched her hands.

Tanny and Fergus's warm, loving smiles were what kept her from turning around and running away. She turned them on, both of them. The way they'd kissed her had told her that. They weren't grossed out because she had breasts, cock, and pussy. It didn't matter if this was going to be only a one-time fling. She wanted them, too.

Fergus kicked his shoes away and peeled off his shirt. The fire blazing on the other side of the bedroom cast shadows across the lean, carved muscles of his belly, chest, shoulders, and arms. Dark hair furred the center of his chest and narrowed down to a black arrow that pointed at the impressive bulge behind his jeans zipper. He grinned at her, then unzipped his jeans and slid both jeans and underwear off his hips.

His cock sprang out, thick and long, and rose to his navel. Pre-cum dewed the bulbous head.

Shannon sucked in a breath. Her mouth watered and she swallowed convulsively. His cock was impressive, alive and warm. Nothing like the vibrators she'd used, and larger than her cock. Would it hurt when he tried to fit all of him inside her?

Fergus bent and pulled both his pants and underwear down to his ankles. He stood and his cock and balls hung heavily between his thighs. He stepped out of his clothing, then went to her and sat down. The mattress sagged under his weight.

Shannon grabbed the edge and maintained her position without sliding any closer to him.

Fergus touched her chin with his finger. "What's wrong, *querida?* Did you change your mind?"

She shook her head.

"My turn!" Tanny strolled barefooted across the carpet. Her toes curled into the thick carpet with each lazy step. She posed beside the pile of discarded clothing, pulled her sweatshirt over her head, and tossed it aside. A lacy bra hugged her taut breasts and glowed a brilliant white against her tawny skin, outlining dark brown nipples and areolas beneath the flimsy material. Her hair tumbled to the middle of her back in a black curtain of waves and curls.

Shannon's gaze stopped at the delicate scar above Tanny's navel marking the location of an anti-fertility implant. She grinned. No distracting worries about getting pregnant for either her or Tanny.

Tanny unzipped her jeans and wiggled them down and off her legs. A white lace bikini barely covered the soft pubic mound. She curved her mouth into a wicked smile and undulated across the carpet to the bed.

Shannon's throat constricted, making it difficult to breathe. She dug her fingers into the bed covers and held on for dear life.

Tanny stopped in front of her. She exchanged a puzzled glance with Fergus and said, "You're afraid. Why?"

Shannon gulped and moistened her suddenly dry lips with her tongue. She didn't know what to say. The moment of truth was here, and all of a sudden she didn't want to take her clothes off. Her clothing was her last barrier, her last shield against rejection.

Tanny leaned down. She kissed Shannon with a hungry need that sent a shock of melting heat straight to Shannon's crotch. When she ended the kiss, Tanny held Shannon's face between her hands and stared at her with wonder. "Is this your first time? Is that why you're afraid?"

Fergus gasped with sudden comprehension. He squeezed Shannon's leg and leaned sideways so he could look into her eyes, too. "There's nothing to be afraid of, *mi corazón*. Everyone has a first time. Even me."

He managed a lopsided grin. "Just tell us what you want and what feels good for you. We have all the time in the world to make this feel perfect for you."

Shannon looked down at Tanny's lovely breasts confined by the lacy cups of her bra. She let her gaze dip lower to Tanny's panties, then sideways at Fergus's cock standing strong and hard at attention between his hairy thighs. "I want to keep my clothes on for a little while longer."

Her nipples ached under her shirt and her cock had become hard as steel inside her pants. Her face was burning up with embarrassment already. If she looked either one of them in the eye, she wouldn't even be able to say what she wanted out loud.

Shannon gestured at Tanny and mumbled past the lump in her throat, "Take your bra and panties off, please. I'd like the both of you to lie down side by side on the bed so I can take my time touching you first."

Fergus squeezed her knee. "That sounds wonderful, *querida*."

Tanny yanked the bedcovers down and plumped up the pillows. Fergus grabbed Tanny's hand, then Shannon's, and the three of them piled onto the bed like kids at a slumber party.

They sorted out their arms and legs and left just enough space for Shannon to kneel between them. They were every wet dream she'd ever had turned into reality. She reached out with trembling hands and touched them.

Fergus's golden-brown skin scorched her hand. His chest was hard, solid muscle. Four black curls circled his nipple. She rolled the hard peak between her fingers and he groaned.

Tanny's rounded breast filled Shannon's hand completely. The whipped-chocolate skin was so soft and warm and her nipples were longer, darker, and harder than Fergus's. She squeezed Shannon's hand tighter over her breast and murmured, "Suck it, please. Suck it nice and hard for me."

Shannon bent her head and sucked. The nipple blossomed under her questing tongue. Tanny whimpered and wiggled under her mouth.

Shannon sat back on her heels again. She ran her hands over their bellies. So similar and so different at the same time. Male and female.

When she stopped, Fergus thrust his hips at her. "Go ahead. I'm not going to break if you touch me there."

So she did. His cock filled her hand with a surprising familiarity. She knew exactly how to squeeze it, pull her hand slowly up the shaft, and then press her thumb over the hole in the tip and rub the pre-cum over the soft skin. She moved her hand up and down his cock with a slow, steady pressure, coaxing him over the edge. He rolled onto his side, giving her an easier grip on him, and thrust into her hand in eager response.

Tanny had shaved her hair down to a narrow strip. The vulnerable pink flesh between the dark skin of her nether lips lay exposed under Shannon's hand, responding to her touch like a rosebud unfolding its petals. No cock hardening between her lips. Only a pink-flushed button of engorged flesh. Shannon touched Tanny's clit carefully. She didn't want to hurt her.

Tanny arched her back and butted her clit against Shannon's finger. "There!" she murmured. "Rub along the left side for now. The right side is too sensitive at the beginning for me."

Warm pussy moisture flooded Shannon's fingers. She smoothed it over Tanny's clit and rubbed harder. The flesh responded like a miniature penis under her touch. So much sensation packed into such a small button.

Tanny whimpered, soft and low, in a keening cry for more. She writhed against Shannon's hand.

Amazing! And humbling to know her touch could give so much pleasure. Shannon caught her breath at the thought of her cock sliding into Tanny. And all the blood in her brain suddenly flooded into the diamond-bright ache at her groin.

Shannon looked up. Fergus held Tanny's breasts in his strong, callused hands. He was carefully sucking and biting her nipples, one after the other.

More moisture flooded Tanny's pussy. Shannon rubbed harder on Tanny's clit while Fergus pumped his cock against the stroking of her other hand.

Then it happened! Tanny threw her head back and bucked against Shannon's hand like a wild woman. Her eyes rolled back, and she moaned and cried her way to a climax.

Fergus thrust faster against Shannon's hand. She tightened her fingers around his cock. The fat vein coiled around the thick shaft pulsed under her hand.

He yelled, "*Diablo!*" and let his cum spill across Shannon's hand and Tanny's pussy.

Shannon sat back on her heels. Her hands were wet with cum and pussy juice. She wiped them on her sweatpants.

Both Fergus and Tanny sat up. Tanny captured her hands.

Fergus said, "Now it's our turn." He tugged at the hem of her T-shirt.

Panic rushed through her. She pulled her hands from Tanny's loose grip and blocked Fergus from lifting her shirt. "I'm not ready yet."

Fergus slipped his hand under her shirt. Tanny grinned and slipped her hand under beside his. They dragged his fingers down her stomach together. Her skin ignited under their touch. Their fingers snagged at the waistband of her pants, then settled on the obvious swelling tenting the soft fabric below. Both hands pressed hard against her erection. Her pulse went into overdrive.

"*Querida*." Fergus spoke in a husky, demanding murmur. "We want to make love to you. Now!"

Oh, yes! She was ready now. Shannon peeled her shirt off and tossed it on the floor.

Two hot hands captured her breasts. Their mouths and tongues tugged and nipped on her in slow, deliberate heat.

She wrapped her hands in their hair.

Pain and pleasure. Sheer ecstasy. So much more than she'd ever imagined it would feel.

They lifted their heads.

Her nipples were swollen and wet from their mouths.

They pulled her down between them. Tanny tugged off her pants and panties with eager hands. Shannon went very still.

Fergus leaned over her and smiled. "You look perfect, Shann." He tucked a strand of hair behind her ear, kissed the tip of her nose, and then ran his callused hands down her body.

Tanny plopped down on the other side. She stroked Shannon's arm and then her belly.

Slowly, teasingly, with the both of them watching her face, Tanny moved her hand lower and circled Shannon's cock in a warm, gentle, experienced grip.

Shannon closed her eyes. *Yes!*

Fergus scooted down. He stopped and brushed his lips across Shannon's anti-fertility implant scar. His hot breath feathered across her belly. "I don't have to wear a condom. I hate wearing them."

When he kissed the head of her cock and swirled the tip of his tongue over the pre-cum, Shannon thought she was going to die from happiness. Now both he and Tanny caressed her cock, teasing her with slow, even strokes.

Shannon braced her heels and dug her fingernails into the sheets. *Yes! Oh, God. Yes!*

Soft mewling sounds escaped from her parted lips.

Fergus slid two fingers into her pussy and wrung a gasp from her with that sudden intrusion. "Do you have a hymen?" he asked. "I can take care of it with my fingers first if you want."

"Noooo." She groaned. "My gynecologist cut it when she inserted my first implant on my eighteenth birthday."

Fergus inserted a third finger and probed her deeper. "That's perfect. No pain for you, then, only pleasure when I ride you for the first time." His thumb pressed against the tight sac of her balls. Tanny milked her cock with her hands and fastened her hot mouth over the head.

Faster and harder, Fergus and Tanny probed and suckled her. It was fantastic. Her balls tightened. Her cock jerked inside Tanny's mouth. Her pussy clenched and dripped around Fergus's long fingers.

Oh, shit! Shannon opened her eyes.

"Stop!" she yelled. "Please! Stop!"

They stopped.

She gasped. "Tanny, I want to come inside you and I want Fergus to fuck me. Now!"

Both of them scooted up. Tanny fit her curvy body into Shannon's arms with practiced ease.

Fergus moved behind her and rolled her sideways her with his strong hands. He ran his hand down her ass and under her thigh, lifted her leg, and eased himself closer. His cock slid between her buttocks and the already moist tip nudged open her pussy lips.

Shannon pushed her cock at Tanny's pussy and bumped into her pubic bone instead. "Sorry," she mumbled.

"That's all right," Tanny drawled. She wrapped her fingers around Shannon's cock, lifted her leg, and guided her inside.

Oh, God! Shannon bit back a gasp. Tanny's pussy was so hot, tight, and wet.

Fergus moved his hand from Shannon's leg, reached over her and took hold of Tanny by the waist, and pulled them both to him. That pushed him inside her in one glorious stroke that went all the way through into her cock.

"Oh, God," Tanny moaned. "It feels like I have two cocks in me at the same time."

Fergus lost control then. He exploded into motion. He pistoned his cock into Shannon.

It was incredible. Even better and more intense than her best fantasy had ever been. Shannon reveled in the sensation of him riding her, showing her how to move inside Tanny, pushing her in and out as if her cock was his. Hard and fast and long he rode them both.

Hot, eager cries escaped from all three of them with each deep thrust.

Oh shit, oh shit, oh shit! Shannon's pussy clenched and squeezed around his cock in wave after wave of excruciating pleasure. Her cock filled Tanny's hot pussy with a long, glorious geyser of cum. Fergus slammed into Shannon one last time and shot burst after burst of his cum into her.

They collapsed in a limp tangle, gasping for air. Legs twitched and trembled. They were so deeply imbedded together, Shannon wasn't sure whose legs were trembling.

Fergus groaned, then pulled himself out and rolled to the side.

Shannon hugged Tanny for a few more moments, breathing in her scent. She tasted salt on her lips. She felt sweat trickling past their breasts and bellies.

Tanny's pussy gave Shannon's half-erect cock one last convulsive squeeze. Shannon's cock slid out as she rolled over on her back.

She closed her eyes. It was over. It was the most fantastic and special Christmas of her life. And she didn't want it to end. *Ever.*

Now that they'd satisfied their curiosity about what it would be like to fuck her, they'd leave and she'd be alone again. They had each other already. They didn't need her.

Finally, she opened her eyes. Fergus and Tanny propped themselves on their arms. They grinned at her.

Fergus rubbed his thumb across her mouth. "*Querida*, you were wonderful!"

Shannon sucked in a deep breath and exhaled carefully. She steeled her heart for the inevitable and said, "Thank you. I guess I better pack your clothes."

Fergus stared at her with a look of astonishment on his face. He frowned. His bushy eyebrows met in the center of his forehead. "Why? Was it that bad for you? Don't you want us anymore?"

Her ears were ringing. Did that mean they wanted to stay with her?

Tanny wrapped her hand around Shannon's breast and pinched the nipple. "Shann, honey," she whispered. "I don't know about you, but what happened here between was very special."

"It was?"

Tanny fastened her mouth on the tender flesh and suckled for a few moments. Then she lifted her head, winked at Fergus, and then smiled at Shannon. "We want to stay with you and be your lovers for as long as you'll have us."

"You do?"

Fergus grabbed her chin and glared at her. "Damn right we do. We love you and we want to stay with you. Are you going to throw us out now?"

Her ears *were* ringing.

They wanted her. They loved her.

She opened her mouth, closed it, and then opened it again. "I love you, too. Please, stay with me."

Fergus's cock stiffened into a hard, solid column against her leg. He shouted, "Yes!" Then he kissed her.

Barbara Karmazin

With over twenty-nine and a half years of experience as a bilingual (Spanish/English) caseworker under her belt, Barbara Karmazin utilizes a unique blend of multicultural knowledge for her Science Fiction. She incorporates the same sense of adventure and wonder to her SF/Erotica stories.

Barbara loves new ideas and is willing to write about all versions of sexuality, both human and alien, while maintaining a fast paced SF adventure plot that will leave you gasping in more ways than one. Affectionately known by the nickname of 'Chainsaw' by her many critique partners, she brings a fresh look and enthusiasm for 'out of the box' SF/Fantasy and Paranormal Erotica and Romance stories.

Feel free to check out Barbara Karmazin's website at http://www.sff.net/people/selkiewife/.

SPIRITUAL NOELLE
(A SISTER Leashed Story)

Jet Mykles

Chapter One

December 5

I thought about my sister Meg during the entire train ride to Buffalo. Not so much about her involvement in not one but *two* deaths out where she lived in California, nor her subsequent exoneration as the cause of said deaths by a tribunal of grand leaders. No, despite the absence of Meg herself from the family festivities in Albany, those subjects had been the main topic of discussion during my Thanksgiving weekend at home, and I was thoroughly over it.

I was intrigued by her sex life. My little sister had leashed two shapeshifters, a rare feat in and of itself. But even more amazing was that, by all accounts, these men were not only gorgeous, but they had been lovers before she leashed them. I'd spoken to Meg myself on the phone on Thanksgiving before the family sat down to dinner. Although my sister was notoriously close-mouthed about her personal life -- when she had one -- I'd gotten enough to know that yes, the men were not only involved but that now all *three* of them were in a sexual relationship. Two men. My little sister had *two* men.

If she could, could I?

Despite a strong urge to do so, I didn't call her from the train. I wasn't sure she could really help in my situation. I wasn't entirely sure I *had* a situation.

But I had to try.

I waited until I arrived at the Depew station before I called the ones who I'd come to see. Timing was key. I'd carefully plotted my route from Albany so that there was no train headed back east after my arrival, figuring that they couldn't turn me away when I'd come so far. I stood at the window, staring out at the lightly falling snow, with my bags at my feet and my parka bunched over my arm, wondering who would pick up the landline.

"Hello?" Deep, rumbling bass. It was Jake.

I put on my "bright smile" tone. "Hi there!"

"Hey, Noelle." My heart warmed at the genuine affection in his voice. "How's things upstate?"

"It was okay." My voice was far more casual than I felt. I hoped. "But I'm back in Buffalo. Can you pick me up?"

"Back in Buffalo? Huh?"

"I'm at the Depew station."

"But..."

"Can you come pick me up?"

"I, uh, well, sure. Sure thing. Uh..."

There was a pause, and I shut my eyes, knowing what was happening. Sure enough, there were mutters off the phone.

The next voice that spoke was not Jake's. "You're in Buffalo?" I swallowed at the sound. Jake's soothing rumble was a welcome warmth, but Daniel's smooth tenor was a hot knife straight in my belly. A hot knife disguised in sumptuous black silk and velvet that popped something deep inside me and let it ooze out warm and wet between my legs. I closed my eyes and took a breath, keeping check on my emotions. "Yes."

"Why?"

"I came back to see you guys."

"Why?"

I need you. Both of you. "I was worried about you."

"Worried?"

I drew pictures with my finger in the dust on the little ledge before me. "You still don't have things under control, Daniel. You're my responsibility until you do."

"We decided that I'd be fine until after the New Year."

"I know." *Darn it!* "But there's all this time between Thanksgiving and Yule anyway. I figured I'd come back."

"I'd think your family would have a million, what did you call them, 'functions' between now and then."

"They do --" *Darn you for throwing my words back at me!* "-- but I've decided to opt out."

"Why?"

"To help you."

"Why?"

I grimaced at the slight reflection of my face in the window. "So you're not going to come pick me up? It's too late to go back." I sighed dramatically. "I'll have to get a room in town."

He let the silence hang for agonizing moments. I hated it. Daniel might very well send me away, and I couldn't come up with a better reason to be there. Well, other than the real reason, which I wasn't ready to tell him. Yet.

"Jake will be there soon. You hang tight."

"Thank you, Daniel."

He grunted. "You guys should pick up some groceries while you're at it. Looks like a storm's coming in."

Chapter Two

It was a good hour before Jake's green salt-and-grit-encrusted Dodge Ram truck pulled up. The station's night lights had come on to try to illuminate the darkening gray twilight. Snow left over from a fall a few days' previous formed blue-lavender mounds out near the street. I bent to pick up my small duffle bag and grab the handle of my big rolling suitcase and took both with me out the front doors.

He saw me, put the truck in park, and got out. Oh, he looked just as good as I remembered. Okay, yes, it had only been two weeks since I'd seen him, but it seemed like a very long two weeks. Big and burly, he almost looked like the bear that was his alternate form, except there wasn't an ounce of fat him. Jake was pure woodsman muscle from the top of his six-foot-three height to the soles of his size-fourteen boots. A riot of thick, deep brown hair curled around his head to about the length of his square jaw, blending into his trim, almost black beard. Today he wore faded, dark blue jeans and a green plaid flannel shirt underneath the open lapels of his olive army field jacket.

He hurried toward me and took the handle of my suitcase with one hand as he gathered me into a big bear hug with the other. Mmmm, no one does bear hugs like a bear, I tell you. He smelled of leather and firewood and musky, comforting man. I'd only known him for three months, and already his smell warmed a piece of my heart that had been lonely during my time away.

I was in trouble. But then, I'd already reached that conclusion.

Flurries had started and the wind was biting, so we didn't talk until we were in the heated extended cab of the truck and he'd pulled out into the street.

"So. We didn't expect you 'til January." Jake's voice held just a touch of gravel. Always made me think of a bear's grumbly sounds.

"I know. But there was no real reason to stick around. Not much is going on that involves me until closer to Yule."

"So you're here for a week or two?"

I stared out the window, the easier to hedge around the truth. "Something like that." Truthfully, I didn't want to leave again. Ever. But he wasn't ready to hear that. Nor was I sure of any extended welcome.

"Your family okay with that?"

"Oh, sure." He didn't have to know that my mother was most decidedly *not* okay with it. I turned back and grinned at him. "Hey, are we going to the store?"

"Yeah. Daniel told you, we need to stock up." He gestured at the mountains of clouds in the night sky. "There's a big storm coming in."

"Good. Can we get some noodles and flank steak so you can make that stroganoff of yours? Please?!" I had discovered that bears -- at least this one -- are marvelous cooks!

He smiled and sent me a sideways glance. My heart swelled. Although he was far more subtle about it than Daniel, Jake was a beautiful man. He had these big, wonderful brown eyes that, while they could be mischievous, were the most honest things you'd ever seen. Top that off with the fact that they were surrounded by thick, dark lashes, and they were simply to die for. "Sure. We can do that."

I stopped at the end of the aisle, staring at the cacophony of red, white, and green Christmas paraphernalia. "Here Comes Santa Claus" was the latest of a string of far-too-catchy Christmas jingles that had been playing in the store since we arrived, and I blamed them for the idea that sprouted in my head.

Did I dare?

Yes.

"Jake?"

He stopped, about to go down the next aisle. "Yeah?"

"Did you guys get a tree?"

"Tree?"

"For Christmas."

He frowned. "No."

I clapped my hands once and beamed at him. "Let's."

"What?"

"Let's get a tree and decorations and stuff." I turned down the aisle, not waiting for him to respond. "My treat."

He showed up with the cart and an unsure look on his face. "Noelle, I don't know that this is a good idea."

"Of course it is. It's a *won*derful idea." I picked up two boxes of the little blinky lights and tossed them into the cart before reaching for a few more.

Jake picked up one box and eyed it dubiously. "I don't think Daniel will want a tree."

"Why not?" I dumped in a few boxes of gold and silver garland.

"I think he's Jewish."

I stopped, staring at the little Santa doorknob hanger in my hand. "Oh." After a beat, I shrugged and restored it to the shelf, then stepped back toward the lights. "So we'll get some blue lights."

"Noelle…"

"It's not the denomination that really counts, Jake." Resolute, I exchanged two boxes of the white lights for blue ones. "The Christmas tree is a holdover of an ancient Nordic belief anyway. Or was that Celtic? Gah, I'm bad at the exacts, but I assure you the idea was around long before a baby was born in Bethlehem." I threw in a few boxes of multicolor lights just to add flavor. "It's the thought that counts. The spirit of the holiday."

I glanced at him. The word *spirit*, of course, had more than one connotation in our conversation. Jake's brown eyes bore steadily into mine and I stared back.

Finally, I sighed. "He needs to lighten up, Jake; I've told you both that. What better than a little holiday cheer? This isn't about any particular religion or belief. It's about a cheery tree that smells good." I leaned on the end of the shopping cart. "It'll brighten up the house and give us something festive to do so we don't have to think about his problem every minute of every day."

Jake grimaced and started to reach for his pocket. "We should call and make sure."

I rounded the cart and grabbed his arm to stop him. "If we call, he'll say no. If we show up with everything, what can he do but pitch in and enjoy?" Okay, there were a few other possibilities, but I was determined not to think of those. "Think positive" was my motto, and I was determined to make this work. Just wasn't entirely sure *how.* "Come now, you want to see him do something as silly as decorate a tree as much as I do."

That got me a reluctant smile.

I leaned against his strong arm, pressing my cheek to the cool fabric of the jacket covering his shoulder. *My,* he had a solid muscle in there! "Please, Jake. It can't hurt, and it could be a lot of fun."

He tilted his head and looked at me out of the corner of his eye.

I batted my own at him.

He laughed. "Do you always get your way?"

I grinned, pushing up on tiptoe to plant a quick kiss to his warm cheek, loving the tickle of whiskers on my lips. "Not always, no."

He snorted, but said no more as I pulled away and proceeded to heap silly Christmas -- and a few Chanukah -- decorations onto the foodstuffs that already half-filled the cart. He even pitched in, laughing with me when we both put in the singing Rudolph doll with the apple-sized red nose that lit up.

It was getting very dark when we emerged from the store, so in the interests of time, we decided to get a tree at a lot not too far away. Jake refused to voice an opinion and merely shrugged when I finally decided on a plump, seven-foot Douglas fir.

We stood by the tree, waiting for the guy to finish with another customer and come take my money. I had my hands dug deep into the pockets of my light blue parka. Jake was less susceptible to the biting cold, so he just stood with his thumbs hooked in his back pockets, gloveless, watching the darkening sky. I envied him. Whether it was being a bear or whether it was the fact that he'd grown up used to it, Jake wasn't that susceptible to cold. His jacket wasn't even buttoned.

I shifted my boots through the thin layer of slush on the ground. Time to get all the information I could out of Jake before we reached Daniel. "Jake, was Daniel's problem with magic the only reason you two left the army?"

Jake dropped a surprised look on me.

I tilted my head to look up at him, brushing a lock of my straight blonde hair from my eyes, though the growing wind whipped it right back in my way. "Daniel told me it was the only reason, but I get the feeling it wasn't." I shrugged. The cold bit at my ungloved hand, and I abandoned my hair in favor of the warmth of my pocket. "I meant to ask you before I left, but there never seemed to be a good opportunity."

He hedged. "If Daniel said…"

"Please, Jake, this is important. With how bottled up Daniel is, he's likely not to tell me the very bit of information I need to know, just because he doesn't want to remember or think about it."

He mulled that over. I'd learned a few other things about him in the short time I'd known him. Chief among those things was that you just couldn't push him to do things. I attributed it to his being a bear. You could suggest, wheedle, threaten, or cajole, but he ended up doing everything in his own time. It was best to make a suggestion or ask a question, then just let it lie. Luckily, he was pretty open-minded and very smart. Daniel was his best friend as well as his witch. He had to work with me here.

The tree guy came up to me before Jake could answer. I paid him, and Jake hefted the fir, showing an impressive amount of strength as he effortlessly carried it back to the truck and tossed it into the bed. He turned, and the look on his face stopped me as I would have rounded the truck to the passenger side. "They thought we were gay," he murmured, then turned to the driver's door.

Yes! I hurried around and climbed into my seat. "They thought you were gay, and that bothered Daniel?"

"Regular humans don't know about the leashed thing, right? And there weren't any other witches or shifters around us, even the officers in charge," he continued as he turned the key in the ignition. He waited for a blue Toyota to pass before he pulled out of his parking space. "It bothered him a lot. They started making comments about how we were always together and how we always had to room together. How we were always going off alone together. We couldn't tell them it was because of the magic." Jake shrugged. "I didn't care. Thought it might be a little easier if they did think we were gay. The whole 'don't ask, don't tell' thing could've worked. But Daniel couldn't stand it. And the more it bugged him, the more they thought it. I guess, when I wasn't around, they teased him more."

Ah, well, that made sense. Jake was Daniel's leashed shapeshifter, which gave them a magical bond that compelled Jake to keep Daniel safe. Long before they met me, Daniel had cast a spell to draw Jake to him, then another to bind them as shifter and witch. It was a mostly one-sided arrangement, in favor of the witch, but most leashed relationships I'd known through my life ended up being an amicable situation, with the involved parties becoming good friends, if not more. Jake and Daniel had one of those relationships. The friendship that had developed between the two men during their time in the army and since almost made the leashing unnecessary. I couldn't imagine Jake ever voluntarily leaving Daniel. Daniel hadn't dissolved the spell, however. The leashing gave them an added metaphysical awareness of each other that was often useful. I sensed, in their case, there was something even *more*, but that would take careful investigation to verify. But I knew from experience that mundanes -- normal humans who aren't witches or shifters -- couldn't understand the closeness of the bond. It was often misconstrued and interpreted as a sexual relationship.

Jake's words confirmed what I'd found out when I'd called and asked their former lieutenant about it. I'd asked now so I could hear it from Jake's own mouth.

"Add to that the special treatment you guys got because of Daniel's abilities -- which you couldn't tell anyone about..." I nodded and sat back in my seat, staring ahead at the snow flittering across the road ahead. "I can see how that would cause quite a bit of jealousy."

"Not to mention the fact that he *is* pretty."

I studied his profile, but Jake just said it like it was a matter of fact. Which it was, but I couldn't tell how the fact affected him. "He is that," I mused. My heart went out to Daniel. True, he was a strong man in the prime of his life, but he was just naturally slim and, as Jake said, pretty. I could imagine that the big lunks in the military could make life miserable for him.

Jake's smile was full of pride as he kept his eyes on the road, hands casual on the wheel. "I called him pretty as a girl when we first met. He gave me a good black eye for that one."

I chuckled, rolling my eyes. Like most women, I just didn't understand the joy men found in the fights they picked with one another.

We drove for a while in silence as I digested what he'd told me. Urban streets began to blend into rural roads as we headed for the densely forested area in which they lived. The wind picked up and pelted the truck with snow.

"It didn't bother you if they thought you two were gay?"

Jake shrugged. "Nah. Not like it was true. We knew it. Who cared what the others thought? Sure, we would've got in a few fights, but that would've passed. Wasn't like they were gonna discharge us or nothing, not with Daniel's skills."

I nodded. The need to keep the knowledge of magic from reaching the broad masses made it impossible for the gifted to be completely free among mundanes. I could only imagine what it would be like in the military when the big brass wanted to use a witch's special abilities.

He'd mentioned the time they first met. I frowned. My short conversation with their lieutenant hadn't allowed me to go into much detail, and Daniel had never been forthcoming with particulars. "When did he leash you?"

Jake's smile dimmed. "They made him cast the spell right after they drafted him."

"They *drafted* him?"

Jake nodded. "They found him when he was still in high school. They won't say he was drafted, and neither will he, but that's pretty much what they did." An edge of anger sounded in Jake's low, easy voice. "But he was eager enough to leave home. He's told you about that."

I nodded. Daniel had been open enough about his childhood. It hadn't been abusive, but it wasn't exactly what you'd call warm and happy. According to him, his dad, the navy man, was rarely around and his Japanese mom was more interested in living her own life in the States than in seeing to her only son.

"Well, after they had him, they decided 'cause he was young and pretty, he needed protection."

"Were you already enlisted?" From what he'd told me, the house that he and Daniel currently lived in south of Buffalo was where Jake had done much of his growing up with his aging grandparents.

"Nope. I was drafted, too. Daniel feels guilty about that, but I didn't mind."

"Your grandparents…?"

"Were already dead. I was alone anyway." He shrugged. "It wasn't so bad for me. I wasn't doing so hot on my own."

"But he still feels guilty about it."

Jake nodded, eyes solemn in the dim light from the truck's gauges. "I expect."

I subsided, thinking. So now I had some answers to questions that had been niggling me. I knew some of the source of Daniel's guilt and fear. He thought he'd forced a life on Jake and likely felt he'd ruined Jake's life with the gay rumors. But Jake didn't seem to be at all upset. If anything, he seemed glad to have Daniel to protect. To have a focus in life.

So I had some answers. Now, what to do with them?

Chapter Three

We spoke of little, trivial things for the remaining drive south. The flurries were still going. Inky night surrounded us, making the snow seem to appear out of thin air as it hit the light from the headlamps. Always reminded me of watching *Star Trek* when they go into warp speed.

As we got closer to where they lived, I began to silently monitor our surroundings for spiritual activity. It was what I'd been sent to Daniel's side to help him with in the first place. He was a spirit witch, like me, but a mostly instinctual one. Before meeting me, he'd had practically no training in our particular form of magic, which was different enough that it did take a spirit witch to teach. But even without training, he could attract more spiritual energy than I could, and I was known as one of the strongest in our specialty. It was even more amazing since he was so young. I was days away from turning thirty-two and had not truly come into my spiritual powers until my late twenties. Daniel, however, was twenty-three, and not only could he wield more raw spiritual energy than I, but his gifts seemed to still be maturing. The strength of Daniel's gift was both a blessing and a curse. He was so strong that attracting and managing spirits had been easy for him during his developing years. His superior officers hadn't thought he'd needed any further training. Trouble was, his power had grown to the point where he simply couldn't contain the amount of spiritual energy around him. His instinctive control was no longer sufficient. It was unwieldy and dangerous, both to him and those around him.

Spirits were not ghosts. They were not souls left over from life, nor did they have true consciousness. Spirits had never been alive and never would be so. They were metaphysical manifestations of nature that imbued everything around us. They were thoughts and feelings repeated over and over by dozens or hundreds of people around one particular area. Spirits were always there, even in places considered "dead." In places where people felt there was an "alive" feeling, they were often reacting to a strong concentration of spiritual energy. Strong, malevolent spirits were sometimes called poltergeists when they inhabited old houses and such. Ancestral homes might have a benevolent spiritual energy that had looked out for the family that lived there for generations. A spirit witch could serve to mass spiritual energy, dispel it, or "talk" to it. Spirits were great that way. A spirit mass that had inhabited a place for a long time knew the entire history of that place. I'd once visited the Parthenon in Athens and spent days just listening to and learning from the amazing amount of spiritual energy. It wasn't always coherent and rarely linear, but -- to me, at least -- always fascinating.

In Daniel's case, spiritual energy amassed around him without conscious thought on his part. Spiritual energy wasn't visible to anyone but spirit witches, and a spirit witch can't see the aura of that type of energy that surrounds themselves, so no one had seen it happening until his control was nearly shot. The army had hoped to have him plant spiritual energy in enemy territory, then either use it to spook enemy troops or for espionage. But they couldn't use him unless or until he could control it. As he was now, he made mundanes uneasy in his presence, because even the non-gifted could feel the pulsing cloud that surrounded him. Instinct had taught him to redirect some of it, but by the time they called me, he'd amassed so much around him that he couldn't do anything with it. He now lived with Jake in Jake's secluded home for a reason. The forest was a better place to accommodate that much energy than a congestion of manmade structures. Abundant plant life or natural mineral formations had a diffusive effect on spirits.

In the three months I'd worked with him, things had improved greatly. When I'd first arrived, I felt the spiritual buzz from miles away. Even someone who wasn't sensitive probably would have felt it when they turned onto the dirt road that led up to Jake's cabin. Daniel, however, must have indeed been doing well, I decided as we made that very turn. I couldn't sense any abnormal spiritual activity on the road, nor as we approached the cabin. At least he hadn't lost any ground while I was gone.

On the one hand, I was proud that Daniel was doing well. On the other, I was anxious at losing my main excuse for being near him and Jake. It made my secret plans for the upcoming days even more important.

The little house was nestled on a gradual slope leading into a valley that cradled a tributary of one of the nearby rivers.

The cluster of sycamore trees surrounding the genuine rough-hewn log cabin helped to keep the wind factor down. At least a foot and a half of snow coated the ground where it hadn't been cleared. Although it was a cabin, it had all the modern amenities: indoor plumbing, electricity from a pretty powerful generator, and a huge satellite for television, phone, and internet access. A born city girl, I'd been deathly afraid of having to rough it when my mother had given me the assignment, but had been pleased to find that was not the case.

He heard us coming, or felt Jake's approach. Whichever, a second, brighter outside light flipped on to augment the dimmer one that turned on automatically as the sky turned dark. Daniel emerged from the door of the covered porch just as Jake parked the Dodge in front of the house.

My heart caught at the sight of him. Even though I couldn't see him very well through the dark and snow, I could well guess his features. I'd memorized them in such detail that they'd haunted my dreams during the weeks I was gone. Just a bit taller than me, Daniel had one of those bodies that could never be massive with muscle. His bone structure simply wouldn't support it. He would always be slim, no matter what he did to bulk up. Which was not to say that he wasn't ripped. I'd seen him once without a shirt in our time together, and the image was indelibly etched in my mind. He had shoulder-length, glossy black hair that seemed to have trapped some merlot wine in it for highlights, and a long, elegant face with the most gorgeous mouth the Goddess had ever created. All this and big, beautiful slanted brown eyes with the thickest lashes I'd ever seen on a man. He'd never told me the ancestry of his father, but the blood of his Japanese mother came through loud and clear.

He hurried forward to help with the groceries, hatless, with an open green jacket thrown over his thick sweater and jeans. His black hair whipped about his head, making him look elemental. Wild. He came to an abrupt halt when he saw the tree dominating the truck's bed.

I stepped out of the passenger side and loaded my arms with bags from the backseat to delay the inevitable. Jake did the same.

Daniel didn't let us get away with it. He appeared at Jake's side and glared at me over the backseat. "What's with the tree?"

"Hi, Daniel," I said brightly. "It's good to see you."

He grimaced, a travesty for those generous lips, but it was his normal expression. He cocked his head. "Noelle, what are you up to?"

"I'm not *up to* anything," I said, keeping my smile as I took my armful around the front of the truck and toward the door. "Other than what I was sent to you to do."

I left them behind, managing the porch door even with plastic bags hanging from my forearm and fingers.

The inside of the cabin was warm, thanks to the fire in the fireplace and the wonderful little pot-belly stoves, one in the corner of the main room and one toward the back to keep the downstairs bedrooms toasty. The place was furnished with typical cabin furniture, nearly all of it made of sturdy cedar, which matched the planked walls. Painted scenes of wildlife hung on the walls between mounted wood carvings Jake's granddad had made. The television was on, but the sound was down. A hallway directly across from the front door led to two bedrooms, a bathroom, and a utility room with another door that opened to the back yard. A staircase dominated the right wall of the cabin, leading up to Daniel's open loft bedroom and its small half-bathroom.

Darn it if I didn't feel like I was coming home! I allowed myself a small sigh since neither of the men could hear it.

I took my bags to the left and dumped them on the heavy dining table that stood half in the kitchen and half in the main living area. The men were only moments behind, two sets of strong arms easily getting the last of the bags.

Jake turned to go back outside.

I kept taking things out of bags and setting them on the table, steeling myself as Daniel dropped his bags on the table and shrugged out of his jacket. "What's with the tree?"

I took a deep breath, then looked up at him, hoping that the flip of my heart didn't show on my face. Goddess! One man should not be allowed to be this gorgeous. It simply wasn't fair to poor little mortal women and their fragile hearts. Even in a bulky gray sweater and relaxed jeans, he was a wonder to behold, despite his skeptical scowl. "I thought it would brighten up the place."

He draped the jacket over the back of a chair. "None of us are Christian."

I tilted my head to the side, widening my eyes. Sometimes the blue-eyed blonde innocent look was enough of a distraction to get me out of conversations that I didn't want to have. "Are you really Jewish?"

He blinked, and some of his anger slid off into confusion. "No. What gave you that idea?"

"Someone told me you were." I glared at Jake as he entered with my duffle bag and suitcase.

"You told her I was Jewish?"

Jake flushed and shrugged, setting my luggage near the couch, then going back to stand by the door, no doubt waiting to see if he was to bring in the tree or not.

Daniel rolled his eyes at him, but shrugged it off and returned his irritation to me. Goody. "Whatever. That's not the point, Noelle. We don't celebrate Christmas."

"What do you celebrate?"

"What?"

"What *do* you celebrate, Daniel? Anything? What time of year do you set aside to just be happy and do silly things? When do you just kick back, take a break, and enjoy the company of those you care for?"

He frowned and didn't deign to answer.

I nodded, calmly balling up one of the empty plastic bags. "Just as I thought. You don't, do you? Ever."

The right side of his mouth lifted in a small snarl. "I don't have a hell of a lot to celebrate."

"That is entirely untrue. You have your life. You live in this beautiful cabin. Most of your expenses are paid for by the US military. You have the best kind of friend and companion in Jake." I picked up steaks wrapped in butcher paper and went to put them in the freezer. "And you've got me."

A glance over my shoulder showed his arms crossed and one slim, jet-black brow arched. That brow was so perfectly shaped that it looked painted on. I wanted to run my index finger over it to see if it felt as sleek as it looked.

Stop that!

"We don't need a tree." From his tone, you'd think he was the oldest of us and not the youngest. But he was definitely the one calling the shots. I'd discovered that early on. Woe to anyone who challenged him.

Like me. "Actually, I think you do."

"Why is that?"

"You need to lighten up."

He cast his gaze toward the beamed ceiling and sighed. "That again."

"Yes. That again." I returned to the table for more groceries. "You've got this dark cloud hanging over you, Daniel, and as long as it's there you'll never bring the spirits completely under control."

"I thought you said my cloud was neon blue?"

It was my turn to glare, even if I knew I wasn't as practiced at it as he. "Ha ha. You know what I mean."

He stared at me, and I forced myself to stare back. He didn't quite believe that it was his emotions that kept the spiritual energy out of whack. We'd been having this argument almost since I'd started working with him. I'm pretty sure Daniel was convinced -- or wanted to be convinced -- that he didn't *have* emotions.

Not surprisingly, I relented first. *I'm a reed; I can bend.* "What can it hurt?" I asked softly, hoping a bit of hurt came through in my voice and manner. Manipulative? Me? *No!* "I'm not proposing the entire Christmas celebration, or even Yule. I just thought it'd be fun. When's the last time you decorated a tree?"

He breathed in, the nostrils of that slim nose flaring. "Not since I was a kid."

"Exactly."

"It wasn't fun then."

His mom even ruined that?! Best not to discuss it. "But it will be this time. This time it's me and Jake, and we care for you. We want to help you." I took a chance and stepped toward him, reached out and put hesitant fingers on the back of his hand. His hand, not his forearm, because I just had to touch that warm, pale skin. "Please, Daniel. It can't hurt and it could help. And it'll give us something to do when the storm throws the satellite out."

He glanced down at my hand, and I braved myself to keep it there. His dark eyes darted back up to my face. He sighed, stepping back, breaking contact. "Okay. Have it your way." He turned to the table and pulled the reindeer doll with the light-up nose from the bag. His look of open-mouthed horror was priceless. "*This* is *not* being hung anywhere in the house."

I laughed and exchanged a happy glance with Jake just before he went to fetch the tree.

Chapter Four

Daniel and I finished putting the groceries away while Jake brought the tree in to the porch. Then they started on dinner. Jake pulled out the flank steak, noodles, and other ingredients for the stroganoff.

Daniel saw the ingredients and raised an eyebrow at me. "Your request?"

I smiled. "What can I say? You have me addicted!"

He shook his head, but made no further comment on the meal as he unwrapped the meat and got a knife to cut it.

I busied myself with first stashing my luggage in the spare bedroom across the hall from Jake's, then moving the tree decorations to the coffee table. I took my time with the decorations, though, because I was really watching the boys.

They worked so well together. Almost like one person. Jake sliced onions, then started them sautéing with the mushrooms. Daniel finished with the meat, then started the noodles. Jake asked Daniel about the football game he'd abandoned to come pick me up, and Daniel filled him in.

While they discussed the finer points of football, I got the teakettle, filled it, then took it to the potbelly stove to heat to avoid getting in their way. Not that interested in the sport, I just listened, enjoying their camaraderie. They were very close friends, which was always a good thing between witch and shifter. There was a deep caring between them. I couldn't quite convince Daniel that Jake's shared strength was probably the only thing that had kept the spiritual energy from tearing him apart. He'd been taught that the leash was a one-way spell to control the shifter. He wasn't prepared to believe some of that could reflect back on or help the witch.

I perched on the stool near the stove to wait for the water to heat. Did they even notice how close they stood to each other? I'd grown up with plenty of men around the house -- my mother's bodyguards and employees, mostly -- and not even the closest of friends remained so far within the other's personal space. I watched Daniel lean in to add the meat to the sauté. His shoulder actually brushed Jake's and neither of them flinched. Yes, it was brief and casual, but such touches were usually solely reserved for lovers. But they weren't lovers. I believed that they thought they were only friends, but their body language said so much more.

Now, if I could only show them that, part of my goal would be reached.

When I went to get a mug and fetch tea and the infuser, Daniel refocused on me. He put his back to the counter, crossing his arms as he propped his tight little butt against the cabinet's edge. Casually, he flipped glossy black hair from his brow, although it fell right back seconds later. "Noelle, why did you really come back?"

I walked away from him toward the water whistling softly in the kettle atop the stove. "I told you. I was worried about you." Truth. I didn't have to admit there was more to it.

"Why? You were okay to leave in the first place."

Could I hope that he was upset that I'd left? I poured steaming water into my mug. "I was sent to help you. You've managed to contain most of your attraction to spirits, but you still don't have much control." I turned with the mug cradled in my hands, breathing away the steam as I crossed the room back to the dining table.

He pushed an exasperated breath through perfect lips. "Have I slipped while you were gone?" He had to ask me because a witch can't see their own spirit aura. It's like trying to see the back of your neck. You know it's there, but you can't twist around to see it. Others, however, with the proper gifts can see it fine.

I looked up at him and deliberately skewed my sight so I could not only see the plainly visible but also the metaphysically visible. To him, it would look like I was kind of looking blankly past him, sort of cross-eyed.

Daniel's spirit aura was amazing. Everyone had a spirit glow to them, even mundanes. This is not the aura that some of the non-gifted have learned to see and even photograph. Spirit energy lends to that aura, but it is, in fact, something different. The non-gifted see auras in many colors, whereas the aura that a spirit witch sees is always in varying shades of blue, from almost greens to deep purples and all through the deep and light blues. I'm told my color was lavender to cerulean blue, depending on my mood. Daniel's color was vivid, neon blue with strange midnight streaks throughout.

When I'd first met him, the roiling blue cloud immediately surrounding him had extended fully ten feet in all directions with a piercing ice blue shot through the farthest edges like a cloud's silver lining. The cloud extended even farther when he was agitated, and it had looked like it had tentacles, reaching out to touch everything surrounding him. On occasion, it would even knock things down, which was the dangerous part. He'd had, in effect, a poltergeist riding him, and it would occasionally reach out to do things to the physical world. Usually it was harmless enough, like knocking things off shelves, but Jake had related one horror story about Daniel's energy throwing the truck Jake was driving out of gear while they were on a particularly serpentine road.

In our time together, Daniel had reined in much of that wild power so that his aura was only about a foot surrounding him and the energy couldn't affect the physical world. He still radiated more than the average person and still did not have it quite under control, but it was far more manageable. I still didn't quite know what the darker blue streaks meant. The research I'd done while away hadn't given me anything other than that they indicated some emotional state.

What was most interesting about Daniel's aura, however, was its active nature. It was the busiest aura I'd ever seen, with very strange behavior. For one thing, the midnight color extended in sinuous tendrils down the glowing yellow leash connecting him with Jake. I'd never seen anything like it. The root of the leash that could only be seen with magical sight was anchored in Daniel's heart and reached in two trails to Jake, the end of one trail winding around Jake's neck like a collar and the other around the base of his cock like a cock ring. The leash was common enough -- although the root in Daniel's heart was not as common; most leashes were rooted in the witch's hand -- but the extension of spirit energy down it was not. During my time away, I'd consulted with a few other spirit witches about it, and none of them had heard of it either, even the two who had leashed shifters of their own. The dark blue vines tapered to nothing before they actually reached Jake, but the fact of their existence was puzzling.

I'd told Daniel about the neon blue with the shots of darker blue through, but I'd kept the fact of it creeping down Jake's leash to myself. I wanted to know what it meant first before I worried him with it. Although I was now under the impression I knew what it meant, I still kept it to myself. For now. "Your aura looks the same as when I left," I told him, blowing on my tea again.

He nodded. "See?"

"But not any better."

His eyes shuttered. "I'm working on it. At least I kept it steady. Besides, I knew you were coming back." He turned to the refrigerator. "I know I'm not there yet." He extracted a bottle of beer and opened a drawer to rummage for the bottle opener. "But you didn't have to come and baby-sit."

I shook my head. If only he knew. "That's not it."

"Then why are you here?"

I smiled at him. "I enjoy your company."

Another arched brow told me he didn't believe me.

I sipped at the tea that was just now cool enough to drink. "I come from a huge, very political family, Daniel. The holiday season with the Grays is spent traveling to various places between Albany and D.C., posturing and showing off. There's very little cheer, and you always have to watch what you say. I'm not a member of my mother's coven, so I wouldn't be participating in the Yule or solstice rituals anyway. To be honest, you're a very welcome excuse to get away from all that." Which was mostly true.

"That must be awful," Jake chimed in, nudging Daniel forward so he could get into the refrigerator behind him.

"It's not horrible, but it can be tiring." I shrugged, noting the casual slide of Jake's hand off Daniel's shoulder as the younger man stepped forward to give him room. "I grew up with it. With my mother who she is and being one of her seven daughters, it was expected of me." My mother was the grand dame of the Northwest United States. It made her the leader of witches and shifters in her region. Where my mother was concerned, it sometimes extended outside of her sixth of the country. Her influence also extended into the realm of the mundane, but we weren't supposed to talk about that.

Neither did Daniel know much about that, other than that the army had called my mother for someone to help him. "So we're an excuse?"

I didn't like the sharp edge to Daniel's voice, but I wasn't sure which part of what I'd said got to him. I smiled and stood, stepping up to reach above the counter to open the cabinet. "Yes. A welcome one." I pulled out three plates and turned back to the table. "To be honest, I haven't decorated a tree myself in over a decade. Mom's trees always had to be just so. I'm looking forward to it."

"You decorated trees as a kid?" Jake asked.

"Yes. We did. Like I told you in the store, the tree decorating was not originally a Christian thing. They just adopted it. Heck, most of the Christmas traditions are like that. Mom didn't see any reason why we couldn't enjoy Christmas just like our friends in school. To the mundanes, we're supposedly a good Christian household."

Jake laughed at that. "I never knew that. But then, my grandparents were devout Catholics and real good at not seeing what they didn't want to know."

I sensed an underlying meaning to his casual words, but didn't press.

Daniel pulled the bag of pre-mixed salad from the refrigerator and stepped up to the cabinet to get a bowl. "Doesn't your name mean Christmas?"

I paused, fingers on the drawer containing the silverware, and smiled at him, delighted he knew it. Well, okay, it was an easy one to know, but still. "Yes, it does. In French."

"More of the front of being a 'good Christian household'?"

I got out three forks and a serving spoon. "No. Mom named me that because my father's French and I was born on Christmas day."

"Christmas is your birthday?" Jake asked as I set out the forks.

"Yes."

"Aw, man, you should've told us. We would have gotten you something." He turned to the stove to stir the sauce. "How old will you be?"

Older than you. I returned for glasses and swatted his arm. "You don't ask a woman her age, silly man!"

"What? You'll be the ripe old age of twenty?"

"Sweet talker."

He winked at me. "You know it." He laughed and bent to bestow a kiss on my cheek. He turned back to the stove. "All right, you guys sit down. This is ready."

"Get off me!"

"Come on."

"Let go, Jake."

Jake completely disregarded the daggers Daniel glared and hauled him off the couch to his feet. He proceeded to shove a shiny red ball into Daniel's hand and force him to the tree. I watched, laughing, fascinated. He did it by stepping up behind Daniel, pressing back to chest, and literally walking him forward with both hands securely fastened to Daniel's upper arms. When they reached the tree, he grabbed Daniel's wrist and lifted his arm, ornament and all, toward the waiting tree bough.

"See?" he said, holding Daniel's shoulders once the ball was hung. "Was that so bad?"

Even Daniel's sulk was pretty, emphasizing the plump curve of his lower lip. "Yes."

Jake smacked the back of his head. "Scrooge!"

"This game is for you two." Daniel scowled, glaring at the ornament. He tried to step away, but Jake held him by sliding one arm about his shoulders. It secured Daniel's back to his chest. While it was a borderline acceptable pose for close friends, it was also a perfect pose for lovers and sent my imagination into overdrive. Daniel showed no reaction to it other than to stare resolutely at the tree and its blinking lights, his arms now crossed over his chest.

Jake leaned in closer to his ear. "It's for you, too, buddy. *Smell* that!"

Since his nostrils were flaring, Daniel couldn't help but pull in the spicy scent of Douglas fir.

Jake stepped back, then slapped Daniel's back, turning to get more ornaments. "Lighten up and help us."

Daniel grimaced, but he stayed where he was beside the tree.

I turned away before he could see my amused smile. Or was it aroused? They looked so good together!

To my delight, he actually came to the table and picked up another ornament. "If I don't help, you'll be all night about it," I heard him grumble. "It's already midnight."

"That's the spirit!" Jake crowed.

The coffee table contained far more than the paltry ornaments Jake and I had purchased at the store. Since Daniel had given in, after dinner Jake disappeared into the storage shed attached to his woodworking shop out back and returned with boxes of his family's Christmas decorations. Much to Daniel's chagrin, there was now a wreath on the inside of the front door -- "where *we* can see it," Jake had declared -- and a few garlands waiting to be strung along the staircase banister.

"Hey, don't turn that!" Daniel protested when Jake grabbed the remote and flipped away from the football game he'd been watching.

"It's recorded. You can watch it later." He flipped to the satellite's seasonal station, but got nothing but static. "Damn."

It looked like the storm had well and truly settled in outside. We could occasionally hear the howl of the wind, but the thick walls of the cabin mostly muffled it.

"See?" Daniel paused by the coffee table, a delicate white filigree angel in one hand and a wire decoration hanger in the other. "Put the game back on."

"No way. I've got a better idea." Jake crouched before the cabinet underneath the stereo. It was where all the CDs his grandparents had owned still sat. Moments later, as Daniel and I continued with the tree, Jake stood with a handful of CD cases in hand. I saw flashes of bright red and green. My suspicion that he'd found their Christmas collection was confirmed when Elvis came on singing "Santa Claus is Back in Town."

Daniel groaned and shook his head, but continued to help decorate, which I found heartening.

Jake, delightedly animated, picked up another item from the storage box and began to unwrap it.

I was beginning to wonder if the tree would hold all that we had for it.

Things became surreal when the CD reached "Blue Christmas" and Jake started to sing. He wasn't horrible, but he wasn't entirely on key. It was worse because he insisted on copying Elvis as closely as he could, complete with a truly pathetic attempt at the King's famous hip swing.

Daniel's reaction was positively comical. He stood frozen beside the tree, staring with wide eyes and jaw agape at Jake.

"What?" Jake asked when he noticed.

"What are you doing?"

"Singing."

"Is that what you call it?"

Jake beamed, pulling up a long rope of gold and silver garland. "Yup."

He started up again and caught me off guard by wrapping the garland around me and pulling me into his arms.

I was laughing so hard that I had to follow his lead or fall to a giggling heap on the floor.

Daniel became engrossed with decorating the tree, careful to keep his distance from us as we danced. Jake and I amused ourselves through Elvis and into a Burl Ives album, but we had to attack Daniel with the light-up reindeer when "Rudolph the Red-Nosed Reindeer" came on. He ran from us, but we cornered him and I almost caught him smiling as he wrestled Jake to the ground for the thing. When he snatched it up and threatened to throw it into the firebox of the potbelly stove, we laughingly surrendered.

Since Jake was tallest, he got to put the angel on top of the tree. It was a lovely, delicate piece with a dress that his grandmother had crocheted by hand. We all stood back, staring at the twinkling lights among the gaily colored balls decorating the boughs, drinking in the singular biting smell of Christmas tree. We hadn't managed to put all of the decorations Jake had found on the tree, but some of them were now scattered across the tables and chairs around the room, giving the room a decidedly holiday feel. It was a satisfying experience.

I slanted a glance at Daniel and twisted my sight. I had to suppress a grin. The bright neon surrounding him was subdued. The cloud wasn't tumbling and rolling over itself so much. Curiously, the midnight blue was like a lining around it, also calm. The tendrils around the leash were thinner but looked more solid, and they extended just a bit farther toward Jake. *Interesting.*

Jake distracted me by taking my hand. Startled, I turned to him and was surprised to be folded into a hug.

Smiling, I hugged back.

"Thank you," he murmured in my hair, sliding his hands across my back. "I haven't done this since…" His breath hitched, and he rubbed his cheek against the top of my head. "…since before they were gone." Judging by his tone, "they" would be his grandparents. From all he'd told me, I gathered that they had been strict but the love amongst the small family had been wholly mutual. He hugged me tighter, then kissed the top of my head. "Thank you. This is the most fun I've had in ages."

I beamed as he pulled back. Before I could say anything, he cradled my face in his big, warm hands and bent to bestow a simple kiss on my lips. It might have lasted just a bit too long. Not that I was complaining.

He smiled as I blinked, then released me. He glanced over my shoulder to where Daniel stood. "I'm beat. I'm gonna hit the hay." He stepped away from me toward the hall that led to the back rooms. "See you guys in the morning."

I turned to Daniel, and the warm fuzziness that surrounded my heart chilled. The look he gave me had a hard edge. I could almost see the blue cloud surrounding him, guessing it was no longer quiescent. But I didn't dare alter my vision. He'd see it, and I wasn't sure what had upset him. Had he taken offense at the hug? The kiss? Or was this something else?

I didn't get an answer. He nodded curtly, said what I think was "good night," and retreated upstairs.

I was left staring at the merry Christmas tree, wondering where the peace of just a little while ago had gone.

Chapter Five

December 13

It was so dark when my eyes opened that my sleepy mind first thought it was still night. But a glance at the alarm clock on the nightstand told me that it was eight a.m. I rolled onto my back, letting my hand escape the warm cocoon of my blankets to rub sleep from my eyes. It was quiet. The storm of the past week had tapered into an on-again, off-again snowfall. This was certainly turning out to be a grand, white Yule season. I stayed where I was, cozy in the warmth of blankets and quilt, and dozed for a little while more.

Eventually, noise in the other room and the smell of coffee woke me. Jake was at his morning routine. The man could be completely silent, but he chose to make little noises in the morning to wake us up. Like me, Daniel was not a morning person. If Jake was actually making noise, however, that meant that he intended to go out for a while. He liked for at least one of us to be conscious before he went outside.

I sat up, yawning. *So, what to do with Daniel today?* I mused as I braved the chill in the air and hurriedly stuffed myself into stretchy Lycra-cotton leggings, a long green skirt, and a gaudy green-and-red-striped sweater. Thick red socks served to keep my tootsies warm.

A week since I'd returned to the cabin, and things had settled back into the same routine as right before I'd left. Jake would get us up, see us fed -- or at least put coffee in one or the other of us -- and then he'd leave for most of the day. He either went roaming the forest in his other form, or if weather didn't permit, he went out back to his woodworking shop. Despite the fact that bears hibernate during the winter, Jake was perfectly fine being awake. Seemed shapeshifter bears had different winter routines. Jake's absence gave Daniel and me a chance to work on "the magic stuff," as Jake put it. Daniel and I would decide how to tackle his training that day and spend hours on that. The only difference now was that when Jake returned, we did something Christmassy instead of watching sports all night.

I smiled, leaving the spare bedroom for the bathroom across the hall. Daniel was not enamored of the turn of events. Over the course of a few nights, Jake and I had dismantled and redecorated the tree twice, had spent a night making and decorating sugar cookies with the ingredients we'd bought that first night I'd come back, and had even spent one hilariously frustrating night with Jake trying to teach me how to carve. I was horrible at it. His wood carving looked exactly like a cute little brown reindeer; mine had turned out looking like a four-legged duck. But I didn't mind. It was fun and kept us amused, especially on the nights that the storm blocked the satellite reception. On the nights when we could watch television, we vetoed most of Daniel's leaning to watch sports and turned on whatever Christmas specials we could find.

After my morning bathroom routine, I put a barrette with a sprig of holly into my short blonde hair. Big blue eyes blinked at me over what I'm told is my characteristic smile. I like to smile. It makes me feel good and seems to have a similar effect on those around me. Most of the time, anyway.

Jake chuckled when he saw my outfit. Daniel, seated on the couch with a cup of coffee cradled in his lap, just glanced up, blank face totally unreadable.

Jake placed a mug of coffee into my hands and kissed me briefly on the cheek, passing me on his way out back. He went, barefoot and coatless, down the hall to the utility room. I squelched the urge to follow him and watch him change. A moment later, the back door opened and then slammed, shut securely by the weight of a bear.

I leaned on the half-wall between the main room and the kitchen, nursing my coffee. "Well," I said after the silence had drawn on. "Should we try some meditation?"

Daniel's profile was to me, sharp and defined as he stared intently at the tree. His black hair was pulled back into a tail secured at his neck, but shorter strands trailed along his temples and cheeks. A dark blue sweater hugged the curves of his chest and arms, and jeans encased the long legs he had stretched out before him. He shrugged and twisted to put his mug on the side table by the couch. As I put my own cup on the sideboard against the back of the couch, he got up and pushed the coffee table from the rug to allow us to take our accustomed places in the center of the woven design.

No sooner had I settled my butt on the rug than Daniel leaned forward to grab my arms and shake me.

"Don't sleep with him!"

I blinked, completely caught off guard. "Excuse me?"

He knelt before me, eyes narrowed. "I've watched you. I figured it out. You came back to sleep with Jake!"

"No, I didn't…" *Not entirely.*

"You're attracted to him. I can understand that. It's just…" He closed his eyes, swallowed, a look of pure anguish passing over his exquisite features. His fingers squeezed my arms, and I'm not sure he knew he hurt me. "Just don't. Please. Not now. Not…" He shook his head.

I leaned into his grip, staring intently into his face. "Daniel." When he didn't open his eyes, I bent my elbows to grab his forearms and shook him slightly. "Daniel."

Sharp brown eyes opened to me.

"Tell me why."

He frowned. "Why?"

"Why don't you want me to sleep with him?"

He released me and sat back on his heels, but I pushed forward to kneel, keeping my grip on his arms.

"Tell me why, Daniel."

He tried to act cool, brushing my hands off. His eyes darted away from mine. "Because I don't want to be around the two of you acting all lovey dovey."

I ducked my chin and tilted my head, trying to reestablish eye contact. "No, there's more to it than that."

"No."

"Yes. I told you, you've got to be open with me if I'm going to help you."

He scowled. "This has nothing to do with the spirits."

"This has everything to do with the spirits. It has to do with your peace of mind."

He frowned, blinked, stared at me. He wanted to deny it; I saw it in his face. But he couldn't. "I am being honest. I'm asking you not to...I..." His voice got steadily softer as he went on until the last was barely a whisper. "I don't want to see you with him. I couldn't handle it. Not...now."

"Why? Because you want to sleep with me?" I paused just a second, wondering if the next sentence was wise. Instinct told me I had to. "Or because you want to sleep with him?"

Anger flared, coloring his alabaster cheeks. He reared up on his knees, grabbing my arms to yank me nose to nose with him. "I'm not gay!"

"Are you sure?"

"What the hell is that supposed to mean?"

I was committed now. "I've seen you around Jake. You guys are so close --"

"We're close, so that means we're *gay?!*"

"Daniel, that's not all there is. The way you two..."

His nostrils flared. His eyes went wide, then narrowed. Quick as a viper, he hauled me up to his chest and forced his lips on mine.

I'd known this was a possible reaction. I'd be a hypocrite to say that a part of me didn't want it. The few touches I'd been allowed on that beautiful body hadn't done anything to lessen my desire to rub against him like a cat in heat. I probably should have backed away and forced him to talk to me, but *oh*, even if his kiss did mash my teeth into my lips, he felt *good*.

At first he was punishing me, pressing his lips to mine and holding me pinned. I think it was when I clutched his waist, or maybe it was when a happy little moan escaped my throat, that the kiss changed. He backed off from the hurt and tilted his head for better access. I went with him, opening my lips to suck in his bottom lip. It was his turn for a little moan as he opened his mouth on mine, disengaging his lips to make room for his tongue to plunge in. Finally he released the harsh grip on my arms, sliding one hand up to cup the back of my skull and slipping the other around my waist to hold me up against him. *Sweet Goddess!* His chest was hard and his arms were strong and he tasted so darn good. I cursed the layers of clothing that prevented me from feeling his hardness against my bare skin.

I wrapped my arms around his neck and desperately devoured his mouth.

He bent a bit and wound an arm around underneath my rear end. He lifted me slightly so he could tilt my body and gently lower me to the rug, without ever breaking the kiss.

I gratefully accepted his weight as he settled on top of me, arms coming up under my back to hold me. I parted my legs and threw them around his waist, that eager to hold him close.

He managed to pry our lips apart, but had to bring a hand up to peel my arm from around his neck to do it.

I whimpered, switching my lips to his neck. I folded my fingers with his to keep his hand from pushing me away. When I bit his earlobe, he groaned.

"Noelle…"

"Please, Daniel, please." I heard the begging in my voice and didn't care. I wasn't above begging for this. "Please."

"We can't…"

"We can."

"Jake…"

"You could call him back."

He raised his head and looked at me clearly. I swallowed, afraid I'd gone too far. But then his eyes shadowed and he lowered his lips to mine again. "Very funny."

I moaned to feel his hand bunching up my skirt at my side.

When he found the leggings, he grunted. "What the hell have you got on?"

"Give me two seconds and I can be out of them."

He took me at my word. He went up on his knees, grabbed the hem of his sweater, and ripped it off.

I lay there, stunned by the pale glory of his hairless chest. A year out of the army's physical regimen had probably softened some of the chiseled edges of his muscles, but not so much that he wasn't still cut. I could count the taut hills of his six-pack quite easily.

His hands went to the buttons of his jeans, but he paused, eyeing me meaningfully.

Oh, yeah, the leggings. I pulled my knees up and shimmied out of them and my socks, all the while trying to watch him as he unbuttoned his jeans and pushed them down his thighs along with the blue silk boxers he wore underneath. I tossed my leggings behind me and pushed up to rip off my sweater. I left the skirt bunched around my waist, not daring to take the time to remove it.

He didn't give me a chance to get out of my bra. He was back on top of me, one arm sliding up under my shoulder and the other pumping the hard, red cock that I'd unfortunately only glimpsed. Our lips met and my legs fell open.

At times like this, I did love being a witch. My magic gave me enough control over my body that I couldn't get pregnant without allowing it. Since he was human, I technically could get a sexually transmitted disease, but I couldn't fathom a situation where Daniel might have caught one. So there was no need for a condom to sheath that wonderful erection as he smeared the head through the folds of my sex.

"So wet," he murmured against my lips. "You want me that bad?"

"Goddess, yes!" I cried, rolling my hips up into him, trying to get him to hurry. "Please."

He set the head at my opening and pushed hard.

I groaned, clutching his back and burying my face in his neck. "Oh, so good," I muttered, winding my legs around his waist so I could push at his tight little butt with my heels. "More."

He muttered something I couldn't translate, but I also didn't care. His fingers clutched in my hair as he slammed home.

I arched back, mouth open to scream. He slapped his free hand over my lips just in time to muffle the sound. I cried out into his palm as he pulled out and rammed back home.

This was every bit as good as I'd imagined.

I lay beneath him, tense as a wire, concentrating on the pool of heat in my groin as I tried to grip him as hard as I possibly could. He snarled and muttered, lips somewhere in the vicinity of my ear as he pushed endlessly into my body, his ass working underneath my heels.

I couldn't stop my ramping orgasm, nor did I try. I exploded under him, screaming then whimpering into his palm.

He cursed, tensing as I tightened around him. He pulled my hair harder, waiting until I stopped spasming, then started pumping again.

I clutched at his back, fingers tearing into his hot, satin skin. The one orgasm had barely subsided before his continual movement sparked another. I chanted his name, turning my head so I could suck at his earlobe, so I could beg him to fill me. Without intending to, my vision skewed and I saw the bright neon blue surrounding him.

No, it wasn't neon. It was all midnight, underscored with a shimmer of violet that I'd never seen before. And his aura didn't extend very far, not the usual foot or so away from his body. It was tight and compact except where, if I didn't miss my guess, it reached down to encompass me.

Now that I was aware of it, I felt the tingling of spiritual energy. Sweet Goddess, he was dripping pure spirit into my body! I opened myself to it, and in it flowed, dark, sweet energy, roiling with decadent power. Strong and almost physically tangible, as I'd only felt spirit energy in Daniel's presence. It instantly touched off my next orgasm.

It might have been my absorption of the spirit energy from him, but he didn't have a chance to hold back this time. With a muted roar, he flung back his head and shuddered, filling me up both with seed and a pure rush of dark essence.

He collapsed on top of me, and we both just lay there, skin wet with mutual sweat and lungs laboring for breath.

I stared at the beamed ceiling far above. I had *never* had sex laced with spiritual energy before. I hadn't known it was possible. Then again, I'd never had sex with another spirit witch, either. Thinking on it, it made sense. Daniel's mere presence attracted spirits; his focused attention could direct the spirit energy. Why couldn't it be used sexually? I couldn't help but wonder what it would do to someone who wasn't attuned to it as I was.

Daniel pushed up on one elbow, gazing down at me. There was something serious in his eyes, a question that I didn't understand until he spoke. "Did you feel it?"

"The spirit?"

Distaste passed over his fine features. "Yeah. I'm sorry. I tried to…"

"What are you *sorry* for?" I grabbed his chin with my fingers and made him face me when he would have turned away. "It was wonderful!"

That surprised him. "Really?"

"Really. Why do you ask?"

He stared at my chin. Strands of his long, silky hair caressed my cheek. "It's freaked out the few other lovers that I've had."

There was my answer. I smiled, smoothing my fingers over the sharp curve of his jaw. "But I'm attuned to it, remember. I loved it."

There was that almost-smile again. It lit his eyes even if it didn't curl his lips. "Really?"

I nodded, hoping he could read my sincerity in my eyes. "Really."

Some tension drained from his face, and there was that ghost of a smile. He pushed back, rolling his hips to press his groin and his softening cock against me.

I moaned, loving the feeling.

He chuckled softly -- how he did that without smiling I'd yet to figure out -- and pulled away. With a sigh, he sat on his heels, then went further until he was sitting with his back against the couch, knees bent before him. Head back, arms on knees, he looked as content as I'd ever seen him. A quick glance through magical sight showed me that his aura was still tightly compact and a dark midnight blue. The violet was gone.

I wondered how to tell him. I was pretty sure we'd just made a breakthrough in discovering the secret to his control, but I was unsure how he felt about what we'd just done. It had started in anger even if it hadn't ended as such.

But as I watched, some of the rolling neon resurfaced and his aura expanded. He brought his head down and fastened his gaze on me. He was outwardly calm, but the aura alone told me emotions were rocking inside.

"Don't tell him."

I let my vision smooth back to normal and frowned. "What?"

"Jake. Don't tell him. He doesn't need to know this happened."

I pushed up to sit cross-legged on the rug a few feet from him. My skirt settled around my hips, hiding most of my legs from view. "But you can't hide sex from shifters."

"What?"

I blinked. "You didn't know?"

"Know what?"

I swallowed. "Jake's a bear, hon. He'll be able to smell what happened. If he didn't feel it through the leash."

His eyes went wide. "What?"

I kept overestimating his knowledge of magic. What had they taught him about his gifts while he was in the military? But I already knew. They'd taught him just enough and nothing more. He'd had teachers who had given him just enough information to understand the basics of magic. They certainly hadn't provided him with a spirit witch as a teacher until they'd sent the request to my mother for help. Throughout the ages, the military had frequently misused the magically gifted. It seemed that present times were no different. But it hadn't occurred to me that they wouldn't have let him know about shifters and sex. "You didn't know?"

"No!"

No. Of course not. And I hadn't told him because, in that moment, I hadn't wanted to give him any reason to second guess what we were doing. In that, I was as bad as the army, keeping information from him to get him to do what I wanted.

He pounded his fists on his knees. "Shit! What have I done? And you knew!"

I flinched. "I don't think Jake will mind."

"Mind?! I just..." He rolled to his knees, snatching up his jeans. "This will make things uncomfortable for him."

"Why? Do you want to do it again?"

I seemed to be surprising him a lot today. He sputtered, tried to frown. "I...don't you?"

"Well, yes. But I wasn't sure if it'd just be a one-time thing with you. I don't know, Daniel. You don't *tell* me anything. I have to pull every little bit of information from you."

"I've told you more than --" He cut himself off with a muttered curse and stood.

Even through the emotions of the situation, I had to admire the beauty of his body. Pale skin stretched taut over smooth muscle everywhere. The slim, toned shape seemed fit more for an angel than a human being. When he turned from me to step into his jeans, I saw that his ass was just as firm and beautiful as the rest of him. He even had those precious little divots just in his lower back that made me want to trace them with my tongue.

Sweet Goddess, I had it bad! "Are you okay with what we just did?"

His back was to me, so I couldn't see his face. I skewed my sight to magical and watched the neon blue energy roil around him. Fingers of it extended out, reaching for anything near to him, including me. The midnight blue was a faint understatement, hanging close to his skin except along the line of the leash that trailed toward the back of the cabin.

He, of course, had no idea. He just continued to step into his jeans. "Yes."

"You don't seem okay."

"I don't want to hurt Jake."

"Jake just wants you to be happy, honey."

I watched the shimmer of midnight blue pulse through the neon, still unsure what the heck it meant. "Yes." But it was strained.

"Come back and lie down with me."

I easily counted to five before he shook his head. "No."

I watched miserably as he gathered up his sweater, very carefully not looking at me. I stayed where I was, trying to figure out if I should push the issue or not.

"You should get dressed," he said as he settled his sweater back around his chest. "We should...get to work."

I nodded dumbly, realizing the discussion was over. To push now would just make him dig in his heels. I'd had some of the best sex in my life with easily the best-looking man I'd ever met, and I felt like someone had just punched a hole through my heart.

I got dressed all right, but I didn't immediately sit down with him on the rug. He sat, and I took my cold coffee to the kitchen, then made a visit to the bathroom. When I came back, I heated up some tea just to give me something to do. He was seated on the carpet, palms on knees, eyes closed, practicing his control. He didn't need me and had effectively excused me. Except for the ache between my legs and the tingle on my skin, you'd never know that we'd just been going at it like teenagers.

I sat at the table, nursing my tea, watching him. I let my sight skew toward the magical and monitored his lack of progress in bringing the neon under control. He'd had a certain amount of success with the method of brute force, trying to rein in the control. It had worked toward the beginning, bringing the ten-foot-plus aura down to the mere foot, but that's where the force had stopped working. It seemed like trying to jam things into a suitcase. At some point, force just wasn't going to cut it. At some point, one had to rearrange or try a completely different tactic.

Like sex. What had it been about our joining that afforded him control? Was it my magic melding with his? Was it an abandonment of his cares into pure pleasure? *Had* he abandoned himself? I certainly had, which meant that I couldn't be entirely sure if he had. If we did it again, I'd have to try and be more aware.

I set the mug down carefully between my elbows and stared into the murky brown depths of my tea. *If* we did it again. He said he wanted to, but whether that remained true was anybody's guess. My skin still tingled. The amount of raw spiritual energy he'd pumped into my body was akin to what I felt when I completely let go of all of my own control and just let the spirits flow through me. I'd felt similar feelings of surging, raw power when I was first coming into my talent, long before I gained true control over it. I had not, of course, ever felt it coupled with sexual arousal. It was quite a heady combination. One I would gladly repeat, if Daniel was at all interested.

I looked up at him again. Magically. There was that darn midnight color. It still snaked out along the ropes of yellow that faded in the distance to where Jake would be. What did the midnight mean? And where the heck had the violet come from? I wondered if it had something to do with sex. I should tell him about it. Maybe we could hash it out together. But I was reluctant. What if he jumped to conclusions and just tried to suppress everything without trying to get to the bottom of what it meant?

I was still in the kitchen, watching him and silently arguing with myself, when Jake returned.

The back door screeched and banged, heralding his arrival. A few moments later, Jake strode down the short hallway, dressed only in the jeans he would have left in the utility room before he'd shifted. I idly admired the furry mat of dark brown hair that covered his chest and trailed in an intriguing love trail down his cobbled belly as he slid on his plaid shirt.

He saw me at the table, then glanced at Daniel seated twelve feet away from me. Brown eyes darted from one of us to the other as he stepped into the room, buttoning his shirt.

I could tell the moment he smelled something. He stopped at the other end of the dining table from me and took a deeper breath. His gaze landed on me, dark brows up in surprise, a silent question on his face. I wished Daniel could see the little smile of hope that curled Jake's wide mouth. His first reaction was pleasure, and it warmed my heart.

Jake didn't say anything, mindful of Daniel's meditation. He moved quietly to my side and leaned down to kiss my cheek. I didn't miss that he took another sniff. "About time," he murmured, rubbing his bearded cheek against mine.

I smiled up at him as he stepped away. He paused, his smile fading, no doubt because my smile was weak. He frowned. Okay, now he knew something was wrong. I shook my head and glanced at Daniel. He grimaced and nodded and said nothing.

He passed by me and quietly started dinner.

Daniel wasn't too long in emerging from his trance. Whether it was Jake's presence or the smell of the potatoes he was frying, I wouldn't know. I used my magical sight to confirm that he had things pretty well under control as far as the spirit energy that surrounded him. I was pleased to see the neon glow was a bit more faded. Oddly enough, the midnight-blue vines about Jake's leashes were pulled up close to Daniel's body, the first time I'd ever seen them like that.

He opened his eyes and turned his head slowly, locating both Jake and me with a glance. Without a word, he stretched his arms above his head, then got up in a fluid motion and came toward us. His eyes were for Jake alone, even though he came to rest at my side.

"Jake, we…"

"Steaks okay with you?" Jake asked, tossing a grin at Daniel before turning back to the skillet. "I'll bet you guys worked up an appetite."

I smiled.

Daniel flushed. "Jake, I…I'm sorry."

"Sorry?" Jake paused, spatula held aloft. "What for?"

"We just sort of…I mean, we didn't mean to…"

"Mean to what?"

Daniel huffed. "I didn't think when it happened. I just sort of…I'm sorry if my having sex with Noelle makes you uncomfortable."

Jake glanced at me.

I shrugged.

Jake smiled, shaking his head. "Doesn't make me uncomfortable, buddy. It shouldn't make *you* uncomfortable."

Daniel was doubtful. "It doesn't?"

"Hell no. *Some*one should sleep with her." He gave me a wink. "Fine woman like that deserves to be made love to. And often."

The warmth in his voice flooded my heart. It floored Daniel.

Jake chuckled at our reactions, clearly getting exactly the responses he'd intended. "But seriously, buddy, don't you worry about me. If Noelle makes you happy, I couldn't be happier."

Daniel pulled himself together and sat around the corner of the table beside me. He finally met my gaze and just stared at me for a moment. I couldn't for the life of me figure out what he was thinking or whether it was good or bad.

When Jake opened the refrigerator and bent down to open the meat drawer, Daniel glanced at him. Was I being far too analytical to think that there was a touch of appreciation in his eyes at seeing Jake's ass presented so nicely?

Then he sat back. "Jake, grab me a beer?" He pulled an air of nonchalance over himself like a veil and turned to me. "So, I've got more of it under control now."

Ah. Business. I nodded. "You're getting better." I wanted to tell him that making love to me seemed to have helped him gain more control. That is, until he started thinking about Jake. I should have told him, but I couldn't. Not with the memory of his body in mine so fresh in my mind. I stood. "Excuse me. I need to visit the restroom."

I felt their eyes on me as I went, but didn't look back. I got to the bathroom and leaned against the sink, sighing in relief.

Sex with Daniel was far more than I'd expected. I'd anticipated wonderful, maybe awkward. I knew his guilt might take over because of leaving out Jake. But I had not at all anticipated the actual feel of that sensuous body in mine, nor the thrill of sharing spiritual energy. My blood still sang from it. I dearly wished I could see my own spiritual aura because I was dying to know if that same violet was shot through it.

I took my time using the bathroom and washing my face, needing to settle my nerves. If I didn't, I might very well scream, and I wasn't sure if it would be inarticulate frustration or a demand for Daniel to take me again. Neither one would help my cause.

When I finally rejoined them, I passed by Daniel and went to offer my help to Jake. The blessed bear started to tell a story about his mother and her "hotter-than-hell" marinade, which he threatened to make for us sometime.

Chapter Six

We put in a DVD and watched the movie *Elf* while eating on the couch. Well, they ate on the couch. The two men took up much of the couch, so I ate in the big recliner chair. Which was fine. I couldn't be that close to Daniel right now and not want to touch him.

Daniel spent most of his time pointing out the inconsistencies of the story, and Jake spent most of his defending. I barely watched. I spent quite a bit of time staring at the Christmas tree, wondering what to do now. I couldn't let sex drive a wedge between me and Daniel, or Jake and Daniel. I very much needed Daniel to be comfortable. Perhaps it was time to tell him about the colors in his aura and how they behaved? Would he believe me? Would he start to draw the same conclusions I had about him and Jake? How would he react to that? I drove myself crazy, thinking in loops. I wished I was much more straightforward about things, like my sister Daphne. If she were in my place, she'd simply tell Daniel the way it was and make him believe that she knew what was best.

I laughed at myself, at the thought. No, Daniel and Daphne would probably not get along very well.

Jake came back to the room from dumping his dirty dishes in the sink and made a big deal about stretching and yawning. "Well, I'm going to hit the hay. Don't worry about waking me up. You know I sleep like a log."

Daniel looked skeptical.

Me? I'd never heard of a shifter that really slept like a log, but then, I didn't know any other bears that well. He didn't hibernate the winter away, true -- thank Goddess! -- but bears might sleep heavier than other shifters.

He left us, and an awkward silence descended.

Daniel aimed the remote and switched off the DVD's vamping menu graphics and music. "Noelle, I don't know if it's wise…"

I nodded and stood, headed toward the kitchen with my own empty plate. "Don't worry about it, Daniel. I know. I'll go sleep in the spare room." Just to be perverse, I went and bent over to place a kiss on his cheek. "Good night."

He remained where he was, staring at the blank television as I left my dishes in the sink. I left him with the lights of the Christmas tree twinkling bright.

I'd changed into my cozy pink flannel pajamas and was just getting into bed when my door slammed open. I had magic at the ready for protection, but let it fizzle when I saw Jake looming in the entrance to the room.

The look he leveled at me was as stern and dark as anything I'd seen on his normally pleasant, calm face. The fact that he wore a pair of sweatpants and seemingly nothing else distracted me a tad.

"Jake? What --? Hey!"

Without so much as a by your leave, Jake stormed across the room and picked me up.

"What are you doing?"

I squirmed, but quickly found out how hard it is to sway a bear with a purpose. The man was just plain strong. I don't even think he heard me or noticed my squirming, and there sure wasn't any getting out of his arms. Of course, they were *nice* arms. I didn't want to hurt him with magic, so I ended up going where he took me.

"Jake, I don't think this is a very good idea," I murmured halfway up the stairs to the loft.

Daniel sat in the middle of his king-sized bed, green sheets and green-and-black-patterned down comforter bunched in the hand he had in his lap. His unbuttoned black silk pajamas provided a nice frame for his gorgeous, pale chest. "Jake! What the hell --?"

His protest was cut short when Jake unceremoniously dumped me onto the bed beside him.

Jake loomed over us, pointing at me. "She belongs *here*," he proclaimed, glaring at Daniel. "You want her here and you know it. Don't be a damned stubborn ass about this."

Daniel glared but said nothing.

I lay very still.

"It'll bother me more to know that the two of you aren't fucking, you cold bastard. You got it?"

I think I heard Daniel's teeth grind, but I didn't dare look to confirm it. "I got it."

Jake nodded, then turned and stormed back down the stairs.

I stayed, frozen and silent at Daniel's side, until I heard Jake's door slam shut downstairs. I very carefully kept my eyes trained on the banister that looked out over the main room and not at Daniel. "I'll go sleep on the couch."

His fingers closed firmly around my upper arm, stopping me. "Don't."

"Daniel…" I protested as he pulled me close.

He buried his nose in my neck, pulling my back up against his chest. "Stay."

I swallowed. "Do you really want me here?"

His arms snugged up under my breasts. "Yes."

"I don't believe you."

He took my hand and pulled it back, tucked it with his under the comforter until he could finally squeeze my fingers around his silk-clad erection. "Believe me now?" He kissed my neck. "I've had this since I came up here."

"You were the one who --"

He squeezed our hands again, clearly liking the feel of it. "I'm not good at asking for things, Noelle," he murmured. "Please. Just stay. Help me."

"No fair appealing to my Mother Teresa complex."

He chuckled, an actual, warm chuckle. Goddess, I wanted to see if a smile went with that! He left my hand around his cock and brought his back up to tweak my nipple. "Help me, Noelle," he breathed, all levity gone. "Warm me up."

I sagged against him. How was I to fight that?

He felt my surrender. Gently, he turned me and laid me down on pillows that smelled of the lavender shampoo he favored. A few tugs got the covers over both of us, creating a hot cavern of warmth. His lips found mine in a soft caress, and for long, agonizing moments, all he did was kiss me and rub his hand lightly on my belly just underneath my pajamas.

I lay quietly as long as I could, not wanting to break the spell. But it soon wasn't enough. I tried kissing more aggressively, sucking his tongue into my mouth and attempting to up the foreplay. He let me do it, but didn't respond in kind. Finally, I reached up to sink my fingers into his silky hair, pulling his head back. I tasted his cheek, his chin. Slid my tongue to the warm spot just under his ear.

He propped himself on his elbow, hovering above me. His hand slid up my torso to one of my breasts, lightly plucking a nipple.

I groaned. "Goddess, Daniel, please," I whispered.

He brought his hand out to quickly undo the four buttons of my top. He laid it open, then bent to suckle my breast. I cradled his head to me, biting my lip over the voluptuous feel of his lips on me, of his hair falling down to caress my chest.

He shifted to kneel over me and started a slow slide down, kissing and licking my skin as he went. My ribs, my belly, the swell just beneath my navel that I hated so much. He breathed into the top of my pubic hair as his hands slid my pajama bottoms down and off my legs. He reared back, letting the covers slide off his back as he tossed my pants aside.

I'd never seen the wicked gleam in his eye before. It was delightful. Almost made it seem that he was grinning. "You smell good," he told me, settling down on his elbows between my spread thighs. He breathed on my curly hair again. "I'll bet you taste good, too."

He bent and I gasped. He was actually going to do it? He was going to put those succulent lips on me and taste me? I could hardly dare believe it and kept my eyes glued to him as that beautiful face tilted over me, as soft, silky hair tumbled down to brush my thighs. Long-fingered hands spread my drenched sex wide, and a sweet pink tongue poked out to drag from entrance to clit.

"Daniel!" I groaned, heedless of being quiet.

It was too good. He was too good. I didn't know where he learned it and frankly didn't care. He set to delicately nibbling me, like a tasty treat that he didn't want to finish too soon. He found my little nub of pleasure and tormented it. He soon had to wrap his arms around my thighs to hold me down because I couldn't keep my hips from helplessly grinding up into that glorious mouth.

"Daniel!" I cried, clutching the pillows above my head. They came forward over my scalp and I clung desperately, suffocating myself in cotton that smelled of lavender and Daniel. I screamed into the pillow as a wave of pleasure crashed over me.

He stopped, and I collapsed in relief, my body tingling. Fingers trailed the inside of my legs and my whole body jumped, attuned to his touch.

The bed moved and the pillow was pulled from my lax grasp. I blinked bleary eyes and actually groaned at the sight before me.

Daniel knelt between my thighs, calmly working his way out of the black silk pajama pants. The overlarge top remained, framing his chest and achingly beautiful groin. How to explain the beauty of the man? He didn't seem at all real. The graceful taper of his chest to narrow hips was a thing to make a sculptor cry. He had those sweet little creases at the sides of his groin, just above his thighs, that formed a perfect V. There was very little hair to hide any of the pale glow of his skin, just a very faint trail from his navel to the light patch that bunched at the base of his cock. And his cock...almost perfection. My only protest was that he was cut and it seemed a travesty to have removed any portion of that loveliness. It jutted forth from its base of black hair, flushed red with arousal, the tip weeping. Fascinated, I reached out to wrap my hand around it.

He groaned, tossing back his head and pushing forward into my grasp.

I sat up and leaned forward, eager to have a taste. I tormented both myself and him by hovering, mouth open just around the tip. The smell of him here was intoxicating. I put my free hand to his hip, sliding it around to grasp his buttock in an effort to steady myself.

"Noelle," he sighed.

Oh, yes! My name. That must be rewarded. I closed my lips around the head of him and swiped my tongue across the slit, tasting the salty cream.

Long fingers curled lightly around the back of my skull, urging me to take in more.

I don't think I could have denied myself. My mouth watered just from that little taste. Slowly I let my lips slide down his length, using my tongue to caress the veins under the velvety smooth skin. I was almost able to take his entire length into my mouth, but not quite. I'm not a deep-throater by any means, so I had to stop before I gagged, but I pushed my own limits, needing to take as much of him as possible. I used my hand to grasp the rest and closed the head of his cock between my tongue and roof of my mouth.

He sighed my name again, and I actually felt my sex get wetter.

I squeezed the root of him as I wetly eased back up the shaft. Lovingly, I nipped and lapped at the head, coaxing more cream to dribble out on my tongue. At the gentle pressure of his fingers on my scalp, I descended down his length again. He let me do that for a while, let me explore him. I lost myself in tasting him as I'd never lost myself in another lover before.

His fingers guided me to a faster pace, and I started to apply suction. His soft cries of encouragement kept me going. I didn't know how far or how long he wanted me to go, but I was content to keep it up, even after my jaw and neck started to ache from the repetitive motion.

But he stopped me. Palms at my temples ceased my movement.

I chanced a glance up his torso and couldn't suppress a groan at the sight. His face was tilted down toward his chest, his loose hair a sleek curtain to either side. Those smoldering eyes were open.

And he was smiling! It was small and darkly seductive, and it was an *actual* smile. For me. I clutched his ass and pulled him forward for another suck, anxious to do anything that would keep the smile on his face.

He hissed, eyes closing and smile turning to a snarl. "Stop." Fingers in my hair pulled me away.

I couldn't resist sucking hard at the end, loving the loud pop as he jerked his hips back, taking himself from my mouth's embrace.

He laid me back in the pillows, following me down. His lips landed on mine, still damp and drenched in the scent of my sex.

I grabbed his head, opening my mouth under his and chasing his tongue with mine.

He groaned, letting me lead the kiss while he reached down to center his cock at my opening.

I wiggled.

He pushed.

We both froze on a shared groan.

"Daniel." I slid my lips down his jaw, sucking on his chin, biting at the soft skin beneath it.

He braced on his elbows above me, eyes closed as he concentrated on shafting in and out of my body.

"Daniel."

There it was again. The spirit energy. It pulsed from his body, bearing down on mine. Heedless of unknown repercussions, if any, I dissolved my own barriers against it and allowed it to flow through me.

"Ah, Noelle," he gasped, dropping his head to rest his face in the bend of my neck.

I held him, hands spread across his back. I kept my eyes shut, enamored with the feel of him and the surging spirits around us. Goddess, the strength of him. If he could harness it, he might well be able to use the spirits as a viable weapon. Unharnessed and uncontrolled, it was certainly taking me over.

But I was a willing victim. And that type of energy recognized me. Amplified in me. As we strained together, a fine sheen of sweat coating our bare skin, I cautiously embraced some of the flow and willfully pushed it back at him.

He felt it instantly. It caught him unaware. He froze.

I pushed some more.

His mouth fell open and a cry spilled out as his body rocked on a wholly unexpected orgasm.

I'd be fibbing if I said that didn't fill me with some amount of pride.

His body shook as he collapsed atop me.

I happily nuzzled his neck and shoulder, content to hold his weight as he recovered.

"What did you do?" he finally asked, voice soft, breath caressing my shoulder.

"Shared the energy with you."

"But there wasn't that much."

"No. I contained it. That's part of what I've been trying to show you."

He pushed up on his elbows so he could look down at me. "You can craft the energy from me?"

I squeezed his biceps. "When you let me."

Ah, that gave him food for thought.

So I added the next part. "If you trust me."

He blinked. "I don't trust easily."

"I've noticed."

The very edges of his mouth tipped up. He leaned in to brush a soft kiss across my lips. "You're winning me over."

I hummed happily as he rolled to his side, bringing me along to cuddle against him. "I hope so."

Chapter Seven

It wasn't easy, despite the fact that I knew Daniel was trying. He was. He tried very hard to trust me. But only one other person in this world had ever given him a reason to trust, and Jake just wasn't helpful in my particular arena.

I kept my theories about Jake to myself for the next few days, waiting for an opening. Daniel was more trusting of me, but he wasn't quite ready to hear that. Nearly every time Jake was in the room with us, I caught Daniel stealing guilty glances at the man.

Yule approached.

December 16

"Will you be going back to Albany for your birthday?"

I snuggled at Daniel's side, head resting on his shoulder, an arm and a leg thrown over him. It was warm and toasty up in his loft thanks to the rising heat from the main room below as well as the fact that his bed was right up against the chimney. His skin was warm, and we were freshly rested from a night of sex. I was feeling good. "I'd rather not, if you don't mind."

His fingers sifted through my hair, breath soft across my forehead. "I don't mind. Will your family mind?"

I let myself feel the pleasure at his first words. He didn't mind. He wanted me near. I had to enjoy that.

"Noelle?"

I shrugged. "They might mind, but they'll get over it. Mom sent me to help you, after all."

"Strange to think that you have such a big family." He paused, chin propped on the top of my head. "Such a powerful family."

I tensed. I had wondered if my family would accept him if I could make a relationship work. But I'd come to the conclusion that they'd be pleased. Daniel, after all, was a wonderfully powerful witch, even if it was only in one specific area. My mother's favorite thing was to bring the powerful under her sphere of influence. But I hadn't thought what Daniel might think. He'd never really had a good family life, and he'd certainly never encountered one like mine. There weren't many like mine.

"They're not so bad." I deliberately calmed myself, sliding my hands over the warm, silky skin of Daniel's chest to remind me of the issue at hand. Nothing to be done about what my family might think. I wanted this, so I had to make it work. "Mom and Talia are bossy, but they're generally fair."

"What about your father?"

"He's not in the picture. Mom provided a different father for each one of her daughters."

"Huh?"

I chuckled and pushed up on my elbow. "My mother is the seventh daughter of the seventh daughter of the seventh daughter, et cetera, all the way back to the middle ages. There's a lot of power in that. She decided to add her own twist to it and chose a different, powerfully gifted man to father each one of us. Only Talia's father got to stay around and be a dad. Sort of."

"Talia is…?"

"My oldest sister."

"Oh." He shifted his weight. The bicep of the arm he had bent behind his head flexed, distracting me. "So, your mom's not married?"

"Hmm? No. Richard's always been around, but they're not married."

"Richard is Talia's dad?"

I nodded. I could see that the conversation was making him think, and I didn't really want him to think. It was time to put in motion a little plan I'd been thinking of for the last few days.

I slid my hand over the sharply defined lines of his collarbone and dropped a light kiss right above the nipple nearest me. "Come on. Get dressed. I have an idea."

"Oh?"

I slapped his belly lightly, punishment for the skeptical look. "Yes." I turned to get off the bed. "But it involves Jake, so I need to get dressed and catch him before he goes out."

I heard the sheets rustle behind me. "What?"

By standing, I narrowly evaded the hand that grabbed for me.

"How does this involve Jake?"

I retrieved my pajama pants and stepped into them. "Get dressed and come downstairs to find out."

He tried to get me to say more as I put on my top, but I refused. I was nervous enough about my little plan. I certainly couldn't let him in on it.

I pattered down the stairs to find Jake in the kitchen. "Jake! Just the man I wanted to see."

He glanced toward me and did a pretty good job of not reacting to the fact that I still wore my bed clothes. I was, however, looking for the telltale reaction. He wasn't completely unaffected by the fact that I wore a layer of flannel and nothing else. The scent of sex on my body surely added to it. I wondered if he liked the bounce of my boobs. My breasts weren't huge, but they were a respectable size and I wasn't wearing a bra. His eyes did widen, and I think his hand trembled a bit as he closed the refrigerator. He had to clear his throat before answering. "Me?"

"Yes. Can you stick around today? I've got an idea that might help Daniel."

Jake glanced up and over my shoulder. I didn't need to look to know that Daniel was on the stairs. Daniel's reaction must have reassured him a bit, though, because he nodded. "Sure. Okay."

"Wonderful. I'm just going to take a quick shower." No sense in drowning the poor shifter in the scent of sex.

When I emerged all fresh and clean in my sweater and long skirt, Daniel passed me to take his own shower. Jake set a plate of eggs and bacon before me, and we both watched the news as we waited. Snowfall was light, so we had satellite reception, although it was a tad spotty.

When Daniel rejoined us, however, the television went off. I directed the men to move the couch and coffee table to make room for us on the rug before the Christmas tree. The smell of pine and peppermint from the candy canes was comforting.

"Good. Now…" I turned to Daniel, who stood with a skeptical look on his face. And didn't he look lovely in a long-sleeved blue flannel shirt and jeans. "Do you feel safe when Jake's around?"

He frowned but eventually said, "Yes."

I nodded. "What about in bear form? More safe?"

"Why?"

I sighed. "Please, just answer the question. I'll explain in a minute."

Daniel glanced at Jake, who shrugged. "I don't know. We haven't really spent much time together when he's shifted."

I nodded. It was surprisingly quite common. Unless the witch was in danger, his or her shifter might not change around them all that often. Some shifters rarely changed at all. "I'd like Jake to stay with us today. I'm hoping that his presence nearby will help you concentrate more."

He frowned.

"I'm never far away," Jake said.

"I know that. And Daniel knows that, but he holds back." I met Daniel's eyes again, but surprisingly, he didn't refute me. "But if Jake's right here with us, you might not feel the need. I could kick myself for not thinking of it sooner. He's your shifter, so his physical presence should help you let go a bit more, knowing he's there to watch your back."

"Are you saying I'm afraid?"

"I'm saying that you've trained yourself to hold everything in. Part of that may be a kind of fear, yes."

Thankfully, he thought about it rather than immediately arguing. Eventually, he nodded. "All right, that makes sense. But why'd you ask about shifting?"

"Your meditative state is largely about the subconscious. Do you think you'd subconsciously feel safer with Jake here in human or bear form?"

Daniel stared at me for a long moment, then shifted his gaze to Jake.

Jake, for his part, just stood there. He grinned at Daniel, obviously willing to go either way.

"Shifted, I think," Daniel said slowly, eyes on Jake.

Jake nodded, then turned to me. "Now?"

"Please."

It's actually a fascinating thing to watch. Shifters don't morph like in the movies. Well, some movies. It's not physics; it's magic. One second they'll be fully human, and the next, they're not. If they're shifting their whole form, there's a flash of what witches tend to dub "not quite light" in between. It's that split second of time which allows any clothing they're wearing to fall to the ground.

So, one moment Jake was there, and the next there was a black bear standing on his fallen shirt and jeans. He wasn't a grizzly, so he wasn't just plain huge, but he was still a bear and plenty big enough. He stood on the rug on all fours and shook, almost as though he was fluffing out his dark, shiny fur.

Something amazing happened. Well, amazing to me. I caught Daniel staring at him. Really staring at him. "Daniel?" He didn't hear me at first, so I had to repeat his name. When he turned to me, I asked, "Have you ever seen Jake in bear form?"

"Sure I have. I just..." He shrugged. "Not often."

"Why?"

"Wasn't necessary. He couldn't shift all that often when we were on the base, and I've never been in that type of danger, so..."

I stepped up to Jake, who lifted his snout into my waiting hands. The short hair around his muzzle was a bit prickly, but the fur around his cheeks was thick and surprisingly soft. I smiled and scratched behind his ears, laughing when he closed his eyes and grunted in what I took to be a happy manner.

I looked up at Daniel, who was watching intently. "Touch him, Daniel."

"No, I...He's not a pet."

I looked down at Jake. "Do you mind if Daniel touches you, Jake?"

His big head shook from side to side, gently dislodging my hands. He turned his rounded, furry body toward his witch and butted the flat top of his head against Daniel's hip.

I laughed. "See?" I stepped up to Jake's side and dug my fingers into his fur. "Touch him."

Reluctantly, Daniel laid his hand on Jake's head. Jake twisted so that Daniel's palm rested near one curved ear. Slowly, Daniel dug long fingers into the fur to scratch.

Jake closed his eyes and wuffed in contentment.

I smiled. I'd had a notion but couldn't be sure until I saw them together. Some witches just never got the hang of the fact that their constant companion literally had an animal side. Daniel had quite obviously never been given the chance. "Most shifters don't mind being petted," I mused, stroking Jake's back. "Not in human form, of course, well..." I laughed, letting Daniel catch my meaning. "But in animal form, they usually like being scratched and stroked just like a full animal. Isn't that right, Jake?"

He grunted assent and rubbed his head against Daniel's side.

Daniel actually had to step back to catch his balance. Instinct had him grab Jake's solid neck, and I was gratified to see him keep his hands there.

"I didn't know bears were soft," I mused.

Jake twisted his head and looked at me through slitted eyes with his mouth hanging open a bit. I figured that was an ursine version of a grin.

"Quite a handsome bear you are, too," I continued. "Isn't he, Daniel?"

"Shouldn't we get on with this? Your plan didn't involve a full body massage for Jake, did it?"

Jake's happy little rumble told me his thoughts on the matter.

I laughed. "No." I thumped Jake on his ample rear. "Lie down, Jake."

He gently nudged Daniel aside, then dropped his heavy body to the rug. He ended up partially on his side, curled to face us.

I gestured at the natural backrest his belly made. "Have a seat."

Daniel sat down and gingerly worked himself back into the curve of Jake's body. It wasn't his normal position for working with me, but it looked wonderfully *right.* Jake rested his muzzle on his paws, and Daniel's hand came up to rest on his head.

"Comfy?" I asked.

Daniel glared up at me.

Smiling, I sat before him, my knees almost touching his. "Okay. Go through your normal routine, but this time be aware that Jake's there." I grinned at the bear's watchful brown eyes. "He's here and he's not about to let anything happen to you."

Jake underlined my statement with a growl.

I chuckled. "Let's see if his presence helps."

Daniel took a deep breath and closed his eyes.

Instinct had me lean forward to slide my hands into the ones he had resting on his knees.

He cracked his eyes open for a second at that, but didn't question before closing his eyes again.

Why didn't I think of this sooner? I berated myself. In half the usual time, Daniel was relaxed and sunk deep into a trance. His attention explored the spiritual energy about us, trying to gain some measure of control over it. I skewed my sight and watched the threads of neon through compact midnight blue and wasn't at all shocked as the violet tendrils began to emerge. The blue and violet reached out and sank naturally into the furry body lying at Daniel's back. Eventually, it looked to my magical sight like Jake's fur was shot through with gently writhing blue and violet. Other tendrils of blue and violet reached out to me, disappearing from my sight before they enveloped me. This was marvelous! Unconsciously, Daniel was binding us. His mind might deny it, but his magic was adamant that Jake and I were necessary to him.

We sat like that for hours, the only movement being mine to lie on the floor and pillow my head in Daniel's lap. I gathered some spirit energy on my own and let it drift toward him, offering him my support. I was pleasantly surprised to feel the gentle pull of him accepting my help. I'd offered this support ever since we'd started sleeping together, but this was the first time he'd accepted.

The house around us quieted.

I dozed. I often did while he was in trance. Even now, offering my magic to aid his, I could let my mind drift without worry.

Daniel woke me by softly sifting through my hair.

I blinked my eyes and yawned, turning from my side onto my back. When I looked up, I couldn't stop my smile from matching his. A real curve of his lips, enough to bunch up his cheeks even.

"It worked," he murmured.

Carefully, I sat up. Jake's head was up, and his brown eyes watched me from right beside Daniel's shoulder. I sat back, keeping my hand in Daniel's, and skewed my sight.

He was right. His aura was down to maybe an inch or so of soft, dark blue glow from his body, a far more normal size. Only a fading thread of neon blue surrounded him. Violet shimmered lightly just over his skin. He'd pulled the glow back from Jake, and an inner check of my own let me know that he'd released the energy I'd offered as support. I was intrigued, however, to see the tendrils of midnight blue that wrapped Jake's leash now actually touched the bear.

"Oh, Daniel." I reached out and ran my fingers through the blue beside his smooth cheek. It was nothing he could see or feel, but he'd know what I was doing.

"So I'm right?"

I nodded, tears in my eyes. "You're right. You've got it as much under control as anyone could."

His smile remained. He tugged my hand as he leaned back against Jake's solid weight. I went willingly and let him curl me into his lap. "It's all thanks to you, Noelle."

"No." I reached around his chest until I could sink my fingers into the thick fur at his back. "It's all three of us."

He let that hang, and I let it go. He was smiling. He was breathing deeply, calmly. Tension eased from his body. I was perfectly willing to let him have his moment.

Chapter Eight

December 19

For whatever reason, he couldn't regain control the next day. He'd maintained the normal aura that evening, even as we watched one of the Christmas specials on television. He hadn't made love to me when he'd taken me up to the loft that night. We'd only snuggled. I'm pretty sure he was afraid of losing control during orgasm. But he lost it during his sleep anyway. He felt the loss of control, and I confirmed it when I saw the riot of neon around him again. That morning, he'd demanded that Jake stay, and we resumed our positions from the previous day. But it didn't come. He kept his cool through that day, and the next. But now it was three days, and he was desperate to get it back.

"Why?" Daniel demanded, pacing behind me.

I took a deep breath and batted at the shiny blue ball that hung from one of the Christmas tree branches. "I don't really know."

"Guess."

"Maybe you weren't relaxed?"

"I'm plenty relaxed."

"You're not."

"I *was*. What was different? You're here; Jake's here. Why can't I do it?"

I shrugged, wondering if he'd listen to my theory. Wondering if he heard himself.

He growled. I heard the couch creak and glanced over my shoulder to see him sprawled out, palms on his face.

I went and knelt beside Jake, who sat quietly in bear form in the middle of the rug. He swiveled his head toward me, a question in his huge, liquid eyes. Smiling softly, I put my arms around his furry neck and buried my face in it. He leaned into me gently, rubbing his cheek against the top of my head.

I turned my neck and peeked at Daniel from underneath Jake's muzzle. He was still sprawled across the couch, fingers pressing at his eyes. His black hair was spread behind him over the back of the couch, and his sweater rode up to display a nice swatch of hard belly between its hem and the waistband of his jeans.

"I have an idea," I said softly.

He dropped his hand and fastened those dark, slanted eyes on me. "What?"

"You probably won't like it."

His eyes narrowed. "What?"

I swallowed and pulled back from Jake, but I didn't let him go entirely. He sat quietly, watching me with a lot more trust than Daniel.

"The other day, you felt closer to us than you ever had, right?"

"Yes."

I watched my fingers sinking into Jake's black fur rather than face Daniel. "It's the closeness that does it, I think. You need to feel the connection to really gain control."

"That's not how it works for you."

"That's how it works for *you*."

I peeked at him. I was right. He didn't like it, but he was listening. "We've been together the last three days."

I nodded. "I think it's time for the next step."

"What are you suggesting?"

I had a feeling he already knew, but he wasn't going to voice it.

I took a deep breath, staring into Jake's eyes instead of Daniel's. It was easier. "I think we should make love."

Jake started.

Daniel was silent.

I stared at Jake, stroking the fur at the side of his head.

"You want to fuck Jake. Is that it?"

I closed my eyes at the bite in his tone. I shook my head. "Yes, but you're deliberately misunderstanding me."

"What? I'm not enough for you?"

"Daniel, would you hear me?"

"What?"

"I want *all three* of us to be together."

He was quiet long enough that I braved looking at him. His nostrils flared, and his eyes were black from between slitted lids. "You get off on being with two guys at once?"

I stayed calm. "I've never been with two men at once."

"Grabbing your chance?"

"I've never wanted to be with two other men at once. But the two of *you...*" I sighed. "Daniel, you refuse to understand how you and Jake are connected."

"Well, sure, he's leashed."

"It's more than that. Most leashes aren't anchored in the heart."

"What?"

"I had a feeling you didn't know that." I sat back on my heels, but I kept stroking Jake's shoulder with one hand. "Most leashes are anchored in the witch's hand, echoing a physical leash. Yours isn't. Yours is anchored in the heart. It doesn't happen often, but when it does, it shows a deeper, emotional bond between shifter and witch. At least on the part of the witch."

He didn't want to believe me. I could tell. But he stayed silent. Jake stayed very still underneath my hand.

"My guess is that it was instinct. You needed someone close, and Jake provided. I don't think he minds." I smiled at Jake, who didn't give me anything to work with. I couldn't read a bear's facial expression. I sighed. "The guardian spell would have provided you exactly the shifter that you needed. The army had you call, and everyone thought Jake was for physical protection, but I think he's really here for emotional protection. He's the shield for your heart."

"Shut up."

"Daniel, I'm not saying that you're gay..." No, he wasn't ready to hear anything like that.

"Shut up!"

"I'm not saying that you want to have sex with Jake. But you might be able to be closer. Through me."

I chanced a glance and winced at his scowl. But I was in for it now. Might as well finish it. "I love you both, very much."

His breathing kicked up. If I'd had the nerve to let him see me look, I'd have bet there was stormy neon blue surrounding him right then. As it was, I could feel the spiritual energy like static cling on my skin.

"That's why I came back. I wanted to be with you. *Both* of you. To help you, yes. I do want to do that, but I want so much more."

He shook his head slowly.

"I want to help you. If it means being the conduit for you to be with Jake, I'm all for it. Use me, Daniel. I offer myself freely."

"None of that's true."

"All of it's true."

"It won't work."

"Why can't we try and find out?"

He leaned forward, about to stand. "No!"

A flash of not-quite-light beside me changed the fur under my hand to warm skin. I was surprised enough to glance over and got my first, full look of Jake in naked splendor.

Splendor it was. Daniel was achingly beautiful, true, but Jake was what you'd call "all male." He had the kind of muscles you don't get from working out. His came from roaming the woods every day and doing actual labor in his woodworking shop and around the house. He was certainly a lot more hairy than Daniel, with a thick mat of dark brown hair across his chest, tapering to a defined line that circled his navel and proceeded lower. His cock was thick and uncut and, presently, half erect.

He sat on his butt, long, hairy legs out in front of him in Daniel's direction, and leaned back on his arms. "Why not?"

I was off guard enough to not quite remember what the question referred to.

"What?" from Daniel, proving I wasn't the only one.

"Why don't you want to find out?"

Oh, yes, my idea. That's what we were talking about.

I glanced at Daniel to see him scowling fiercely at Jake. It was ruined by the fact that his eyes kept casting downward to the impressive organ jutting proud and full from Jake's crotch.

"Buddy?" Jake prompted.

"What? You want a threesome?"

Jake grinned. "Why not? What could it hurt? And it could help, just like Noelle said."

"You just want to sleep with Noelle."

I faced Jake to watch his reaction to that.

Jake's grin remained, open and honest. "Well, yeah. But I wouldn't mind seeing you fuck her. In fact --" His dark eyes took on a wicked glint. "-- I've been thinking about that all week."

"What?"

Jake laughed, shaking his head. "Damn, man. You don't understand. You two smell *good.*"

I licked my lips, trying to hide my smile.

Jake winked at me.

Daniel snorted. "I don't believe this."

"Why not? What's so hard to believe about a threesome? Like she said, you and I are close. Lots of buddies do it, if the woman's willing."

Lots of buddies would do it if the woman *wasn't* willing, but that certainly wasn't the case here. I stayed quiet, realizing Jake was going to be a lot more convincing in this than I was.

Daniel said nothing for a long time.

Jake finally switched his balance to one arm, freeing a hand to reach up and brush his fingers against my cheek. His look was achingly tender and amazingly hot at the same time. I felt moisture dribble from my sex in reaction, and a long inhale from him, followed by a lazy grin, told me that he knew it.

"I'd love to watch you suck his cock."

I heard a strangled cry from Daniel, but I was enthralled by the lazy seduction in Jake's eyes and couldn't look away. I licked my lips, delighted when the move drew his gaze to my mouth.

He brought one big finger around to trace the lower curve of my lip. "Please?"

Well, he asked so nicely. I smiled and nodded. I wanted to kiss him, but didn't, not sure Daniel would accept that. I wasn't sure Daniel would accept *any* of this, but at least he was still seated. I turned and crawled the short distance to the couch.

Daniel watched me like I was a python slithering toward him. There might have been some similarities, because I certainly wanted to squeeze the life out of part of him.

I reached him and put my hands on his knees, edging them further apart. Our gazes locked. His was negative, but his legs fell open just the same. I dropped my eyes so I could watch myself unbutton his jeans.

There was movement behind me. Out of the corner of my eye, I saw Jake sit facing us on the other end of the couch. He was out of arm's reach, but close enough to see everything clearly. And he was still, of course, quite naked.

I swallowed as I continued my work. I'd never been an exhibitionist, but the thought of Jake watching us had my hands trembling in excitement. I eased down the zipper of Daniel's jeans, then carefully pulled the waistband of his boxers out and down, exposing him. I had to wrap my fingers around the shaft and carefully pull it out to lie, flushed and red, on his flat belly. I flipped my hair to one side, away from Jake, and bent my head so I could suck the smooth head of Daniel's cock between my lips.

Daniel groaned.

Jake echoed him.

Sweet Goddess!

I curled my fingers in the waistband of Daniel's boxers and jeans and tugged them down his hips a little farther, freeing more of his flushed cock. Our talk of threesomes must have done this to him, because he was amazingly hard. The removal of the clothing had to be a relief.

I slid my lips up and down his shaft a few times, letting the moisture in my mouth make him gleaming wet. I hummed happily when his hand came to rest on the back of my head, gently brushing loose hair away from my face, making sure Jake's view was unobstructed.

*Speaking of whom...*As I sucked, I glanced to the side and actually wiggled at the sight. Jake leaned back against the arm of the couch, one leg folded before him, the other hanging off the edge. He had one arm draped over the back of the couch and the hand of the other wrapped around his fully hard erection. His eyelids were at half mast, and he winked at me when he caught me watching.

Daniel's fingers pushed, and I remembered what I was supposed to be doing.

I yanked at his pants again, and he obediently pushed up to let me pull boxers and jeans down around his knees, then to his ankles. We had to shift a bit so he could get them off, but I refused to take my lips from his cock. We finally managed, and he collapsed back in relief, the fingers of one hand holding a knot of my hair tight at the back of my neck. He used it to control me, and I let him, wrapping my hand around the base of his cock so he couldn't push past my gagging point.

It was a heady thing, doing this with someone watching me. I wasn't sure I could do it with any other two men, but I'd meant what I'd said to Daniel. I loved them. *Both* of them. It was a relief to me to be able to express it in any way.

The audience proved to be a strain on Daniel's control. Sooner than usual, his breathing grew ragged and his mutters intensified. His fingers jerked my head faster, and I just concentrated on keeping my lips as tight as I could around his shaft. All at once, he yanked my head back and wrapped his free hand around the top of the shaft. I watched his hand and hips twitch and tremble; then creamy fluid spurted from the tiny hole at the tip. Some of it painted my lips and chin. I tilted my head up and let him have the rest of his orgasm while watching my tongue lap the semen from my lips.

He subsided, and I brought my hand up to wipe away most of the rest. He groaned when I put my fingers in my mouth to suck them clean. "I would have swallowed," I assured him.

His eyes darkened with promise.

I turned my head to look at Jake.

His smile was broad and happy, his hand still slowly stroking his erection.

Without looking back to Daniel, I moved from between his thighs and crawled toward Jake.

He watched me come, but when I would have climbed up onto the couch to take him into my mouth, he used his free hand to stop me. I looked a question up at him and was caught off guard when he leaned forward, securing my head with his hand, and devoured my mouth. The kiss was wonderful on its own, but it was only when his tongue lapped at the edges of my mouth and my chin that I realized he tasted the residue of Daniel's cum. Did Daniel realize it?

Jake's eye twinkled when he pulled back. He smiled. "Can we get you naked?"

I matched the smile. "I think we could manage that."

I stood and grabbed the hem of my sweater. A glance at Daniel as I removed sweater, stretchy pants, and underwear showed me that he seemed content to watch me. His face was calm, his eyes half closed in that sleepy, sated look he got after orgasm. By the time I was nude, the hand he'd had on his thigh was on his mostly softened cock, beginning to stroke it back to awareness.

I stood before him naked. "What will you allow?"

His movements stopped. "What?"

"You're calling the shots, Daniel. You're the one who doesn't want to do this."

He frowned. "It's not that I…" He trailed off.

I waited.

Daniel glanced at Jake, who just shrugged.

Daniel grimaced, and I had a horrible moment thinking that he would, indeed, call a halt. But then he dropped his gaze to Jake's rampant, flushed cock. His looked back at me with dark purpose. "Ride him."

I stopped the "You're sure?" that wanted to spill from my lips. Questioning him didn't seem like a good idea. Instead, I simply obeyed. It wasn't as though he'd suggested something awful. Indeed, he'd suggested something that nearly made my knees give out. I stepped toward Jake, who held out a hand. Gratefully, I took it and let him help me straddle him.

"Goddess, you're big," I murmured, feeling the stretch in my inner thighs as they spread over his.

"Too much?"

I smiled up into his caring face, certain that this sweetheart of a man would stop if I was at all hesitant. I put my hands on his shoulders and brushed a soft kiss on his lips, loving the tickle of his mustache. "No. Just noticing, that's all."

He had to help me manage. His hands cradled my butt as I reached down to take hold of his thickness. He growled at my touch, and I pumped him once, just because I could. I laughed when his fingers tightened. He lifted me, supporting nearly all of my weight with his hands, and, after I'd aimed him, lowered me onto his cock.

I shuddered, unprepared for the friction of his thickness. I pushed down and fell forward against his chest, gasping as burning shivers washed through me.

"You okay?" he asked, palms sliding over my bare back.

I nuzzled the wiry mat of hair over the hot satin of his skin. "Oh, yeah."

I peeked at Daniel. He was watching with hooded eyes, his fingers playing idly with his renewing erection. Part of me was scared to let him see how good this felt, but I had to be honest and open if I expected the same from him in return.

It took me a few minutes to find my stride, during which I rolled and twisted my hips enough to make both Jake and me groan. Then I just curled my hands around his neck and hung on as I started to ride.

I slammed down hard on him, grinding groin to groin, and had to smash my eyelids closed as another tremor took me. Jake just hit all the right places. Or maybe it was the position. I'd never done this with Daniel or my few previous lovers. I'd been on top, but it hadn't been comfortable and I hadn't liked it. And Jake was just plain big, bigger in all ways than any other man I'd been with. But his hands were strong and supportive, and truthfully, I just couldn't get enough of the feel of him. Helpless little mewls pushed from my lips as I slammed down on him, making sure that the friction was just right. I could only hope that this was good for him, because I was galloping toward orgasm and couldn't afford to wait.

When it came, I screamed, arching my back, trusting Jake to hold me. His growl echoed my scream, and I sort of noticed his body shook along with mine.

Jake pulled me back against him as we came down, and I happily snuggled on his furry chest, listening to his heart race.

When I opened my eyes, I was startled to see Daniel up close, his face in mine, just inches away from Jake's arm. It looked like he'd been waiting for my eyes to open. "You really want both of us?"

"Yes," I answered, without hesitation.

I felt his hand, a hot brand on my back. Without taking his eyes from mine, he slid that hand down over the swell of my butt, his fingers trailing down the crack until one teased my back opening. "Really?"

I swallowed. "I've never done it before, but yes."

"Daniel, wait," Jake said.

But Daniel was up off the couch with a hurried "Be right back."

Jake cupped my chin and made me look up at him. "Are you sure about this?"

"Yes."

"He's never --"

I smiled. "Neither have I."

He shook his head. "It could hurt."

"Yes."

"You don't have to." His concern was written all over his features.

"Yes, I do. He's testing me."

Jake scowled.

"It's okay. He needs to know he can trust me." I smiled again, reaching up to smooth the lines from his face. "He won't hurt me on purpose."

"You trust him?"

"Don't you?"

I searched his face, realizing belatedly that his feelings for Daniel may not be as open and deep as I'd thought. *Good Goddess, don't let me be wrong now!*

He said no more. Gently, he lifted me from his lap and set me beside him on the couch. By that time, Daniel had returned from upstairs with a bottle of lube.

Jake stood, hand to Daniel's chest to stop him.

Only because I was watching did I see the surprised, wide-eyed gulp where Jake did not. Daniel was all scowls when he looked up at Jake.

Jake just stared him down. "We should clean up some."

"Why? We're just --"

"'Cause you should show some respect for the lady who just brought both of us off." His tone reminded Daniel that he was older and presumably wiser.

Of course, I was older than either of them, but I chose not to dwell on that.

Daniel stood, shell-shocked, while Jake turned from him to head for the downstairs bathroom.

I reached up to smooth a hand down Daniel's forearm. "It's okay."

He swallowed. "Are you...?"

I smiled. "Really. I'm okay. Although --" I waved a hand at the semen dribbling down my thighs. "-- cleaning up a little isn't a bad idea."

He shut his eyes. "Noelle, this is --"

"Shhh." I pulled him down to the couch beside me, stroking his arm, his shoulder, his chest. "I want this. I want you. I want you both."

He let me kiss him and hold him close. We were still in a clinch when Jake returned with a wash towel. He started to wipe me clean, but I broke from Daniel to do it myself.

Jake took the towel from me and jerked his chin toward the stairs. "We should move up to that big ol' bed upstairs, don'tcha think?"

Daniel and I stood, both in agreement.

I preceded them upstairs and sat on the edge of the bed as they joined me. "How do we do this?"

"I'm too big," Jake declared baldly. He crawled onto the bed beside me and twisted to sit with his back against the headboard. "So you should ride me while he takes you from behind. Besides --" He stared coldly at Daniel. "-- you're pushing this."

"I'm not --!"

"Please!" I stopped them, kneeling up and holding a palm out toward either of them. "I don't want you to bicker. I *want* this." I stared at Jake. "I do." I turned to Daniel. "But I will admit to being a little scared."

Daniel softened. Not much, but I could see the subtle shift of his emotions now. "Noelle, we don't have..."

"You're not hearing me, Daniel." I put some sternness in my voice. "I *want to do this.*" I reached out, thrilled when he came to the edge of the bed to allow me to touch him. "I'm just asking that you go slow."

He slid his hands along my hips, nodding. We kissed, a slow, thoughtful promise.

I pulled back and turned to face Jake. His anger was gone, visibly anyway. He smiled and reached for me.

I glanced down to see he wasn't quite ready for a ride. So I crawled over and positioned my knees between his spread thighs. "You're beautiful, Jake," I murmured, sliding my hands over his chest.

He chuckled. "Not me. That's Daniel."

The bed behind me sank. "No, man, she's right. You're beautiful."

I didn't dare turn, so Jake's pole-axed look had to serve for us both.

Daniel chuckled. "Hey, I'm not allowed to realize you're a good-looking man?"

"With all your 'I'm not gay' talk..." Jake protested.

Daniel snorted. "I'm not gay. But I'm not blind."

Unsure how best to react, I chose to distract myself. I moved down and kissed Jake's chest, right above the heart. He hummed, a hand coming up to stroke my hair. I kissed my way across surprisingly soft hair and hard muscle to the flat nipple trying to hide in the dark fur. His sigh told me he liked that.

Daniel's dry, warm hands slid over my butt, squeezing, massaging gently. He didn't seem to want to hurry things along, so I made my leisurely way across the great expanse of Jake's chest toward his other nipple.

I heard the distinctive pop of the cap of the lube bottle.

"Make sure you use lots of that," Jake's voice rumbled underneath my lips.

"I will," Daniel assured him softly.

Warm fingers slid down the crack of my butt to tease my rear opening.

I took a deep breath.

Jake's hands slid up and down my arms. "Relax, Noelle. You say the word, we stop."

"No," I murmured into his ribs. "I'm okay."

Daniel's finger circled, tickling, soothing. His other hand continued to massage my cheek. Slowly, he sank part of his finger in.

I bit down on Jake's chest.

He jumped. "Ow!"

I smiled and lapped at the hurt.

"Oh-ho, that's how it is, huh? Hey, buddy, you hurt her and she'll hurt me."

The finger inside me wiggled gently. "Ah, you're tough. You can take it."

I couldn't help it. I laughed.

I was delighted when they -- both of them -- joined me.

We played that way, leisurely, slowly. I distracted myself with laving and nipping at Jake's chest while Daniel accustomed me to one finger, then slowly two. When he added the third, I had to call for a pause, resting my head on Jake's sternum.

"You okay?" Jake asked.

"It hurts."

"Want me to stop?" Daniel asked, breath and lips whispering over my lower back and the top swell of my buttocks. His voice was just as soft and caring as Jake's.

I shook my head. "No."

"Noelle…" Jake started.

I gasped. I felt it. Daniel. Spirits. Energy. I braced up on Jake's chest and looked over my shoulder.

The light was behind Daniel, but I could see the glint in his eye and the small smile of…triumph? I matched the smile. "Daniel!"

"You feel it?"

"I do."

His wrist twisted slowly, and my entire body shuddered. "Make it better?"

My eyes rolled back in my head. How to describe? Yes, he'd filled me with spiritual energy before, but it had always been in the throes of passion, a wild, barely controlled flood. This was different. This was like a caress. Yes, that was it. He was caressing me with his magic, with the spirits he attracted. Since it wasn't physical, it filled my being and seeped through my skin. It warmed me, coaxing my own control to weaken. I sank down on Jake's chest, sighing happily, pushing back onto Daniel's fingers. What Daniel had done had relaxed my body, convincing it to accept the invasion. "Oh, yes!"

"Whoa." Jake laughed softly. "What did you do?"

"I'm not sure I can do the same to you."

"Don't try. Not yet, anyway." Jake caressed my back. "Make her feel good."

I sighed happily, wiggling my butt to indicate that I was feeling just fine.

Daniel kept open the controlled conduit between us. I helped from my end, kind of grasping his hand and holding it, spiritually speaking. Along that "handhold," the most marvelous warmth surged between us.

At first it was simply nice, but then it became more, until finally I was wiggling with excitement. "Daniel."

He slid his fingers out of me, despite my whimper of protest, and I felt his lips caress my butt. "Ride Jake, baby."

Oh, yes! Happily, I squirmed up and pretty much allowed Jake to lower me down over him. I hummed, pleased to feel him fill me as Daniel's directed spirit energy tickled my skin.

"Noelle," Jake breathed, rocking his hips to shuttle his cock slowly in and out of my wet channel.

"Mmmm, Jake," I answered, braced above him, just enjoying the feel of him.

"Did you make her drunk?" Jake asked.

Daniel chuckled, and I felt his mirth echo through the spirits. "Kind of." I felt movement behind me; then his hands were on my buttocks, gently pressing them apart, exposing me. "Noelle?"

"Yes!"

He gasped as the spirit energy rebounded back on him. "Damn."

"You okay?" Jake asked, still slowly sliding through my sex.

"Oh, yeah." The smooth head of Daniel's cock rubbed my opening. He carefully pushed into me, both physically and with his magic.

I gasped. It still hurt, but not nearly as much as the three fingers had. This was a dark hurt that somehow went along with the amazing heat that was bubbling just below my belly. He forged ahead, and Jake held still, supporting me as I took both of them inside my body.

"Oh, man." Daniel stopped when he could fit no more and simply breathed.

"Oh, yeah." Jake groaned, starting a slow exit from my body.

I cried out, nails digging into Jake's chest.

"Noelle?"

"Don't stop!" I pounded an ineffectual fist on his chest. "Goddess, don't stop."

That's pretty much when I lost track. It felt too good. The fire in my skin was fed by the violet energy that Daniel pressed into me as he and Jake found a synchronous rhythm in my body. I could do little more than be there, between them, taking them, making us whole. I cried, tears streaming down my face and spattering Jake's chest. I vaguely recall his worry at that and have no idea what I said or did to reassure him. I only know that they didn't stop. They took me, they filled me, and at some point I burst. And burst again when they didn't stop. It turned into one long, agonizing orgasm that shattered my mind and soul before they finally found their completion.

Chapter Nine

December 24

I watched them make dinner on Christmas Eve, torn. On the one hand, it was a grand view since Jake only wore boxers and Daniel his black silk pajama bottoms. On the other, something was missing.

They didn't touch each other.

They stood side by side at the counter, Jake humming to "The Little Drummer Boy" as it played on the stereo, Daniel mashing the potatoes. Both were relaxed. Daniel even wore the small smile that had become an almost frequent feature on his face since the three of us started sleeping together. But when Jake moved to open the oven to baste the turkey that'd been driving us crazy with its smell all day, Daniel moved aside. Earlier, when Daniel had been peeling the potatoes, Jake had calmly enough moved around him, but there was none of the casual brushes from before all the sex had started.

I doubted either of them noticed.

But I did. They did it when we had sex, too, so very careful to only touch me and not each other. So very careful not to give even a hint of an impression that they were attracted to each other. I suppose that would be ideal for most women in my situation, but it wasn't what I wanted. *Have I brought us closer together or further apart?* I nursed my tea, wrapped up in a quilt on the recliner. "Can I help?" I offered for the umpteenth time.

"Sweetheart," Jake drawled, crossing the room toward me, "you need your rest."

I grimaced ineffectually at him as he leaned down to my level, hands braced on the arms of my chair. "I'm rested."

His eyes twinkled. "Sore?"

I squirmed. "Well, yes."

He nodded. "You've been taking a lot lately. Let us take care of you." With that, he leaned in to briefly kiss my nose and then walked back to the kitchen.

As soon as Jake's bulk moved aside, I could see Daniel. There was no doubt in my mind that he had been eyeing Jake's butt, although he hid it well, transferring his gaze to me, smiling slightly because he knew it dazzled me.

I sighed, mind reeling. How could I make them *see?*

Frustrated, I grabbed the universal remote. I switched off the stereo and punched on the television. I did have to get up to find a DVD, since the heavy snowfall outside had yet again thrown out the satellite. I found and put in *It's a Wonderful Life* and returned to my nest in the chair.

Dinner was ready to eat by the time the dance scene and the fall in the pool happened. We arranged ourselves on the couch, the boys on the outside and me curled up between them, to watch the rest of the movie. Before we'd been sleeping together, we wouldn't have fit, but lovers can find wonderful positions that involve a lot of touching to make such close confines work. We finished eating shortly after Clarence and George met up, and the boys wouldn't let me help with the dishes, so I lay staring at the Christmas tree until they came back. We watched the rest of the movie with me lying between them, my head on Daniel's lap, with Jake gently rubbing my feet. I actually started to doze, but woke with a start when George started yelling "Merry Christmas" while running up the street.

Jake shut off the television after the end, and we sat for a moment, listening to the soft crackle of the fire in the stove. All the lights were out except for those on the tree.

"Do you ever wonder?" I asked softly, staring at the white and blue twinkles.

"What?" Jake asked.

"What life would be like if you'd never been born?"

Daniel sniffed, but kept stroking my hair. "Useless to wonder. My parents would have been happier."

"I wouldn't have been," Jake said. I glanced over to see him with his head tilted against the back of the couch, eyes closed. "With you gone, I mean."

"Thanks," Daniel said. "It's been okay having you around, too."

Jake snorted.

I smiled.

Again silence descended. I wondered if I dared the idea that came to mind, but then I figured it was now or never.

I sat up, startling both men. They watched as I swung my legs over the edge of the couch, then turned so I was seated on the coffee table. I faced Daniel. "There's something I need to tell you."

His relaxed expression tensed, and I was sorry for that, but this needed to be said. I think.

"Your aura has changed. You've gained control, and it's down to a manageable level around you, but the colors are different than when we first met. It's still neon blue some, but it's faded into this midnight blue."

"What does that mean?"

"I think it means you're more settled. Like I've told you, not everyone's colors are the same, and the colors don't mean the same on different people."

He nodded. "Settled is good, isn't it?"

"Yes. But there's something else that's strange about the darker blue." I had to pause. Here started the part that he'd either accept or deny. "It reaches down your leash toward Jake."

He frowned.

Jake tilted his head, eyeing me carefully.

"Is that normal?" Daniel asked.

I shook my head. "No. I asked around while I was gone. I even asked some spirit witches I've been in touch with who have shifters. They say it's not normal. Of course, their leashes are based in the hand, not the heart, like yours."

I left that. I could see by the look on Daniel's face that he was drawing his own conclusions.

"There's more."

"Why have you waited to tell me this?"

"I didn't think you'd want to hear it."

"I take it you have theories on what this means?"

I nodded.

He stared at me.

"Do you want to hear the more?"

"Sure. Why not?"

"There's a violet color that's come into your aura since you and I made love. It's gotten stronger since the three of us have started sleeping together. I can't see it when it melds with my aura, but I'm pretty sure it's that color that you push into me during sex."

"And?"

"And the violet has been reaching for Jake in the last few days."

He stared at me, showing me no reaction whatsoever.

"Noelle?" Jake asked. "What are you saying?"

I didn't answer. It wasn't for me to verbalize the conclusion. That was Daniel's decision, both to acknowledge what I was implying and to say it aloud.

Daniel's eyes narrowed. His lips twisted into the grimace that I'd hoped he'd lost. "She's saying that I want to fuck you."

"Huh?"

Daniel stood, his face a cold, beautiful mask. "But she's wrong. She's projecting what she wants to see onto me. Am I right, Noelle? You one of those women who gets off on watching two guys fuck?"

I kept my gaze steady, even though my heart hurt. I knew he'd lash out at me if he didn't accept. That was his way. "I wouldn't mind."

"Well, it's not going to happen. We're not like that." He turned away. "She's all yours tonight, Jake."

Jake turned on the couch as Daniel rounded it on his way to the stairs. "Hey, wait, hold on a minute."

"No," he said calmly as he reached the stairs. "Noelle's obviously not content with having two of us. She wants something unnatural."

"I want what *you* want, Daniel," I called after him. "If you're honest with yourself, you'll know I'm right."

He froze, glaring at me over the banister. "Are you *determined* to ruin what's between me and Jake?"

I shook my head. "I don't want to ruin it, Daniel. I want you to be true to it."

"You're a perverted bitch, that's what you are."

"Daniel!" Jake barked.

Daniel shook his head, starting up the stairs again. "Forget it. Merry fucking Christmas."

Jake spun back to face me, face intent. "Explain this to me."

I glanced at Daniel, but he didn't stop. Sighing, I lowered my face into my palms. "Maybe I was wrong."

Big hands grabbed my shoulders and shook me. "Noelle, explain."

I lifted my head to look at him. "You've heard us talk about auras."

He nodded.

"His has been doing exactly what I said. It's been reaching for you. I don't know how else to explain it."

"Are you sure it's about sex?"

"The violet only appeared after we had sex the first time. I don't see what else it could be."

Jake stared up at the loft. Daniel's hearing was merely human, and his magic powers outside of manipulating spirits were sadly neglected, so there was little chance he heard our low voices.

I grabbed his arm. "I'm sorry, Jake. Maybe I should have just told him and left you out of it. It just seemed...I was so certain I was right."

"But you're not sure," he said softly. Thoughtfully.

"No." I watched him as he stared upstairs. "Jake?"

Quite suddenly, he grabbed my arm and pulled me up to my feet.

"Jake? Eeep!" The last because he picked me up and headed for the stairs. "Jake, no."

Daniel appeared at the top of the staircase, glaring up a storm as we climbed toward him. "Get the fuck away."

Jake just kept right on climbing. "No."

"Jake, she's not right."

"Okay, she's wrong. Doesn't mean *I* have to be punished, does it?"

Daniel frowned.

Jake pushed past him with me, toward Daniel's big bed.

"What do you mean?"

Jake dumped me on the bed -- relatively gently, but I still bounced -- then turned to Daniel. His fingers landed on the waistband of his boxers. "I'd rather have sex with the three of us." He yanked them down.

Distracted by Jake's tight, bare butt, I missed Daniel's initial reaction. By the time I thought to look, he was scowling.

"We're not gay," he insisted.

Jake waved the notion away, sitting on the bed. "I know that." He leaned back on his elbows, displaying his mostly hard erection. "But we've been having plenty of fun, the three of us. Why stop?"

Daniel kept scowling.

"C'mon, buddy. Just 'cause she said what she did about your aura thing doesn't mean we can't fuck, does it? She told you what she thought." He shrugged. "She's wrong. You okay with that, Noelle?" He turned to me and smiled.

I matched the smile. "Yes."

"See?" He turned on the bed, putting his butt toward Daniel as he crawled over me. "So let's have some fun."

I lay back under Jake's looming presence and glanced at Daniel as Jake's fingers started on one of the buttons of the pajama top I wore. He watched, skeptical, until Jake had the top open and had leaned in to take one of my nipples into his mouth. Whether it was Jake's lips sucking at my breast or my arched back that got to him, I don't know. But Daniel's hands went to his pajama pants and he dropped them, revealing that gorgeous erection.

He knelt on the bed by my head and sank his fingers into my hair. Eagerly, I opened my mouth as he guided it to his cock.

"I'm not gay," he told me, locking gazes with me as he slid between my lips.

I nodded, humming happily as my eyes slid shut. After a bit, my neck started to hurt, so I tried to turn toward him to ease the sharp twist. The bulk of Jake's body had me pinned, though, so I couldn't shift far.

Jake decided that we needed to move. He reared up and, with two strong hands, flipped me over onto my belly. "Daniel, sit up there," he directed, nodding toward the headboard.

Daniel complied, and Jake positioned me on my hands and knees, face right over Daniel's lap. Happily, I took him back into my mouth, much more comfortable in this position. Daniel's fingers sank into my hair, guiding me again as he settled back in the pillows.

Jake trailed hands and lips down my spine, licking the top of the crack of my butt before he licked his way back up. He took hold of my hips, adjusting them, then reached down. I groaned around Daniel's cock when I felt Jake pressing at my sex. He sank inside, torturing me by going slow. I squirmed, trying to get him deeper faster, but he held on and refused to alter that slow, brutally wonderful slide inside my body. But finally he was in, and I took Daniel as far into my mouth as I could to mirror the feel for him. The men echoed each other's groans. I pulled up as Jake pulled out and chanced a look up at Daniel to see his head thrown back, a sure sign of his pleasure.

Jake set a steady rhythm, stroking inside me, twisting a little as he slammed home to make sure he caused the most friction. I moaned and sucked Daniel, rewarding him for how good Jake was making me feel. I came, my scream muffled by the cock in my mouth. Daniel hissed, clutching my hair and shoulder, tense as he held back his own orgasm. I sighed as I came down, releasing Daniel's cock with a gasp.

Another hand gripped my hair over Daniel's and pulled gently but insistently. Head muzzy from a fierce orgasm, I fell aside with only a small cry of surprise as I was shoved slightly forward by the weight of Jake's body draping heavily over my back. My cheek pressed into the side of Daniel's hip, just under his belly.

"Wha-- Shit, Jake!" Daniel cried out.

My eyes bugged out to see Jake's mouth descend over my shoulder and take in the head of Daniel's cock. Flushed, pale skin eased past Jake's dark pink lips. Jake's eyes were closed, his expression showing every indication that he enjoyed what he was doing.

Daniel's hand in my hair fought with Jake's, but Jake kept both hands right where they were. Daniel's other hand shot toward Jake's head, but for all I could tell, Jake caught that one, too. He was stronger and heavier than either of us and had both of us quite effectively pinned.

"Jake!" Daniel cried out, hips thrusting up as he tried to wiggle out from under us. "Fuck, Jake!"

Jake hummed and shook his head sharply.

A ragged groan pulled from Daniel's chest at the move. "Shit, Jake, what are you doing?" His voice was hoarse, ragged.

I looked up, concerned. I realized that Jake could very well be doing this just from what I'd said and that I really could be wrong. Daniel's mouth hung half open, and his exquisite face was deeply flushed. His nostrils flared, and his eyes glittered from beneath half-closed lids. He frowned, confused, conflicted. "Jake, *Goddess!*" Jake must have done something particularly wonderful because Daniel's eyes closed completely and his bottom lip disappeared between his teeth.

Jake thrust his hips, vividly reminding me that his huge cock was still buried in my body. I shook as he started his rhythm again, this time sucking Daniel's cock himself.

Caught between them, I could only watch and feel. This had to be good. This had to be right. I convinced myself of that, knowing that the leash between them made it impossible for Jake to really do something Daniel didn't want. At any time, with a mere thought, Daniel could throw Jake off of both of us and keep him away.

But he didn't.

"No!" Daniel cried. His hips bucked beneath me, but I don't think he was quite the master of their movement. "Damn it all, Jake!" His voice was husky, the tone making a mockery of the words. "Fucking stop!" His hand fell from my hair, but Jake kept a grip on his wrist.

Jake didn't stop. He held Daniel's wrists to the mattress, trapped his legs with our bodies, and pounded me into an orgasm that hit seconds after Daniel roared and shot semen into Jake's sucking mouth. I tried to watch, even as I was coming, because the sight of Jake's bearded cheeks hollowing, of Daniel's hips pumping helplessly, was too amazing to miss.

Jake sucked Daniel until he was soft, then finally slid his lips all the way up to the tip and off. A dribble of semen that Jake hadn't managed to swallow still connected cock and lips before Jake tilted his head back to look at Daniel.

I looked up, too. Daniel's eyes were half closed and slumberous, his pale cheeks flushed. It was a look I'd grown fond of. It was Daniel's sated look and one I worked hard to put on his face. To know that Jake had put it there…

"Why?" he asked, eyes locked on Jake's. He didn't look mad, but he did look confused.

Jake grinned. "You said you weren't gay. I never said *I* wasn't."

Daniel's eyes went wide; his mouth fell open. "But you…"

Jake sat back, carefully releasing Daniel's hands. He put his hands on my hips, easing out of me as he went.

He was still hard, but he ignored his erection for the moment, staring at Daniel. "I saw from the start that it bugged you if anyone thought we were gay, so I figured I wouldn't say anything."

Daniel swallowed. "But I thought…" His voice trailed off as he stared at Jake in helpless confusion.

Jake's smile was dark as he carefully lifted my leg and eased me to my side. "'Scuse me, sweetheart." He winked at me before turning back to a dumbfounded Daniel. "You think too much."

I scooted aside and lay very quietly to watch Jake lean in to Daniel. He kept eye contact the entire way as he slowly closed the distance between their mouths.

Daniel's only movement was the more rapid rise and fall of his chest as his breathing sped up.

Jake stopped with his lips a breath away from Daniel's. "Buddy?"

Daniel swallowed. He closed his eyes. Then, very slowly, he tipped his head to the side and up.

Jake closed the distance.

They kissed.

I fought not to squirm at the gorgeous sight. Two men kissing had never really turned me on before, but *these* two men kissing…This was what I'd hoped for. This was what I was convinced Daniel needed.

At first it was a simple meeting of lips, a soft how-do-you-do. Then Jake parted his lips and pushed a little. Daniel's head tipped farther, and his jaw fell open slightly. I actually saw Jake's tongue slide from his mouth into Daniel's before he pushed in a little more to seal their lips. It lasted forever. Daniel lay quietly, moving only in response to some sign from Jake.

Jake moved forward so he could balance on his knees between Daniel's legs. His huge hands came up to frame Daniel's face. Only then did he allow their lips to part. Eyes closed, he continued to nibble and lick at Daniel's lips, tasting and exploring them the same way I had the first chance I'd been given permission to do so.

"So beautiful," Jake murmured. "I've wanted to do this for years."

Daniel swallowed and squeezed his eyes shut. Despite that, I saw the trickle of tears down the cheek I could see. Jake must have felt it hit his hand because he angled Daniel's face so he could trail his lips up the younger man's cheek to kiss his eyes.

I felt like a peeping tom, but I couldn't have moved from my spot if I'd wanted to.

Jake inched forward again. He nudged his knees under Daniel's thighs, forcing him to move them up onto Jake's legs.

Daniel's eyes shot open. He reached up and grabbed both of Jake's forearms. "Jake!"

"Shhhh," Jake soothed, kissing his lips lightly. "I'm not going to do it. Not if you don't want me to."

Daniel sagged a bit, his watery eyes locking with Jake's. "Jake?"

Jake grinned. He released one hand from Daniel's head and dropped it to Daniel's cock.

Daniel groaned, his eyes falling shut.

"Yeah," Jake crooned, fondling Daniel's renewed erection. "I've been wanting to do this forever."

Daniel squirmed, his hands reaching up to clutch at Jake's shoulders. "Shit."

"Easy, baby." Jake glanced at me, a huge, delighted smile on his face. He winked, just to let me know he remembered my presence, then returned his attention to Daniel. Gently, he rubbed his bearded cheek against Daniel's smooth one. "Easy."

Daniel moaned. He switched his hands from Jake's shoulders to his head and yanked Jake's lips back to his.

I squeezed my thighs together, trying in vain to ease the empty ache between them.

Jake nudged forward some more, curling Daniel's body before him. I didn't realize why until he took hold of his own cock and held it in the one hand with Daniel's. *Goddess, that's hot!* He used his hand and rolled his hips. He freed his far hand momentarily to scrabble on the nightstand for the bottle of lube. Blindly, he poured some on the cocks he had imprisoned in his tight grip. Daniel grunted, no doubt at the feel of cool liquid dribbling over hot skin, but when Jake started to pump their cocks, he went wild. His hips started to buck, and his kiss at Jake's mouth grew sloppy. Jake thrust as well, clearly losing control. They strained together until they fell away from the kiss and landed cheek-to-cheek as they both thrust into Jake's fist. Daniel came first, splashing cum onto his belly. Jake followed within seconds, moaning low into Daniel's neck.

Jake held them there as they caught their breath.

Daniel recovered, moaning. His hands fell down beside him, and he tried to push up. His eyes came open, and he twisted his head so he could see me.

I smiled huge. Only then did I realize tears were streaming down my cheeks, matching the ones that streaked his own.

Jake eased back, giving Daniel room to unbend from what must now be an uncomfortable curl.

Suddenly thinking to be useful, I rolled off the bed and hurried into the bathroom to run a washcloth under some warm water. It took a while for the water to warm, so by the time I got back to them, they were in a completely different position. Daniel lay on his back in the center of the bed. Jake was propped on his elbow at Daniel's side, his big hand spread over Daniel's heart. They were kissing lightly.

I stopped at the edge of the bed, unsure. On one hand, I very much wanted to keep watching. They were so beautiful. On the other, I felt like an intruder.

Jake broke the kiss and sat up. "Thanks." He smiled, reaching for the cloth.

I remained standing at he wiped pools of milky white from Daniel's cobbled belly. "Should I...?" I cleared my throat. "I should go downstairs and leave you two alone."

Jake chuckled. "You don't want to go all the way down there."

"Well..."

Daniel reached for my hand. I met his gaze. He still looked shocked, confused, but momentarily content. "Please stay," he said softly.

Jake nodded, rising from the bed with the cloth as I knelt. I watched him cross around the foot of the bed toward the bathroom.

Daniel took my hand and drew me down. Our gazes met. He shook his head. "Not right now." He closed his eyes. "Please?"

I nodded and lay down beside him.

Jake came back. He made us move so he could pull the covers down; then he got into bed on Daniel's other side and pulled the sheets and quilt over us. He twisted to turn off the lamp, leaving us with only the dim light from the Christmas tree below for illumination. I watched him settle beside Daniel, one hand spread across Daniel's chest. Eyes still closed, Daniel brought his hand up to lie over Jake's.

Jake smiled and winked at me over Daniel's body.

Not sure what to make of this, I simply closed my eyes and slept.

Chapter Ten

December 25

The sight of Jake devouring Daniel's mouth was my first sight when I woke up Christmas morning. Sweet Goddess, what a gift! Daniel's pale hand stood out against the darker skin of Jake's shoulder. The sheets and quilt were draped low over Jake's hips as they lay pressed half atop Daniel. Jake's hand was wrapped firmly around Daniel's morning erection, pumping it slowly in time to the gentle rhythm of his hips grinding against Daniel's thigh.

It took me a moment to realize that Daniel was protesting. Weakly. The hand on Jake's shoulder was pushing, not pulling, and the movement of his head indicated that he was trying to free his mouth.

He finally managed it by twisting his head toward me. His eyes were closed. "Jake, stop."

Jake bent his head to nip at Daniel's neck. "No."

"Jake, damn it." Daniel reached down to wrap his hand around Jake's wrist.

Jake didn't stop. "Why?"

Daniel gritted his teeth. "Jake."

For the first time since I'd met them, Daniel used the leash. I wasn't looking magically, so I couldn't see it, but I saw the immediate effect. One moment Jake was half draped over Daniel, the next he yanked back, eyes wide, making a choking sound.

Daniel scrambled forward, shooting off the foot of the bed as Jake landed on his back.

"Daniel!" I called, sitting up.

He didn't look at me. He snatched up the jeans and sweater he'd worn the day before from the chair by the head of the stairs and took them with him on his mad dash to the main room below.

I glanced at Jake. "Are you okay?"

The corner of Jake's mouth curled in a rueful grin as he fingered his neck. "Yeah. He hasn't done *that* for years."

I turned to start off the bed. "We should go after…ah!"

I fell across Jake's chest as he yanked me down. His hand closed around the back of my head and drew me into an engulfing kiss. I was helpless to do anything but respond.

"He's not the only one I want," Jake huffed when he released me. His gaze bore into mine. "You hear me?"

I swallowed and nodded.

He nodded and released me. "Let's go."

He stormed naked down the stairs. A bit more modest, I grabbed Daniel's oversized pajama top and put it on as I followed.

Daniel sat in one of the chairs by the dining table, pulling on socks that must have been stuffed somewhere in the clothing he'd picked up. The jeans were already on, the sweater waiting on the table. His boots and the front door were not far away.

"Where do you think you're going?" Jake demanded.

"Away from you."

"Running?"

Daniel spun in the chair and reached out to grab his boots. Underneath the fall of loose, silky black hair I could see the panicked look in his eyes. "Yeah."

I stopped Jake halfway across the room.

He frowned down at me, but stayed put as I approached Daniel.

"Daniel," I said softly.

He didn't look up, stomping into one boot.

"Daniel, the storm picked up last night. You can't go anywhere."

He froze, hands hovering over the laces of his boot. Hands that trembled violently.

I stepped closer and reached out to brush aside some of his hair. "Daniel --"

He jerked away from me, back ramrod straight against the back of the chair. Wide, panicked eyes looked at my hand like it was a viper. "Don't."

I pulled my hand back and took a step in reverse.

He glanced at the window in the kitchen, clearly seeing the haze of gray and white. Yesterday Jake had told us we were pretty well snowed in, and he certainly hadn't taken any time to shovel us out since then. Daniel knew that. Clearly, his panic had made him forget.

His hands closed into fists on his thighs, but that didn't stop the trembling. "You've felt like this all along?" He continued to stare out the window.

It was obvious he wasn't talking to me. I glanced at Jake, who stood naked not far from the staircase, arms over his chest and feet braced apart.

"Yes," he answered.

"Why didn't you tell me?"

"And have you react like this?"

Daniel shut his eyes, pushing new tears down his cheeks. Given their positions, I don't think Jake could see the tears. I could, though, and it sparked tears of my own.

"You never gave any indication…"

"No. I didn't. You made it obvious that you weren't gay, so there was no hope."

Daniel's chin tilted down, and he brushed at one cheek with his bare shoulder. "I've seen you with women. We've dated *women.*"

"I like women, too."

Daniel shook his head. "That doesn't make sense."

"Why not?"

"You either like men or you like women. You can't like both."

"I'm sorry, buddy, that's just not true."

Daniel swallowed. "Have you...been with a guy since we...?"

"I haven't been with a guy since you leashed me, no."

"Because there wasn't a chance? Have you...wanted...?"

"No. I met you and pretty much found what I wanted in a man."

Daniel cringed. "Me?" his voice was barely a breath.

"Yes."

"Even though...?"

"Even though."

Daniel's face crumpled, and his mouth opened in a silent sob. His fingers clawed into his thighs, and he bent over, silky hair falling forward to hide his face from view.

I wanted so very much to take the two steps between us and wrap my arms around him, but I didn't. This had to happen. This was important, painful as it was to watch. I glanced at Jake to see him a few steps closer, tears slowly tracking his cheeks into his beard. He met my gaze, and I saw that he knew it, too.

I clutched Daniel's pajama top closed between my breasts and turned back to him just as shuddering sobs started to tear from his chest. I chanced to look at him with magical sight and nearly gasped. A three-foot aura surrounded him, ablaze in midnight blue and pulsing purple. Tendrils writhed halfway down Jake's leash, reaching for him, then retracting. I saw the ghost of similar tendrils reaching for me.

"It's not right!" he gasped, voice broken. "It's not...right. You...can't..."

I swallowed a soft sob of my own. "Can't what, Daniel?"

He propped his elbow on the table beside him and dropped his face in that hand. "You can't feel this way about two people! And one of them *can't* be a guy. It's just not --" He broke off, and the sobbing took over. Groaning, he brought his other hand around and tore at his temples with both hands, succumbing to the teary storm.

As one, Jake and I closed the distance to him. I knelt beside him, sliding one hand up his side and the other over his thigh. Jake came up behind him on the other side, arms wrapping around his shoulders. The move forced Daniel up against the back of the chair, exposing his face and the wreck the pain had made of his sculpted features. I grabbed his hands and held them when he would have brought them up to claw at his face. Held between us, between the two people who loved him most in this world, he completely fell apart. I put my face to the hands I held in mind, the hands I held on his thigh, and cried with him.

There's only so long a person can cry, however. No matter the pain, there's only so much time the body can succumb to body-wracking sobs. His wailing eventually ceased and the tremors subsided. I looked up to see Jake's arms still banding his chest, Jake's face buried in the side of his neck. Daniel's face was turned the other way, hair partially hiding his features as his cheek pressed Jake's arm. He was a mess. I'd never seen him look so awful. From what I could see, his eyes were puffy, his cheeks and nose were red, and snot and tears drenched his face.

I released his hands and stood, using the cuff of the pajama top to blot at my own tears as I turned to the sink. Quietly, I grabbed a few paper towels and ran half of them under the water. The men hadn't moved by the time I returned to the table. Gently, I brushed damp hair from Daniel's face and used one of the wet towels to blot at his cheeks and nose.

He sniffed and opened his eyes.

I smiled, knowing it was watery.

He reached up and wound an arm around my waist, pulling me close. I went gladly and wound my arms around the head that he buried in my cleavage.

Jake lifted his head. His cheeks and beard were damp from tears.

I offered one of the towels, and he unwound one of his arms from about Daniel's shoulders to take it. He blotted his eyes and nose.

I reached out to comb my fingers through the curly hair at his temple.

"I love you."

Jake and I both froze, unsure we'd heard the words from Daniel's mouth, muffled as they were by my cleavage.

Daniel reached up with his free hand to clutch at the forearm Jake still had banded about his shoulders. He rolled his head aside some so his voice was more recognizable. "Goddess, I love both of you so much. How is that even possible?"

Unsure how to answer, neither Jake nor I did.

But Daniel didn't seem to want an answer. Not yet anyway. "Noelle, you're such a pushy woman."

I barked a laugh. Jake grinned at me.

Daniel continued. "Always making me do things. Think things." The arm around my waist squeezed. "I wanted you before, but I didn't think it was right. I didn't think you'd want to…stay."

I bit my lip and sifted through his hair. "I want to stay," I assured him softly.

He squeezed Jake's forearm. "And you." Daniel reached up and found Jake's cheek, his ear, the hair behind his ear. He grabbed hold and dragged Jake's face down closer. "I've always..." He swallowed. "From the first...Gah! But wanting another guy is wrong."

"Who told you that?" Jake asked softly.

Daniel laughed. *Laughed.* He tilted his head back, resting it on Jake's shoulder, and couldn't stop.

I exchanged an alarmed glance with Jake, but we stayed quiet. The maniacal laughter, like the sobbing, was clearly a needed release.

"My mother!" Daniel finally managed to tell us. "My mother. My father. The army. Goddess, why would I listen to *them?* My parents have never been right about anything. *Anything!*"

Jake used his free hand to brush at the renewed tears on Daniel's cheeks. He kissed Daniel's temple. "I love you, buddy."

Daniel's laughter subsided, and he tilted his head to rest against Jake's, eyes closed, his face almost peaceful. "Goddess," he breathed, lips brushing Jake's beard. "I love you, too."

Jake straightened up, beaming

Daniel opened puffy eyes. Smiled.

Jake chuckled. "You know, beautiful as you are, you look like shit."

Daniel laughed softly. His eyes turned to me.

I smiled. "He's right. You do."

Daniel rolled his eyes and tried to lean forward.

Jake and I both released him and stepped back, allowing him to get to his feet.

He accepted one of the paper towels I offered and blotted his nose. He leaned on the table briefly to balance while toeing off the unlaced boot he'd managed to put on before. "I'll be right back."

I watched him walk down the hall until he turned in to the bathroom.

Jake came up beside me and gathered me into his arms. "You sure you want this?"

I tipped my head back to look up at him. "It's a bit late for second thoughts now."

He grinned. "Yeah." His eyes searched my face. "Goddess, you're beautiful. Are you sure you're all ours?"

I absolutely adored the way he said that. No doubt that this was a three-way deal. I went up on tiptoe to brush his lips with mine, loving the tickle of his mustache and beard. "As long as you're sure that you're both mine."

He held me against his chest, arms firmly banded around me to hold me up. Our kiss deepened to a meeting of tongues.

The bathroom door opened, but neither Jake nor I broke immediately from the kiss. We took our own sweet time about it, reluctant to part...just yet.

When we did, I glanced over to see Daniel leaning in the arch that spilled the hallway into the main room, a smile on his newly washed face. "That was hot."

Jake chuckled, pulling the pajama top up my back to expose me below the waist. "It can get hotter if you come over here."

Daniel pushed from the wall and sauntered over. "I can do that."

He came up behind me, his hands going to my hips to fit my rump against the crotch of his jeans. In front of me, Jake's cock twitched and poked me in the belly. Jake's hands left my back, and I can only assume they found Daniel's shoulders or back. Jake leaned in over my shoulder, and I twisted my neck to see him take Daniel's mouth.

"Mmmmm," I purred, pressing my cheek to Jake's chest. "Merry Christmas and happy birthday to me."

They broke on a laugh, but we stayed in that marvelous three-way hug for precious moments.

Daniel's hands wandered first. They slid around the front of my hips. Jake hissed when one of those strong-fingered hands wrapped around his cock and pulled.

"Let's move upstairs," Daniel suggested.

No one argued.

I dropped the pajama top at the head of the staircase, and Daniel quickly doffed his jeans and socks while Jake pulled the covers down from the bed. We all crawled on the mattress and met in a jumble of hands, mouths, and bodies. Jake ended up on his back with both Daniel and me attacking the wealth of skin that covered his hard muscles. I dove for his cock, eager to have the thick, steely length in my mouth.

Daniel hovered over his mouth, then eased down to explore his chest. Then -- I think to everyone's surprise -- Daniel crawled down beside me. I popped Jake's cock from my mouth and, still holding it, ducked down to gently suck at the hairy sacs of his balls. Daniel's hand closed around mine, and I glanced up to see him lick his lips to wet them before sliding his mouth over the head of Jake's cock.

Jake's moan was like to rattle the rafters. I saw his fingers thread through Daniel's hair as Daniel sucked him down.

I freed my hand from underneath Daniel's and used both hands to spread Jake's thighs just a little wider so I had more room to torment his balls and the sensitive skin behind them.

Jake rocked under the dual assault, muttering and pumping underneath us.

I gave in to an impish desire. Thoroughly wetting my index finger, I trailed it down and found Jake's tight little opening.

"Noelle!" I heard my name on a gasp.

I wiggled my finger in to the first knuckle.

"Oh, shit, yeah!"

I wiggled it around, searching for something I'd heard about, not sure what I'd find since I'd never done this before.

"Goddess, I'm --"

I glanced up at Daniel, whose eyes were on me even as his cheeks were hollowed from sucking Jake hard.

"-- gonna come!"

I think I found what I was looking for. If not, whatever I did, combined with the suction of Daniel's mouth, did it for Jake. He roared and came. I was amazed at how tightly his back hole clutched my finger, pumping rhythmically.

Daniel sputtered, clearly not expecting either the taste or the amount of cum that spurted into his mouth. He caught some, but lost hold on Jake's cock in the middle so that salty sperm splashed both his face and mine.

Jake sagged beneath us with a sigh.

Daniel and I grinned at each other.

I yelped when Daniel dove at me, pushing me down on the bed safely away from Jake's thighs. "Time to fuck you, birthday girl," he told me.

I giggled, happily splaying my legs. "If you insist."

He aimed and sank his entire cock into me in one hot glide. "I insist," he groaned, settling on top of me.

I framed his face with my hands and lapped at the cum spattered on his chin and cheeks, groaning from his near frenzied attack on my pussy. Not that I minded. I happily writhed underneath his assault. The conduit between us flared open and pumped spirit energy into me, making my skin sizzle with awareness. I came in a rush of blue-white heat and yanked Daniel into bliss right with me.

We lay together an hour or so later, still in bed. We'd barely bothered to rearrange ourselves before falling into a doze. I lay on my back with Daniel pressed against my side, head on my chest. Jake lay pressed against his back, his arm long enough to drape over my waist.

I wasn't really asleep, just happily drifting. I don't think I'd ever been so happy in my life. I had not one but two wonderful men in my life when I'd begun to think that I'd never find anyone I wanted to be with forever. And I did want to be with them.

Forever.

Daniel stirred, his hand lazily coming up to cup my breast. I looked down to watch the hand, slightly paler than my medium tan, curl around the handful of my flesh and squeeze.

Things low in my belly tingled.

Jake's hand moved, sliding down my belly to the curls between my legs. I shifted my far leg away to give him room, and he obligingly sought further. His fingers easily slid into my wet depths.

I groaned.

"I want my Christmas present now," Daniel announced solemnly.

Jake and I froze.

"We didn't do presents," I said.

"Mmm, not that kind."

He shifted, and Jake had to take his fingers from my sex to allow Daniel to get to his knees. He moved until he was kneeling between my thighs and shifted his dark gaze from Jake to me and back. "I want both of you."

Jake chuckled. "You've got us."

Daniel smiled, and it was a beautiful, unfettered thing. I wondered if Jake's heart thumped like mine at the sight of it. "No. I want to have sex with you --" His eyes locked on Jake's. "-- both. I want you inside me."

I glanced at Jake, who stared intently at Daniel.

"Are you sure, buddy?" Jake asked quietly. "We don't have to."

Daniel's eyes dropped to Jake's cock. He reached out and quite deliberately wrapped his fingers around it.

Jake hissed.

"I want it." His eyes flew up to Jake's. "I've wanted it for years."

Jake grabbed his wrist to stop him. "What?"

Daniel licked his lips. "I've wanted you; I just didn't *want* to want you. I was..." He shook his head. "I thought there was no way you'd return my feelings and if I mentioned what I felt, it could make our relationship...bad. And I'd already done so much to ruin your life."

Jake pushed up to sit, his hand going to Daniel's shoulder. "Fuck, man. You've never done anything to ruin my life."

Daniel slid his hand from Jake's cock up his chest to finally thread his fingers in Jake's beard. "Fuck me. Fuck me while I'm fucking Noelle. Let me have you both at once."

How could either of us deny that raw plea?

Jake pulled Daniel into a kiss that lasted forever and for brief moments. I got wetter just watching Daniel's plump lip disappear into Jake's mouth and the brief glimpses of their tongues as they devoured each other. Not to mention that they were both growing hard just from the kissing.

Just as I was contemplating sitting up and taking hold of both of their cocks, Daniel pushed away. "Get the lube," he rasped.

Jake nodded and turned.

Daniel leaned in over me, grabbing hold of my thighs to press them open further. He slid gentle fingers through my sex, finding and rubbing my clit. "This okay with you?"

"Oh, yes!"

"You really want both of us?"

I held open my arms, and he came into my embrace. "I *love* both of you. Please believe that."

He kissed me gently, guiding his cock to my entrance. "I'm trying to believe it," he murmured against my lips, slipping into me. "Work with me?"

I giggled, wrapping my arms around him. "I'll do that."

He rolled his hips, kissing me as he filled me. The conduit between us opened and established contact through spirit magic, making my skin tingle. I dragged my nails over the smooth muscle of Daniel's back, smiling when he moaned.

Jake came up behind Daniel, bottle of lube in hand. "You two are fucking hot," he assured us, pouring clear liquid on his fingers. "How did I get so lucky?"

Daniel's movement slowed when Jake's hand lowered. I felt him tense and decided Jake must have put a finger in. "Must be that bear dick of yours," Daniel answered, tossing his head to clear his silky hair from one side.

Jake chuckled. "Is that so?"

Daniel sighed and pulled back from me, which must have pushed him onto Jake's fingers. "Yeah."

Jake leaned in, bracing his dry hand on the mattress beside my shoulder. He kissed Daniel's shoulder. "Been wanting my bear dick for a while, have you?"

Daniel twisted his neck so he could look at Jake. Tendrils of his hair brush my cheek. "Oh, yeah."

Jake's eyes lit with fire. He grinned.

Daniel tensed, hissing.

The spirits between us jolted, making me gasp.

Jake glanced at me, his grin growing. "Oh, yeah." He leaned in until his mouth was right beside Daniel's ear. "You pumping Noelle full of magic, buddy?"

Daniel groaned, his hips twisting. "Yeah."

"Goddess, Noelle. Dick and magic. What do you need me for?"

I reached up to grab his hair, making him look at me. "I need you to fuck him."

That got to them. I rarely, if ever, used the word. It wasn't one of my favorites. But I did realize that it could be quite effective in the right circumstances.

Like now.

Jake's eyes lit up and his nostrils flared. He shoved forward.

Daniel hissed, arching his back as Jake's action pressed him into me.

Jake groaned and leaned down as I lifted up so we could devour each other over Daniel's shoulder.

I'm sure Jake was doing a pretty good job finger-fucking Daniel, because the man between us started to rock and whimper. The cock inside me hit that spot that made me writhe, and I moaned into Jake's mouth. The spirit energy between me and Daniel simmered.

"Now, Jake," Daniel begged. "Please, Jake, now, Jake, please!"

Jake tore away from me and reared back on his knees. As Daniel pumped into me, Jake snatched up the bottle of lube and poured a generous amount on his palm.

"Jake, please!" Daniel begged.

"Please!" I echoed, picking up Daniel's desperation.

"Fuck," Jake groaned.

I heard the wet slapping of palm on cock as Jake leaned in.

Daniel froze.

"Push back, buddy," Jake murmured. "It'll hurt less."

I don't think Jake meant for Daniel to push *quite* as hard as he did.

Daniel arched on a cry.

Spirit energy surged between us.

I gasped.

Jake growled. "What the *fuck?!*"

I stared up at Daniel, unable to see much of Jake. Daniel's back was arched, his head thrown back, his eyes closed. I couldn't decide if the look on his face was pain or pleasure, and it probably didn't matter. Slowly, he pushed his rock-hard, swollen cock into my depths, then just as slowly pulled out. I can only imagine what it felt like to have his cock leave the warm confines of my pussy and his ass fill with the steely heat of Jake's cock.

"Oh, shit!" Jake cried.

My eyes dropped to stare in amazement at Jake's hands where they grasped Daniel's hips. It wasn't my imagination. His fingernails had changed to thick, black talons, and fur coated his fingers and hand, extending up his forearms as far as I could see. I'd heard that shifters could lose it during particularly good sex, but I'd never seen it.

Daniel's head dropped down. He was breathing hard as he pushed forward and pressed back again. Was he seating himself on Jake's cock?

"Goddess, Daniel, what…?"

"Magic," Daniel growled.

My eyes opened wide. Was Jake feeling the spirit magic? But that made sense. It happened whenever Daniel was inside of me; why wouldn't it happen when Jake was inside of him?

Daniel rolled his hips again, his movements a bit freer. He still moved slowly, but I was pretty sure he'd gotten a feel for as much of Jake's length as he could take and was now figuring out how best to move.

I groaned.

Daniel peeked up at me, his face flushed with pleasure. His dark eyes sparkled above a wicked, happy grin.

Jake fell forward over us, banding an arm around Daniel's chest. Claws threatened the skin just above one of Daniel's nipples, and the feel of it pushed a cry from Daniel's lips.

"Sorry," Jake muttered, and I felt the jolt of his hips bucking into Daniel's. "I can't --"

"Don't be," Daniel snapped, shoving back at him. "Love it. Fuck me."

Daniel bent his forearms, dropping both of them down on top of me.

I grunted happily under the weight, writhing as the position scraped Daniel's pubic bone against my clit.

Spirit energy sizzled around us.

"Fuck me," Daniel demanded.

"Don't want to hurt you," Jake muttered, but I felt the pump of Daniel's hips into mine that didn't feel exactly like his movement.

"Hurt me," Daniel growled. "Want it. *Fuck* me."

Jake couldn't hold back. The fur of his forearm brushed my nipple as he held on to Daniel and started an achingly slow, pounding rhythm that pressed Daniel's cock into me as he pressed his cock into Daniel's body.

"Yes, Jake," Daniel moaned.

I cried out, writing beneath them in a mini-orgasm as spirit energy burbled beneath my skin.

"Fuck." Jake growled, his voice lower than a human's could possibly go.

Jake picked up the pace, breathing heavily. Daniel gasped and groaned, clutching the pillows beneath me, braced between us.

My eyes crossed, and violet lit up the air around us. It pulsed and writhed as Jake strained at the top of the heap.

"Can't hold..." he grumbled.

"Don't!" Daniel snapped.

Spirit energy erupted.

I screamed, clutching at Daniel's shoulders.

Jake roared, rearing back, talons digging into Daniel's shoulders as he held on.

Daniel shuddered between us, mouth open on a painful, silent sob.

We stayed in that tableau for trembling, aching moments, afraid to move, still overcome by shattering release.

With a small groan, Jake pulled back. His arms and hands were again fully human as he sat on his heels, then toppled over onto his side.

Daniel sagged over me, his hair trailing over my chest.

I lay trying to remember how to breathe.

Spirit energy settled back down, and I skewed my sight just in time to see Daniel swallow up and dissipate the extra energy as he slowly pulled out of my body.

He sat back on his heels, raising trembling hands to brush damp hair from his cheeks. He was disheveled and flushed, and I thought he'd never looked so beautiful.

He glanced from me to Jake and back, smiling. A wide, possessive smile. "That was the best damn Christmas present I've ever had!"

We all laughed.

Epilogue

December 26

"It's something, isn't it?"

"It is that."

"Who would have thought?"

"Certainly not me."

Meg's chuckle came through my cell phone. "So what now?"

"I'm going to take them to a solstice party Aunt Henri's throwing the day after tomorrow." I settled into the recliner, warm and toasty with the comforter wrapped around me. "I figure it's as good a time to introduce them as any."

"How do they feel about it?"

"They're surprisingly game." I chuckled. "I don't think they realize what they're in for."

Meg laughed. "Yeah, well, you're lucky."

"Yours don't want to meet the family?"

She was silent long enough for me to prompt her. "Meg?"

"They want to meet them. I'm not sure I want the family to meet them."

"Why not?"

She was quiet for a long time again. "Meg?"

She sighed. "Oh, nothing. It's just they're all going to get excited because of who Michael is, that's all."

"Meg, you'll have to deal with it sometime."

"I know. I know. But not now."

"Maybe we'll come and visit."

"That'd be nice. I'd love to meet the two men you think deserve you."

"Likewise."

We laughed.

"Noelle, I'm happy for you."

"Thanks. I'm happy for you."

"Happy birthday."

"Thanks. And Merry Christmas to you."

She laughed. "And happy flippin' New Year."

Jet Mykles

Jet's been writing sex stories back as far as junior high. Back then, the stories involved her favorite pop icons of the time but she soon extended beyond that realm into making up characters of her own. To this day, she hasn't stopped writing sex, although her knowledge on the subject has vastly improved.

An ardent fan of fantasy and science fiction sagas, Jet prefers to live in a world of imagination where dragons are real, elves are commonplace, vampires are just people with special diets and lycanthropes live next door In her own mind, she's the spunky heroine who gets the best of everyone and always attracts the lean, muscular lads. She aids this fantasy with visuals created through her other obsession: 3D graphic art. In this area, as in writing, Jet's self-taught and thoroughly entranced, and now occasionally uses this art to illustrate her stories, or her stories to expand upon her art.

In real life, Jet is a self-proclaimed hermit, living in southern California with her life partner. She has a bachelor's degree in acting, but her loathing of auditions has kept her out of the limelight. So she turned to computers and currently works in product management for a software company, because even in real life, she can't help but want to create something out of nothing.

Printed in the United States
123824LV00003B/40/A